THE Determined MISS RACHEL

ALSO BY LAURA ROLLINS

Daughters of Courage

The Audacious Miss Eliza

The Determined Miss Rachel

The Fearless Miss Dinah (coming August 2021)

The Tenacious Lady Blackmore (coming Spring 2022)

Lockhart Regency Romance

Courting Miss Penelope—available at LauraRollins.com

Wager for a Lady's Hand

Lily for my Enemy

A Heart in the Balance

A Farewell Kiss

A Well-Kept Promise

A Dickens of a Christmas

The Hope of Christmas Past

The Joy of Christmas Present

The Peace of Christmas Yet to Come

THE *Determined* MISS RACHEL

~ DAUGHTERS OF COURAGE ~

a regency romance by

LAURA ROLLINS

For Sara and Jake,
Thank you for the inspiration and encouragement to find my own happiness.

PROLOGUE

A knock sounded at the library door and Seth's hands tightened around the book he had been pretending to read.

"Enter." His voice remained firm; he wasn't sure how his daughter was going to take this conversation, but regardless of how she responded, staying levelheaded would no doubt help.

Dinah slipped in. She'd always looked best with her blonde hair curled about her face and in simple pink. But since coming to London for the Season, she'd positively bloomed into a radiant lady —one flirty enough to catch any blackguard's attention. Seth motioned for her to take the seat opposite him. The sooner they left London the better.

"You wished to speak with me, Father?" she asked as she sat.

"Yes, it is regarding my sister."

"Aunt Grace?" Dinah's brow creased. "Should I go get Rachel? Surely if you have news of her mother she would wish to hear it."

"No." Seth held up a hand. "She is to know nothing of this. Is that clear? Not a hint, not a whisper, not any notion of what I am about to tell you."

It wasn't often he took such a firm tone with any of his three girls—three *young ladies* they were now. Lud, sometimes he wished he could spirit them all back to seven years ago, back to when they wore their hair in pigtails and there were no cads wishing to court them.

"Very well, sir," Dinah said, sitting back further in her seat. "I promise not to say anything to her."

"Not to Eliza either."

Dinah looked even more baffled. "If you wish it."

"You must promise me, Dinah. Even if you do not care for what I am about to say, you must swear never to breathe a word of this to anyone."

She rocked back slightly at his tone. "I said I wouldn't."

He hoped she was in earnest. The last thing he needed was for her to go running to Eliza and Rachel and telling them all. But he couldn't in good conscious proceed without her knowing what they were about to do. After all, she was the one who would most feel the weight of the consequences.

Seth closed the book completely and placed it on a small, nearby table. There was no easy way to say it. Best to just come right out with it. "My sister, your Aunt Grace, has found herself in a delicate situation and is in need of additional funds immediately."

Dinah remained silent.

His youngest daughter had grown. Normally he could trust she'd interrupt and pester him with questions he couldn't answer because she never stopped to draw breath long enough to give him time. Instead, she waited patiently. She was not the same impetuous little girl she'd been not long ago. They'd all changed since he had been knighted. Now, instead of being a tradesman with two daughters and a niece to raise, they were associating with the *ton*. No one could experience such and not have it change them in some way or another.

"The amount is substantial," he continued.

"How much?"

"We will still be accompanying Lady Blackmore to the country to stay with her friend, the Dowager Fitzwilliam, for the next month or two. But once we return . . . there will not be much left."

Dinah's mouth pursed. "We'll have to cut the Season short."

Seth already hated that he was putting his girls in such a situation—pushing all three to find a match in a single London Season. It was utter madness. Now, if he helped his sister, Dinah and Rachel would have even less time than they originally thought. Eliza, at least, had already secured her own happiness. Lord Lambert was a good man and Seth was happy that soon he'd call the viscount son-in-law. But oh, how he worried for his other two girls.

"This isn't forever, Dinah. We will be able to return to London at some point," Seth said, even as Dinah's look of curious uncertainty was quickly changing to one of insulted petulance.

"If funds are running low *now*, why not stay in London where both Rachel and I have the best opportunities to find a husband? Why go to the country at all?"

Seth lifted an eyebrow. "I raised you smarter than that. You know quite well that staying in the country will not cost nearly as much as being here in London. Furthermore . . ." This was the part he'd debated telling her. It would either soothe her or anger her more. With Dinah, he often had a hard time knowing which way her emotions would land. Well, in for a pound and all that. He drew himself up in his chair. "Furthermore, the Dowager Fitzwilliam's grandson, the current Lord Fitzwilliam, has just returned from his Grand Tour. Lady Blackmore is convinced he and Rachel would suit."

He watched Dinah closely, trying to judge how his words sounded in her ears.

"So," she began slowly, her jaw tight. "We have nearly no funds left, and you are using what we do have to see that Rachel is perfectly positioned to catch the eye of a baron?"

She was angry. Hang it all. What he wouldn't give to return to life before his knighthood. Where there were no barons to be impressed, no gentlemen who spent more time improving their clothes than their brains, no blackguards eying his daughters.

"There's always a chance," he said evenly, "that you will find someone you can respect while we're in the country as well." Just so long as Dinah didn't choose to 'respect' any of the untrustworthy gentlemen who had been paying her so much attention as of late.

"I don't want a country bumpkin," Dinah said, her voice growing in volume. "I want a London Season."

Seth sighed. He'd been worried she wouldn't take this news well. "You're having one now."

"I want to meet someone *here*, among society."

Seth focused on keeping his own tone steady. "There will be plenty of society in the country; Lady Blackmore assured me."

"This isn't fair." Dinah shot to her feet.

Life wasn't fair—none of it was. It was ridiculous to expect otherwise. "We have already accepted the Dowager Fitzwilliam's invitation and we will stay long enough for Rachel and the baron to court and wed if they find one another to their liking."

Dinah shook her head. "But there will be *no one* there for me!"

And here he'd been thinking only moments ago that she'd grown up a bit. Well, she *had*. Only, it seemed she still had a bit *more* growing up to do. "Come now, Di—"

"No." Her hands curled into tight fists at her side. "You've always put me last." Her voice caught. "All I ever get is Eliza's and Rachel's cast-offs. Their old clothes, their old hats. Now, I won't even get my own chance to secure a future, not unless I can snag a cast-off suitor from one of them."

"That's nonsense," he muttered. He'd never known a young woman to have as many prospective suitors as Dinah; unfortunately, not a single one of them would suit, and Seth would never part with his girls for anyone less than a respectable gentleman who would treat them right.

At his words, Dinah's brow dropped, and she sent him a stare that could set an old barn ablaze. Seth inwardly sighed. He was making a hard situation even worse. Why the good Lord had decided to bless him with three girls he would never know. He was terrible at this.

Seth drew himself up and tried again. "You've been given as many opportunities as Eliza and Rachel. Every ball they've attended, so have you. Every outing, you were there. Goodness knows you've requested *even more* husband catchers than either Eliza or Rachel."

Dinah pursed her lips. "Stop calling my dresses that."

He waved off her frustration at his cant. "A short London Season is far more than any of us ever expected."

"So I should just be content with what I have? Is that it?"

Yes . . . that was exactly it. Why, then, were warning bells going off in his head, repeatedly telling him *not* to agree with her?

In his silence, Dinah shook her head, speaking as though only to herself. "I don't know why I expected any different. Now that Eliza is settled, you can see to Rachel. Once Aunt Grace and Rachel are taken care of, no need to worry about Dinah. She'll be fine with the cast-offs. Surely that's good enough for her." Dinah spun on her heel, Seth just catching sight of a tear before she rushed toward the door.

"Remember," he called after her, "you promised. Not a word."

She paused before the door but didn't look back at him. "Oh no, I would hate to say anything that would put a damper on our trip to the country."

"Dinah, please." Seth did his best to keep his tone soft. He truly did. But frustration forced its way in all the same. "Rachel needs us right now. There is more at play here than I can tell you, but she needs to find a match, and soon. Lord Fitzwilliam is her best chance. Give her this one thing, and then I'll figure out a way to bring you back to London."

Dinah didn't respond right away. But she wasn't rushing off either. He let her have some silence to think through all he'd just dumped on her.

At length, she spoke. "How long?" Her hand swiped at something on her cheek. "If we return to London, how long would we have?"

Seth let out a long sigh. "If we retrench, four weeks, possibly?"

"Four weeks?" Her hushed words were filled with disappointment.

He wished he could give her more. But he couldn't. Grace needed funds immediately, and no matter how much he crunched the numbers, each pound could only go so far. "I know it's asking a lot," he said, "which is why I felt you needed to know." He'd have much rather not say anything at all regarding Grace to any of his girls.

Still standing by the door, Dinah slowly turned and faced him. "Rachel and Aunt Grace *truly* need this? There is no other way?"

He shook his head. "There is no other way—and yes, they do truly need this." Once things were made known, she'd understand. She hadn't been wrong in stating that she was often last. Blast, but Seth hated that she always felt as though she were last in his affections. Dinah was the youngest, after all, and as a single father with three girls, he simply could not be all things to them all the time. He had to prioritize. Perhaps he should have prioritized her first more often. But even looking back over the past few years, he still couldn't see how he might have.

If only he'd been at liberty to tell her *why* he was asking her to cut their Season short. But that was far too big a secret. He'd had to tell her something—his conscience had demanded it since Dinah would be forced to pay in the form of a shortened Season—but he couldn't tell her all.

Once all was done, once everything had come to light, she'd understand.

She'd agree that it had been the right thing to do.

Dinah drew herself up. "Very well then." She was calm, but there was still an edge of hurt in her voice. "Let us go see if we can't pair Rachel up with a baron."

Seth's heart warmed at her goodness. Dinah was often prone to dramatics. With her, everything was the best or the worst, the most glorious or the most hideous. But for all her antics, she had one of the largest hearts he'd ever seen.

Dinah opened the door, her demeanor changing with the swing. Her chin lifted and she shot him a glance that portended trouble. "If I have so little time left to secure my future, then I suppose I ought to make the most of my dance with Lord Down in two days' time."

Seth opened his mouth—she would do *nothing* to encourage that blackguard—but Dinah didn't give him time to respond. Instead, she slipped out the door and shut it firmly behind her.

Seth blew out a hard breath, staring at the door she'd just left through. If he didn't know any better, he could have sworn that last comment about Lord Down was more a jab at him than an actual declaration to secure the idiot's affections. At least, he hoped it was only a jab. He'd far prefer that to Dinah sincerely pursuing such a dishonorable man. Dinah may have a big heart, but that didn't mean she wasn't also a handful.

He rested back against the chair, his eyes wandering to the ceiling. Heaven help him if she actually *did* choose a man like Lord Down. Just the thought left Seth feeling as though he'd eaten a plate full of rocks. Or suppose Rachel and Lord Fitzwilliam didn't suit? Or suppose Grace met with disappointment? Blast it all; so many things could go wrong.

Shifting about, he pulled Grace's letter from his jacket pocket and flipped it open. Though he'd read the words dozens of times before, he skimmed them once again. How long he'd waited to see Grace heal. How long he'd wished his money and efforts in helping raise Rachel could somehow be enough. But when was financial support ever enough to fill a hole in one's life? Taking on raising Rachel had helped; Grace had repeatedly told him so.

But never before had he been able to gift Grace such a huge sum of money all at once. When Seth had been knighted, he'd had to leave trade, selling his contracts and trade agreements. It had left him with a large sum, more money than he'd ever had. Most men would have used it to set themselves up with some land and begin a new life of luxury. But Seth had chosen to use it for a single London Season—and now, to also help Grace and Rachel find peace in their life.

He hardly dared hope all would be well. But if this new endeavor worked, Grace and Rachel's life would be forever changed for the better.

Seth shut his eyes. He could do this. He would take his girls to the country and see Rachel happily connected to Lord Fitzwilliam. Then he would bring Dinah back to London and *somehow* keep the many jackanapes away while steering her toward gentlemen of honor and respectability. He rubbed a hand roughly over his face and then folded the letter once more, tucking it away. As wonderful as Grace's news might prove to be, there was no guarantee. And until there was, he was determined *none* of his girls should know. Rachel had endured enough heartbreak in her young life. Until things with Grace were fully settled, he wasn't about to speak about any of this.

He placed a hand atop his jacket pocket, feeling the hidden letter inside crinkle softly beneath the pressure. Dinah only needed to trust him a bit longer, then he could devote *everything* to her. But, for one last time, Rachel had to come first.

CHAPTER ONE

The trees and grass passed by at an alarming rate—just like life was wont to do. Forever streaming by, and never slowing down. Forested woods changed to open fields. The rocky road changed to smooth dirt. The clear sky changed to dark clouds.

Miss Rachel Chant let the curtain drop back down over the carriage window and rested back against the squabs. It never mattered how much one wished for life to just *stop*. It continued, relentless, revolving, ruthless. No matter how cherished one moment was, the next was forever hanging over her head, just waiting to descend upon her and sweep the moment away.

And once a moment was gone, it was gone for good.

Dinah snored loudly from the other side of the carriage. Rachel glanced at her blonde-haired cousin and pulled her lips to the side. Would that *she* could lie down and sleep away her anxiety so easily. Then again, Dinah hardly knew what anxiety was, she experienced it so infrequently. Frustration, yes. But then Dinah grew upset, shouted at times even, and then it was all over.

"Would you care to lie down as well?" asked Lady Charlotte Blackmore, the only other person in the carriage, even as she scooted further away from Rachel, making space for her on the bench.

"Thank you, but I don't believe I could sleep just now."

The dear woman reached out and patted Rachel's hand. "You needn't worry. You will adore Curio Manor, I dare say. My lovely friend, Lady Fitzwilliam, is quite the hostess if a little eccentric. We are assured to have all that is comfortable and enjoyable."

Rachel only nodded as she pushed aside the curtain and once more returned to watching the vista pass her by. She could hear the soft clopping of horse hooves even over the rattle of wheels. She hadn't been surprised when both Uncle Seth and Eliza had chosen to ride on their beloved horses instead of inside the comfortable carriage.

"I am sure you have heard stories regarding the happenings at Curio Manor," Charlotte continued. "But I can assure you nothing truly scandalous happens there."

"I am not worried," Rachel said, not looking away from the passing fields and occasional tree.

No matter the rumors she'd heard concerning Curio Manor— and she'd heard plenty—she wasn't afraid of either the baron or his grandmother. No matter that they were rumored to be eccentric. No matter that some claimed they served strawberries on potatoes or that they'd once dressed in roman togas while receiving morning callers. It wasn't what she would find at Curio Manor that bothered her. It was that they were going at all.

Because life was forever doing that to her.

Going.

Changing.

Pulling her further and further away from anyone she cared for, anyone she loved.

The road grew familiar. She had known they would pass over this stretch but hadn't expected it for another hour at least. Either it was later in the day than she'd realized, or they were making excellent time.

"Charlotte," Rachel said, "what would you say to a wild, impetuous change in plans?" Rachel looked over at the woman beside her. Charlotte was sporting a few wrinkles around the eyes and a touch of gray in her hair, but her expressions were forever youthful, her wit undimmed by years. Though Rachel had only known Charlotte for less than a year, she'd known the elderly woman to do wild and impetuous things in the past. Might she prevail on the woman to do so now? At this point, Rachel had to try; Charlotte was her last chance.

"I had not thought you, of all people, would ever ask for something wild." Charlotte smiled, her eyes sparkling. "What is it?"

Rachel's hopes lifted. Perhaps she should have started with Charlotte and not bothered with Uncle Seth or Cousin Eliza at all.

"Do you see that turn up ahead? There, beside the large oak." Rachel pushed the curtain even further aside, pointing toward the spot.

"I do."

"Why not take it?"

Charlotte's brow dropped. "What, instead of going on to Curio Manor?"

"Wouldn't it be fun?" If she opted for an enthusiastic tone, perhaps she would sound as though the idea had only just now come to her. But how exactly did one do that? "We could explore for a time, and perhaps arrive at Curio Manor tomorrow, or even the next day." She wasn't at all confident her tone was right.

Charlotte's expression changed from one of excitement to a sad sort of sweetness. "Rachel, dear, I know you talked to your uncle about stopping by your mother's along the way."

Drat. Thwarted before she'd even begun.

"Sweetie," Charlotte began again, "you know it would add at least two days to our travels."

"I know." Rachel repeated the same words she'd used when Uncle Seth had denied her request. It *was* pointless to add two days' travel to a trip that should only be six hours long to begin with.

"I am sure she is well," Charlotte continued.

Rachel wasn't at all sure. Mother had promised she would write Rachel when she'd come with the Mulgraves to London for the Season—but she hadn't. Not once.

"She has been written to and will know where you are should she need to reach you or any of us."

Clearly, Charlotte and Sir Mulgrave had discussed Rachel's request for she'd listed the exact same arguments as her uncle, even going so far as to list them in the same order. Which meant Rachel knew what was coming next.

"Perhaps we can visit her on our way back to town in two months' time."

"No, we won't," Rachel muttered. She hadn't voiced the thought aloud when speaking with Sir Mulgrave. Truth was, though he'd taken her in ten years ago and treated her as his own daughter all this time, Rachel was still a bit frightened of the silent, gruff man. She hadn't even voiced the thought when she'd tried to get Eliza on her side.

Perhaps it was just that Charlotte was so easy to talk to, or perhaps it was the fact that the turn-off was racing toward them, and if Rachel didn't do something soon, she'd miss the opportunity completely.

Either way, she turned toward Charlotte and faced her directly. "We won't, though. We won't go visit her when our time at Curio Manor has passed. Either it'll be straight back to London, or . . . or *something* will happen. No matter what everyone says. We won't be going back." Rachel's sight turned blurry. She blinked a few times, and a hot tear ran down her cheek. She hadn't meant to become overly emotional. She tried very hard to always keep such things to herself; it was frightfully embarrassing to cry in front of other people.

Charlotte scooted closer once more and draped an arm across Rachel's shoulders. With a gentle tug, she pulled Rachel close. Rachel let out a little sigh and rested her head against the woman.

"I know you miss her," Charlotte whispered, her hand gently rubbing up and down Rachel's arm. "But she wants you to be happy."

"I would be most content *with* her." She just needed to see for herself that Mother was all right, that she was healthy and whole. Granted, she'd visited Mother not long before they all left for

London. She'd been well enough then, but she hadn't seemed happy. She hadn't seemed . . . at peace. As if that wasn't enough to cause her worry, Mother hadn't written to Rachel since that last visit.

"She wants to know your future is secure. She wants you to find *your* happiness, not be forever concerned about hers."

"I'm only asking for a short visit." Rachel's hand went to the simple chain about her neck and the locket hanging from it.

"This is your Season, Rachel. Right now. You may never again have an opportunity to meet so many eligible young men. I am sure your mother understands this and is only keeping away so that she might not prove a distraction."

Rachel cupped the locket in her fist and held it gently. Mother was proving a far worse distraction by *not* writing. But she didn't feel like admitting to Charlotte that she hadn't received even a single letter. She'd told Eliza once, and though her cousin had been sympathetic to her plight, Rachel didn't feel like telling Charlotte. Not now, anyways. She didn't want the pity such a pathetic truth would surely elicit.

"I'm not asking to toss away my entire Season. I just need to know she is all right and then I will gladly participate in balls and musicales and the like." Though she felt horridly guilty every time she did—it was wrong for her to be enjoying life so much while her mother was alone.

"I would argue," Charlotte said softly, "that you have already tossed away such opportunities."

Rachel scowled. "I have participated in as many outings as either Eliza or Dinah."

"In body, yes, but not in heart."

If someone in Charlotte's family had been refusing to write her back, she would feel the same way. She would understand that Rachel *couldn't* enjoy the Season, not until she knew her mother was all right.

Charlotte continued in Rachel's silence. "I would just hate for you to look back on this opportunity and realize that, though you were here in person, you missed out on the *friendships* that were available to you."

A true friend would support her in her endeavors to see her mother.

"Promise me you'll make more of an effort while at Curio Manor?" Charlotte asked.

Rachel didn't respond. Was reaching out and forming friendships even something a person could do while so caught up in worry?

Without lifting her head, Rachel's gaze moved back toward the window. The large oak—the one which was burned in her memory —sailed by, barely filling the window for more than the blink of an eye.

They'd passed the turn.

Her last small bit of hope that she might prevail on *someone* to allow her to visit her mother snuffed out. Rachel let her head droop more heavily against Charlotte. How she prayed she and her family were all correct in assuming her mother was well.

"Rest if you can," Charlotte said softly, apparently choosing not to press the issue further. "No doubt these next couple of months will be quite exciting."

Rachel closed her eyes, willing the rocking of the carriage to carry her away from all the changes. First, she had been forced to leave home to live with her uncle, then she'd been forced to go to London. Now she was being forced to leave once more.

Squeezing her eyes shut, Rachel solemnly vowed that she would somehow make her way back to her mother.

She didn't know how she would manage, but she would do it. She was done being forced away from the people and the places she cared about. For all her life, others had decided for her what her happiness should look like. Lady Blackmore was certain Curio Manor would hold the key to her future. Before that, Seth had decided they should all attend the London Season. Even before that, her own mother had believed Rachel should leave home and live with her uncle and cousins—that somehow living away from all she'd known and loved would lead her to a better future.

But all it had done was create an empty hole inside Rachel that nothing had ever filled.

No more. No longer would she allow others to decide what happiness meant or where and with whom she could find that happiness.

It was time Rachel took a stand.

CHAPTER TWO

Mr. Christopher Dunn nodded slowly, his gaze moving over the trees around them, his horse plodding along at an even gait, even as Lord Fitzwilliam, the most peculiar baron in all the county, continued his rant on the superiority of the English breakfast, especially when compared to that which was found on the continent.

Christopher hadn't particularly cared for breakfast on the continent any more than he did here in England—unlike most gentlemen his age who started their days with ale, eggs, toast, or even plum cake, Christopher asked only for coffee. That was all he ever felt like first thing in the morning.

"And that barmaid in Dozza?" Fitzwilliam let out a low whistle. "It's a shame she couldn't be prevailed upon to come home with us along with all the other keepsakes Grandmother demanded we bring back."

Christopher chuckled. "You can't bring a lady home like you do keepsakes."

Fitzwilliam nodded. "We would have needed a far bigger trunk, for one thing."

Christopher only looked up toward the sky and shook his head.

Though Fitzwilliam talked like a scoundrel, Christopher had never known him to actually do anything dishonorable, and they'd been together nearly every minute of every day for the better part of the past two years.

But that was all about to end. Christopher felt the coffee in his stomach turn over in a nauseating wave. He drew in a breath and focused on the road before them. He would deal with his uncertain future soon enough. For now, he was still at the mercy of his employer, the Dowager Fitzwilliam, who'd hired him as her grandson's tutor and traveling companion for his Grand Tour.

"Do you remember the way her eyes sparkled as she showed us the night sky?" Fitzwilliam said, his tone turning wistful. "They outshone even the stars."

Christopher pulled on his horse's reins, placing a bit more distance between himself and Fitzwilliam as the path widened. The man, with his blue eyes and hair so blond it was nearly white, could smile and have every woman in a fifty-foot radius batting her lashes and plying for a dance. Whether or not he could keep them around after he opened his mouth was quite another story. The gentleman was prone to say the most ridiculous things. Christopher sighed inwardly. He was going to miss Fitzwilliam when he had to leave.

"Perhaps," Christopher said, "if you had offered for her to travel with us *as a person* instead of inside a piece of luggage she would have been more open to the idea."

Fitzwilliam scoffed. "Where would the fun in that have been?"

As they neared the top of a small incline, the sound of a carriage rattling toward Curio Manor's front door reached them.

The men shared a look, though Fitzwilliam spoke first. "Were Grandmother's guests arriving today?"

Christopher nodded. "Today is the day." Then again, there were other aspects of this position he was not going to miss. When Christopher was hired to see after a man the same age as himself, he'd thought he'd be more friend and companion and less nursemaid and personal secretary. But he was paid to be what Fitzwilliam needed, and that often included remembering the baron's many obligations.

"Why did you not remind me this morning before we set out?"

"I reminded you last night, my lord." After which, Christopher had promptly retired and spent the next several hours before bed searching the newspaper for available positions. Then he'd tried to sleep, only to have strange dreams of being hired to look after the monkeys at the Royal Menagerie—little devils who crawled all over him, poking at him and scratching his head. His poor sleep was undoubtedly another reason why his typically reliable cup of coffee was not sitting well today.

"I am sorry, my lord," Christopher said. "I will try to remind you in a more timely manner in the future." Though that future would not be a long one.

"I wish you would," Fitzwilliam said, urging his horse forward to where he would have a clear view of the carriage and his home. "If I'd known they were arriving today, I would have had Cook pack us enough food for the day so we might not return until well after nightfall."

Christopher pulled his horse up next to Fitzwilliam's. "Do you not care to meet your Grandmother's guests?" He hadn't shown any signs of reluctance thus far.

Fitzwilliam shifted about in his saddle, a clear sign of discomfort. But not from horseback riding, Christopher would guess. Fitzwilliam rode often and hard.

Christopher turned his gaze toward Curio Manor. As expected, a large carriage was just rolling to a stop near the wide, elegant stairs that led to the front door. Two individuals on horseback rode nearby: a gentleman whose age Christopher could not tell from this distance and a young woman. As they dismounted, the footman opened the carriage door. First out was a woman Christopher thought he recognized. He squinted a bit to better make her out. If he wasn't mistaken, that was the esteemed Lady Blackmore. Gads, when the dowager had said she had guests coming, Christopher hadn't realized the party would include the widow of a marquess. Christopher tossed a glance toward his friend, who was also watching the party's arrival. Fitzwilliam was moving up in the world to be entertaining such a well-respected lady.

But did Lady Blackmore have any idea what kind of house she was stepping into?

Another young lady followed Lady Blackmore out, rubbing a hand over her face and pushing blonde curls back into place.

The four of them began to ascend the stairs. Halfway up, Lady Blackmore looked about, then turned toward the carriage. She called to someone, and though Christopher could hear her voice, he couldn't make out exactly what was said.

The carriage shifted slightly, and a fifth individual stepped out.

A lady, her hair darker than anyone else's present. She wore a purple dress, which she smoothed as she stepped out. She didn't hurry to catch up but instead took her time looking up and over all of Curio Manor. Even from here, Christopher could see the gentle turn of her neck, the gracefulness of her figure.

His heart gave a sudden jolt, one he felt across his whole chest and deep in his stomach.

Christopher rocked back, forcing his gaze away. Never before had he experienced such a reaction to any woman. What was his illogical heart about? He could barely see the lady, she was so far away. No doubt, once he saw her up close, it would be only to realize she was nothing out of the ordinary. Christopher pushed his lips to the side; too much time in the sun, that's what it was.

He pulled on the reins, turning his horse away from Curio Manor. Fitzwilliam fell into step beside him.

"You know," Christopher said, "if you are determined, there is a small pub an hour's ride away. We might find enough food and drink there to hold us well into the night."

"Capital idea," Fitzwilliam said, urging his horse forward. "Last one there pays for the drinks."

CHAPTER THREE

As the soft rays of morning's first light danced across her eyelids, Rachel woke. Drat, but she wasn't used to waking up so early. Her pillow was so soft, and her new room truly was all that was comfortable. Her eyes flitted shut once more.

No.

Rachel forced them open. She was *not* going to lay about. It had taken her late into the night, but she'd finally landed upon a plan. One that required an early start. Sitting up, Rachel blinked away the last bit of sleep and then swung her feet over the edge of the bed. Curio Manor truly was a magnificent country home—nothing at all like either home she'd grown up in, the first with her parents and then, after her father was taken to debtor's prison only to pass away soon thereafter, at her cousins' home two hours away.

Rachel stretched, willing alertness to flood into her arms and chest. She hadn't been able to visit her mother nearly as often as she'd wanted these past many years; their regular visit once a month had never felt like enough. How could one content themselves with seeing the person they loved most in the world only a few short hours ever thirty days? But Mother had, out of necessity, begun to take in not only wash and mending but boarders as well. It wasn't a home that a girl could be raised in, not if she wished to make a respectable match to a tradesman or shopkeeper. At least, that's what Uncle Seth had said, and Mother, too, the few times Rachel had pled to return home.

Rachel stood and moved over to the curtains, throwing them open. Still, there had always been a feeling, an impression that niggled at the back of Rachel's mind. Mother always appeared happy—overjoyed, truly—to see Rachel. Mother's smile was always bright and her words always positive. But her smile was never big enough to hide the bags under her eyes or the fact that she was frightfully thin. Her words were never upbeat enough to hide the exhaustion that ran like a forceful undercurrent just beneath the surface.

Uncle Seth frequently sent Mother money—Rachel knew that— and Mother was working hard making money herself. Yet, to look at her, one would think she hardly ate, hardly slept, hardly stayed warm in the winter or cool in the sweltering summer.

Rachel's eyes moved, unseeing, over the vista before her. Mother should be living comfortably. And if she wasn't, why not come live with Uncle Seth and Rachel? It didn't add up.

What weren't they telling her?

Rachel let out a long breath and leaned her forehead against the glass, shutting her eyes. Rachel's maternal grandmother had died quite suddenly while working in the fields. Too much exertion over too long a time, the doctor had said. Her husband passed on not nine months later when his heart gave out. Rachel had always believed that he simply didn't care to live without his wife. They, both, had not even been thirty. Far too young to be taken from their loved ones.

Would Mother die like either of her parents had? Either from working herself to the bone, or simply from loneliness and heartbreak?

It wasn't as though she hadn't spoken of her concerns. Many times over the previous years, Rachel had asked Uncle Seth why Mother could not just come live with them. And she'd asked Mother countless times if she was truly all right or if she needed more help. But both of them gave her the same lines they always did.

Mother needed to work to keep food on the table.

She was busy but perfectly healthy.

She didn't care to come live with Uncle Seth; she wanted her own home, her own life.

All was well.

Rachel didn't need to worry.

Unfortunately, all their words only made Rachel worry more.

During their last visit, just before leaving for London, Rachel had never seen Mother looking so fragile. Her cheeks were sunken, her wrist bones plainly visible. Even her smile was worn. It had always shone so brightly for Rachel, but it had been little more than a soft lift of her lips.

Rachel had returned to Uncle Seth's home more afraid for her mother than ever before.

And since then?

Mother had simply stopped writing. She had *always* written to Rachel in the past. They couldn't visit more than once a month, but at least they could write. Losing that had felt like the last bit of hope tying Rachel to the woman she loved most dearly had snapped. Rachel was floating, alone and without direction. Mother was sinking, slipping away from her desperate grasp.

For years, she'd trusted both Uncle Seth and Mother when they'd told her all was well. She'd ignored that prick in her gut that said things weren't how they seemed.

But she couldn't do that any longer. It was apparent, now more than ever, that Mother was not all right and that she needed someone by her side—someone who would see to her health and wellbeing. Someone who could help Mother realize she had to take care of herself as well as the sewing and laundry and boarders.

Simply put, Mother needed Rachel.

Which was why Rachel *wasn't* sleeping in today.

Rachel straightened and hurried over to the door which led to a closet so big, it was its own small room. Though she now owned more clothes than she ever had before in her life, her items looked paltry when hanging in the space. Her few things only took up one wall of the room, leaving all the rest empty. Still, she would gladly give up three rooms this size, bursting with clothes, if only she could see Mother once more.

Rachel pulled on her simplest dress then put some extra clothes in a small handbag. Her hand went to the locket about her neck. Ought she take it off? Nothing would be worse than losing the piece. Her hand moved around to the clasp at the back. Then again, it had never come loose before. Not once had she fretted over it slipping off her neck. No, she would keep it. After all, she would need the courage it gave her to complete her plan.

Rachel tugged on her riding boots, then she hurried back through her room and pulled open her bedchamber door. The corridor beyond was silent and empty; a few of the candles in their wall sconces still burned low.

Moving as silently as she could, Rachel stepped out into the corridor, shutting her door noiselessly behind her.

She looked across the hall, eying both doors which stood before her. One led to Eliza's room and the other to Dinah's. While she adored both her cousins—truly they were more sisters than cousins —Eliza would never condone Rachel's plans for the morning. Dinah, on the other hand, would most likely jump at the opportunity.

Only, which door was which? It had been so late last night when they'd finally retired, and yesterday had been nothing short of extremely overwhelming.

"May I be of service, miss?"

Rachel whirled around, hand going to her mouth.

"It is only me, Lorenzo the butler," the tall man said, bowing low.

Rachel breathed out a sigh of relief. "You scared me half to death."

"My deepest apologizes, miss." He didn't move to leave, but stood, waiting, the same orange cat she'd seen about his feet yesterday nearby once more. Rachel had never seen a cat who followed a particular individual about all day. Yet, she'd been told

Curio Manor was a unique household, unrivaled in its peculiarity by any in all of England.

Rachel turned away from the slightly unnerving glare of the cat's eyes. Her plan rested on her and Dinah getting out of the house unseen. "I am quite all right now, thank you. I only wished to speak with my cousin, Miss Dinah Mulgrave."

"The room on your left."

"Thank you." Rachel moved up to the door and turned the handle.

"That is what I am here for." He offered another bow and turned and left.

Rachel pushed the door open and stepped into the dark room. Hopefully, the butler wouldn't see her movements as anything unusual or worth noting to other members of the staff. Either way, at this point, Rachel wasn't going to change her mind. She tip-toed over to Dinah's bed and placed a hand against her cousin's shoulder.

"Dinah," Rachel said, shaking her softly. "Dinah, wake up."

Dinah's brow creased deeply, and she rolled onto her back. "Rachel?"

"How would you like to do something wild this morning?"

Dinah pushed herself up on her arms. "You know I'm all in."

Rachel smiled and stepped back as her cousin pulled herself out of bed and hurried to her own closet.

"What shall I wear?" Dinah called.

"Something easily stepped out of," Rachel responded.

Dinah's head appeared from around the door frame, her expression one of mixed curiosity and excitement. "What on earth are we doing?"

"We're going for a swim."

Dinah stared at her.

"Did you not notice the obliging lake just up the way? We passed it just before arriving yesterday."

Still, Dinah didn't say anything, neither did she move.

"I think a dip this morning shall be just the way to start our visit here."

Dinah stood up straight. "Are you sure you're my cousin, Rachel Chant?"

Rachel pursed her lips. "I could always go ask Eliza if you aren't up for it."

Dinah disappeared inside her closet once more. "You know I'm up for it," she said, her voice floating out, "I'm only shocked to hear you suggest such a thing."

"It isn't as though we're doing anything truly scandalous," Rachel called back. Just something a bit unseemly. If her uncle believed she was becoming too much to handle, perhaps he'd take her request to see her mother more seriously. "At this early hour, no one will be there to see us."

"Let us hope not," Dinah said, hurrying out of her closet even while pulling papers from her hair and sending random curls bouncing about her face. "If anyone does see us, this might be the shortest trip to the country anyone has ever taken."

Rachel could only hope for as much.

It took them no more than half an hour to sneak out of the manor and make their way down the empty road toward the lake.

It truly was a most lovely sight. The water was still, all except for off to Rachel's right where a few ducks paddled about. The sun was just stretching past the tree tops, chasing the last bits of darkness away from the western sky. The day was already promising to be warm. Nonetheless, the water could be wholly different.

Rachel slipped off her boots, not allowing herself time to hesitate, and lifted her skirts before dipping a toe into the water.

She pulled it back out immediately.

"Don't tell me you're getting cold feet now," Dinah teased.

Rachel shot her a glare. "If you're so brave, you can wade in first."

"Me? This was all your idea."

They both quickly removed their dresses and stood staring at one another in only their chemises.

Dinah took Rachel's hand. "We go in together."

Rachel nodded and they faced the still lake. Stepping together, they approached the water.

They each put one foot in. Rachel ground her mouth shut at the biting cold even as she heard Dinah inhale deeply.

"No backing down," Dinah chanted. "No backing down."

Rachel repeated the words in her head as they took a second step. The lake floor was rocky but blessedly, none of the rocks seemed particularly sharp.

They took another step, the water freezing Rachel's lower legs up to her knees.

"No backing down," Dinah continued, her teeth starting to chatter. "No backing down."

Rachel drew in a breath and then moved forward. The water deepened suddenly, rising up fully to their waist.

Dinah let out a squeal and Rachel clutched her cousin closer.

Cold. It was so intensely, freezing cold.

"No backing down." Rachel repeated the words.

Dinah nodded.

They both reached another foot out, but the rocks shifted below them. Rachel pulled back, keeping Dinah close to her.

"It gets deeper quite fast, it seems," Rachel said, turning and facing Dinah but not letting her go. Rachel wasn't sure if their hands bumped because Dinah was shivering so hard or because she was.

Dinah nodded again. "We should just dunk ourselves."

"What?" Rachel said, though her teeth knocked against themselves. "Completely under?"

"Y-y-yes. Get it over with."

Rachel was still reeling from her decision to come for a dip at all. She wasn't sure she was ready to be *this* brave.

"I'll count to three," Dinah said, pulling back slightly. "One." She held Rachel's gaze with a firm one of her own. "Two."

"I don't think—"

"Three!" Dinah dropped beneath the water, pulling Rachel down with her.

Rachel let out a scream as she was dragged under. Water filled her mouth before she could close it. As quickly as Dinah had dunked them, she let go of Rachel and stood up fully once more.

Rachel also pushed her head back above the water, sputtering and wiping furiously at her face. "I never agreed to that!"

Dinah was laughing, though. "This is what we came to do, isn't it?" With another laugh, she took off, swimming deeper into the lake.

Rachel wrapped her arms tightly around herself. She *was* already adjusting to the cold water, and she had to admit that going completely under had helped.

Halfway to the far side of the lake, Dinah stopped and turned back. "Come on, already," she called.

Rachel hesitated. The water directly next to her was warming. If she moved, it would only grow colder again.

Dinah waved to her, beckoning her to come.

Rachel shut her eyes for a moment, then steeled herself and dropped below the water's surface of her own accord this time. Pushing off the rocky lake bed, she propelled herself toward Dinah. Though ladies of the *ton* rarely learned to swim, it wasn't as though Rachel, Dinah, or Eliza had been *raised* by a knight. Uncle's new title was just that. New. Rachel had been born the daughter of a shopkeeper, and later had become the ward of a tradesman. As such, and with a lovely river in easy walking distance from her cousin's house, she, Dinah, and Eliza had all become quite proficient swimmers at a young age.

"This was a grand idea," Dinah said as Rachel drew near. The lake bed was too far below Rachel to stand, so she swirled her arms and legs about to keep herself afloat.

With a sigh, Dinah floated onto her back. "We should start every morning this way."

Perhaps they should. It might take nothing less than that for Uncle Seth to see he needed to send Rachel back to her mother. Rachel moved to roll onto her back herself, only a flock of birds took flight suddenly, their cries drawing Rachel's attention. They appeared to have been startled by something on the road.

Rachel turned herself about, facing that direction. There—the sound of horse hooves.

Drat.

"Dinah," she whispered. "Do you hear that?"

"Speak up. I can't hear you."

"Dinah!" Rachel gave her cousin a firm shove on the shoulder.

Dinah flailed a bit but managed to keep her head above water. "Be a bit more careful."

"Hush," Rachel said. If only she could cup her hand over Dinah's mouth. But she needed both her hands to keep afloat herself. "Do you hear that?"

Dinah, far from looking worried, only smiled all the brighter. "Someone's coming," she said with a giggle.

Rachel scowled. "The idea wasn't to get *caught* out here."

They both looked about.

"There," Dinah said after a minute. "We'll hide underneath those low-hanging branches."

Rachel eyed the trees. The branches did protrude most blessedly over the lake. But hiding there would take them quite close to the road.

"Are you certain?" Rachel asked.

Dinah was already swimming that way. "We're closer to those trees than the ones on the far side."

Rachel looked behind her. Dinah was right.

"Hurry up," Dinah called, now quite far away.

Rachel pushed with her legs and arms, quickly catching up to Dinah, and together they swam as quickly as their many years of experience granted them.

CHAPTER FOUR

"The hardest part will be sneaking in without Lorenzo knowing," Christopher said. Turning atop his horse, he looked over at Fitzwilliam. "Any ideas?"

Fitzwilliam slumped in his seat. "Blast this bright sun."

Christopher tried his best to hide his smirk. Though truth be told, his friend's headache was bad enough this morning, he probably wouldn't have had the wherewithal to notice a smirk. "I told you not to drink so much last night."

"I didn't drink *so much*. I only drank what was necessary." Fitzwilliam pushed his hat further down over his eyes. "Didn't you hear the lass talking of how her father would lose the pub soon if they weren't able to turn a better profit?"

"So?"

Fitzwilliam shrugged. "I was only doing my part to help them out."

Christopher chuckled.

"Please." His friend let go of his reins with one hand so that he might wave it at Christopher. "Not so loud."

"That's not me," Christopher countered. He had been laughing, but he could rarely be blamed for being boisterous.

"*Something* is being loud."

Christopher glanced about them. They'd scared a flock of birds moments ago and the fowls were making their annoyance known even as they flew off. There was a bit of splashing coming from the lake as well. Several pairs of ducks roosted there, so that was easy enough to explain.

"It's just the birds," Christopher explained. "Sparrows in the trees and ducks from the lake."

"The lake," Fitzwilliam muttered. "Lud, but I could do with a dunk about now."

"It won't make your head ache less."

"Might be worth the gamble to try." Fitzwilliam pulled too hard on his reins and his horse had to skip.

"Ho, there." Christopher caught up to his friend and took hold of the reins himself. "Be a bit gentler with your mount. The last thing either of us needs is for you to be thrown."

Fitzwilliam muttered beneath his breath, then dismounted.

Christopher followed suit, pulling both horses behind him as they neared the edge of the lake.

Fitzwilliam quickly removed his boots and stockings and stepped into the water. Immediately, he skipped back out again, declared it far too cold for any man, and sat down to pull his stockings back on. Christopher watched wordlessly all the while; there had been a time when he'd first been hired on to travel with Fitzwilliam that such actions would have annoyed Christopher. Now, knowing that such events would soon come to an end, Christopher only wished he could prolong their acquaintance.

"Hold up." Fitzwilliam's head snapped up. "This isn't my boot."

Christopher left the horses near a tree and walked over. "It has to be."

Fitzwilliam shook his head, holding the offending boot up. "Not unless it shrunk. And I may be hung over, but I'm certain *I* went into the water, not my boots."

Christopher took the black boot and turned it over. Clearly, it wasn't Fitzwilliam's. Not only was it too small, but it was a lady's boot, not a gentleman's. Where the blazes had it come from?

"Here they are." Fitzwilliam nearly fell off the log on which he sat as he reached over and grabbed his much larger boots.

Christopher looked over the lake and all about him, but he saw no one. "It must have been left here by someone yesterday, or even the day before." The boot didn't look like it had been out in the elements long, but it hadn't rained the past few days so one never knew.

With his own boots on once more, Fitzwilliam stood. "I know what to do." He motioned with his hand for Christopher to give the boot back.

The minute Fitzwilliam had hold of the boot, he turned toward the nearest tree and tossed it up. The boot sailed well above their heads and lodged itself near the top-most limb.

"What the blazes?" Christopher said, his gaze jumping from the stuck boot to his friend and then back again.

"The man who successfully reaches the boot and brings it back down first wins." Fitzwilliam began undoing the buttons on his jacket, stripping it off quickly.

"Why the devil would we want to do that?"

Fitzwilliam unfastened the buttons about his wrist and pushed up his sleeves. "Why not?"

Christopher placed his hands on his hips. "This wouldn't have anything to do with you avoiding returning home, would it?"

"Of course not." Fitzwilliam scowled. "But if it delays us another half an hour . . ." He waggled his eyebrows. In two large strides, Fitzwilliam was at the base of the tree. "I may have let you win on our race to the pub yesterday, but I won't go easy on you today."

"Let me win?" Christopher tugged his own jacket off. "I won fair and square, and you know it." He unbuttoned his sleeves, then carefully rolled them up and out of the way; it wouldn't do for them to start falling back down around his hands when he was halfway up the tree.

Taking a running start, Christopher kicked off the trunk of the tree, throwing himself up high enough to wrap both hands around a sturdy branch. With a heave, he lifted his torso up and onto the branch. Fitzwilliam laughed heartily as they both scrambled upward. Though they were on opposite sides of the tree, as they rose up, they drew closer to one another.

"Don't fall," Fitzwilliam said with a laugh. "I'm sure I drank too much last night to carry your sorry carcass back to the manor."

"I'm sure you drank too much to win," Christopher replied, passing Fitzwilliam.

With a playful grunt, Fitzwilliam stopped climbing.

Christopher, nearly to the boot, paused and looked down. "Don't tell me you're stuck."

"There are too many small branches above me; I can't get any higher this way." He reached a hand around the trunk, now much smaller than at its base. "I'm coming up behind you."

"The devil you are. There isn't space on this side for both of us."

"Sure there is." He pulled himself so that he was directly beneath Christopher. The tree swayed dangerously in their direction.

"Blast, I think I may still be drunk," Fitzwilliam called. "I could have sworn the tree was tipping."

"It is, you idiot," Christopher called down. "Get back over to your side. We're too high up to both be pulling the tree this direction."

Fitzwilliam said something that sounded quite like, "perhaps you're right," but Christopher didn't ask him to repeat it. He was just relieved the tree righted itself as soon as Fitzwilliam returned to the opposite side among the topmost branches.

"Well, can you reach the boot?" Fitzwilliam called up.

Christopher placed a hand against a branch and pulled himself up, but the footwear was still just out of reach.

"It seems not," he called back. "Let me try again." He angled himself around to the left a bit, stepping on another branch at knee height, and pushed himself upward.

The branch beneath his foot snapped. His stomach flew into his throat. Christopher clutched the tree tightly with his left hand, catching his fall. He placed his other hand against the main trunk and steadied himself.

"Good heavens, man," Fitzwilliam called. "A silly boot isn't worth your life."

No, it wasn't. Christopher shot his friend a quick smile to let him know he was all right and then began climbing down. As he passed Fitzwilliam, the gentleman reached out and clasped his arm.

"Remind me next time I'm hung over to not go around throwing boots."

Only Fitzwilliam would think there could ever be a 'next time.' Still, he didn't like leaving the boot in the tree. He wasn't used to leaving messes for others to clean up. Even as he followed Fitzwilliam, he glanced back up at the lady's boot. He couldn't like leaving it there—he'd forever wonder if they hadn't been the cause of much distress.

Together, they made their way down. The horses grazed calmly where Christopher had left them. It only took a moment to roll their sleeves back down and pull on their jackets.

Fitzwilliam mounted first. "Perhaps we ought to return to the pub. A man could certainly do with a good drink after a near fall like that. I'll buy you one."

"I think," Christopher said, mounting his own horse, "it's time we return to the manor and you greet your grandmother's guests."

"Very well," Fitzwilliam said with an exasperated breath. "But I'm only doing this for you because you almost died this morning."

Christopher chuckled even as they started forward; the mood never stayed heavy for long when Fitzwilliam was around. "That is quite generous of you." Nonetheless, despite his friend's attempt at levity, Christopher couldn't shake his unease over leaving the boot in the tree.

"Most certainly. For all we know, Grandmother has invited long-winded, decrepit old friends to bore us with stories of their childhood."

"Just so long as you don't tell the dowager *she's* old and decrepit." Though Fitzwilliam and his grandmother had a close and caring relationship, Christopher had known Fitzwilliam to speak his mind a little too freely on many occasions.

Fitzwilliam laughed loudly; it seemed his hangover had been

cured by the fear of them both falling from the tree. "I did one time, you know. When I was only a boy."

"I can't imagine she took it well."

"It was just after . . ." His smile slipped a bit. "She'd only just come to live at Curio Manor."

Christopher nodded his head in understanding. There was only one thing that made Fitzwilliam less than jovial—the memory of his parents' unexpected passing. It was then that the dowager had come to live at Curio Manor. Had come to raise Fitzwilliam, in all honesty.

Fitzwilliam's smile returned quickly enough. "I was upset, though I don't recall why, and I called her old and withered and I don't remember what else." He chuckled. "She gave me such a talking to."

"Even worse than when you secreted two frogs into church in your pocket?"

"Most certainly. She was even madder than when one of the gossips told her I'd kissed all the girls in the neighborhood—all on the same day."

Christopher turned in his seat. "I haven't heard about that one."

Fitzwilliam waggled his eyebrows again. "It was a good day."

"One can only hope you didn't leave a few dozen broken hearts in your wake."

Fitzwilliam scowled. "I believe in having a good time, but I would never be so careless as to do so. Though I suppose it *wouldn't* have been a good time for one so gallant as you."

"Lay off." How could a man such as himself ever be considered gallant? A man whose entire worldly possessions could fit into a single trunk, whose entire life was made up of going from job to job and doing whatever his current employer asked of him, who had no standing among society?

"I am in earnest," Fitzwilliam pressed. "I don't think I've ever seen you inconvenience a soul if it was within your power to avoid it."

Christopher slowed his horse to a stop, his father's voice floating through his mind. *Never leave a person worse off for having crossed paths with you.*

"Actually," Christopher said, "I think I will try for that boot again." Though he didn't see himself as anything so ideal as "gallant," Fitzwilliam had been accurate on one point. Christopher didn't like to leave work for others that truly should be his own.

"You prove my point," Fitzwilliam said with a shake of his head as he reined in next to Christopher.

"Regardless, suppose the owner comes back looking for it?"

"Why would the owner come back? If she'd wanted the boot, she would have taken it with her and not left it by the lake in the first place."

"It is possible she lost it and will come back to look again." Christopher turned his horse about. It was probably pointless but leaving the boot in the tree just did not sit right with him. It wasn't something his father would have done; it wasn't something his father would have wished *him* to do. Though Christopher couldn't claim to have received anything in the way of wealth or social position from his father, he had received frequent lessons on how a gentleman comports himself. It was the best sort of legacy a father could leave, and Christopher had no desire to part with it. "Do not wait for me. I know your grandmother will be anxious to see you."

"But you couldn't reach it last time," Fitzwilliam called, even though Christopher was already riding back. "What makes you think you'll reach it this time?"

"I'll carry a stick up with me and knock the boot from its perch." Not waiting for his friend to say more, Christopher rode back toward the tall tree and the small boot.

***

The moment the two gentlemen climbed atop their horses and turned to leave, Rachel let out a long, pent-up breath.

"Gracious," Dinah said, managing to giggle even as she shivered. "I truly thought they were going to pull the entire tree down with them."

Rachel glanced about once more, but the gentlemen were gone for sure. She hurried out of the freezing water. Once she and Dinah had secreted themselves beneath the low-hanging branches of the tree, they'd had to remain quite still to avoid making any noise. At least they hadn't been caught. Hurrying up the bank, Rachel grabbed her dress and pulled it on quicker than she ever had before.

"I suppose we were lucky all they saw was one of my boots," Rachel said, tugging her dress fully into place.

"I just about died when they found that much," Dinah said, halfway into her own dress. "What a disaster it would have been had they found our dresses and the other boots." Though Dinah used such foreboding words, her tone made it sound as though she would have welcomed such an occurrence.

Rachel tugged on her stockings and then picked up her untouched boot, carrying it with her as she moved toward the tall tree.

Dinah hurried up to stand beside her. "I fear it is a lost cause."

"If I don't return with both my boots, someone will start asking questions." If she'd had multiple pairs, perhaps she could lose one and no one would be the wiser. As it was, she needed these boots.

Dinah slowly turned her gaze on Rachel. "Don't tell me you are *actually* considering . . ." She fell silent, instead choosing to merely point toward the boot suspended above their heads.

"I must." Rachel sat the boot she'd been holding near the trunk and reached above her head for the lowest branch. "Come, give me a lift."

"I do not know what London has done to you, Rachel," Dinah said, moving over and dropping to her hands and knees. "But I think I like this new version of you better."

Rachel stepped onto Dinah's back and easily reached the lowest branch. She pulled herself up. Her wet chemise beneath her dress clung and stuck most uncomfortably. But she only needed to tolerate it until they were back at Curio Manor, then she could change. Before that could happen though, she needed her other boot.

She climbed from one branch to the next, quickly rising higher and higher.

She neared the spot where the two men had stopped. Though she hadn't been able to make out most of what they'd said to one another, she had heard the jest in their tone, the easy manner they had with one another. She'd never seen either gentleman in her entire life, though that was hardly surprising. The one with light hair was, perhaps, more striking. But it was the other who had drawn her attention most. His voice had been quieter, more confident. His features were more becoming as well—a straight nose and well-defined chin; the morning sun had revealed a bit of auburn in his brown hair. When he'd first taken her boot, he'd turned just enough that she'd caught sight of his blue eyes. It wasn't often one met a man with dark hair and light eyes. But Rachel found she liked the combination quite a lot.

Rachel could easily see her boot now. She reached a hand up, but her fingers were still several inches away from the footwear. She had to get a bit higher. Lucky for her, she didn't weigh as much as either man, certainly not as much as them combined, and the tree didn't sway with her movements. She turned about the trunk a bit and continued up to her right, finding better branches up that way.

Two more attempts and she had the boot in her hand.

Relieved, Rachel glanced down to toss the boot to Dinah. Only, Dinah wasn't anywhere to be seen. Rachel searched all below her; where would her cousin have gone? Still holding her boot, Rachel carefully made her way down the tree, pausing once she was nearly to the lowest branches. Still, she could not see Dinah.

There was the sound of footsteps and a man's head came into view.

Rachel sucked in a breath. Oh, how she hoped he wouldn't look up. If only he continued on his way, she could get down after he left and be safe.

No such luck. He continued to look about the forest floor for several minutes—though what he was hoping to find, she couldn't imagine. Rachel eased herself more fully onto a thick branch, tucking her skirt tightly around her legs and allowing her arms some respite. Comfortably seated, she watched the man closely.

Why—it was the same brown-haired, blue-eyed gentleman who'd been here before.

What reason could he have for returning now? Certainly he wasn't hoping to find the other boot. Perhaps she and Dinah hadn't remained as unnoticed as they'd believed.

He bent down and picked up a long, thin stick. "Just the thing," he said softly, turning the stick over in his hand. He approached the very tree she was in and, being taller than her, easily took hold of the lowest branch.

He must be attempting to get her boot again. Rachel looked about, but she was undeniably stuck. It wasn't as though there was anywhere to go. The gentleman hoisted himself up with admirable ease, but with his gaze focused on his hands and feet, he hadn't yet looked up and spotted her.

Rachel peered down toward the forest floor. Perhaps if she simply jumped . . .

No, that was utter foolishness. Of course he'd see her as she fell past him, and she was much too far off the ground to land without bruising herself or worse, breaking something. As the man climbed nearer, Rachel felt the moment he would become aware of her creeping closer as one feels a spider crawling up one's leg.

Unable to await the inevitable any longer, Rachel coughed softly.

The man's head snapped up. He saw her, his eyes going wide. In his shock, his foot lost its perch and he slipped, catching himself almost immediately, much as he had the first time he'd climbed the tree.

Regaining his footing, his gaze came back to Rachel.

He was only a couple of feet away, and from this close, it was clear his eyes were even bluer than she'd originally realized. The red in his hair was more prominent as well.

"Good morning to you, sir," Rachel said calmly.

His brow creased. "Good morning to you as well, miss."

There was a silence as they both did no more than look at the other.

"It is a most pleasant morning, isn't it?" Rachel asked at length.

Still appearing quite confused, the man nodded. "We have been enjoying a rather long stretch of fine weather."

Again, they both fell silent.

The man's gaze fell to the boot in Rachel's hand. "You retrieved it."

She lifted it up, tipping it first one way and then another. "As you see."

He crossed his arms and rested them atop a branch, hanging heavily on it. "However did you manage?"

"I suppose there are benefits to being smaller and of a lighter weight than a man."

"Then you saw my earlier attempt?" Though he still looked wholly uncertain as to why he'd just found a woman in a tree—could he be blamed?—Rachel could hear the smile in his voice.

"Guilty," she said, feeling her own smile surface.

"Then it is your boot we so rudely put in harm's way."

"I am afraid so." She nodded politely, the movement sending a trail of water from her still soaking wet hair down her back.

The corner of his lips ticked upward. "Please accept my apologies for the inconvenience my friend and I unknowingly caused you."

"It is quite all right."

"And please," he reached a hand out, "allow me to help you down."

"Very well." She took his hand only to realize after her fingers wrapped around his glove that her own was bare. Gracious, could this moment get any more embarrassing? Surely he must think her a country bumpkin. Then again, just over a year ago, that's all she'd been. He helped guide her from one branch to another, which was truly helpful since she was so mortified at having been caught dripping wet and in a tree, she didn't believe she could have thought clearly enough to get herself down safely.

Eventually, the man helped her sit on the lowest branch of the tree.

"Hold on," he said and dropped to the forest floor himself. He looked back up at her. "Go ahead; I'll catch you."

41

"You certainly shall not, sir," Rachel called back. Of all the mortifying things. Her only consolation at this moment was that at least she did not blush so easily as Eliza. "I am certain I can jump from this height without injuring myself."

"Or you can just trust me to catch you."

Rachel shook her head. "Step back or I shan't jump at all." She waved a hand, indicating that he should step away.

The gentleman stared at her for a moment, and Rachel gave him her firmest, most determined stare back. Finally, with a sigh, the man moved away. Rachel shifted about on the branch, readying to jump, and the man leaned forward.

"Don't even think about trying to catch me," Rachel said, motioning again for him to back up.

With another sigh, the man did, taking three long steps backward, and folded his arms.

Content that he was much too far away to interfere with her shameful drop from the tree, Rachel slipped herself off the branch. The ground rushed up faster than she'd expected. She hit and couldn't keep her balance, tumbling to her knees.

The man was beside her instantly, a hand at her arm, helping her stand. Twigs and leaves along the forest floor bit easily through her stockings, pricking at her feet.

"Are you all right?" he asked.

"Yes, quite." She pulled her arm from him. No doubt, even though he was wearing gloves, he'd noticed how wet her sleeve was. "Nothing strained or bruised." While she'd hit harder than she'd expected, she didn't feel she'd injured herself in any way. Bending down, she retrieved her other boot from beside the tree. "Now if you will excuse me, sir, I shall be on my way."

"May I see you back home?"

"No." The word rushed from her far too quickly. Rachel took a deep breath. "I am quite all right and do not wish to trouble you further."

"Very well. I bid you good morning."

"You as well, sir." Rachel curtsied as he bowed. She remained standing where she was as he turned and left. Only after he was well out of sight did she move to sit and replace her boots.

"Wasn't he handsome?" Dinah said, emerging from behind a tree.

"Fat lot of help you were," Rachel grumbled.

"I couldn't let him see me all dripping wet." Dinah motioned toward herself.

Rachel cringed—oh, how she hoped she didn't look as soggy as her cousin. "I think this may be my first and last foray into the slightly scandalous."

"I hope not." Dinah twisted about, looking in the direction the gentleman had gone. "Not when your forays end so beautifully."

"You call dripping wet and stuck in a tree beautiful?"

Dinah sighed. "*He* was."

"Then next time, *you* are more than welcome to chase my boot." The gentleman, kind though he had been, had no doubt guessed she'd been swimming. What must he think of her? Swimming first and then climbing trees. Her only hope was that she never saw him again.

CHAPTER FIVE

"A lovely morning, is it not?" the dowager asked, smiling at Fitzwilliam as brightly as the yellow ribbon in her hair.

Christopher couldn't help but smile as well. There was something about the elderly lady that always made him want to smile. Perhaps it was how cheerful she always seemed, or that no matter her years, she still wore ribbons in her hair at breakfast.

"Quite fine, quite fine," Fitzwilliam agreed, stabbing a bit of ham with his fork.

They sat in the dowager's sitting room, same as they did every morning for breakfast, a fine spread of food on the table between them. Christopher had been rather surprised that the dowager was not taking breakfast with her guests. But apparently, she'd been told by the maids that her guests were all still tired from the day before and taking breakfast in their own chambers, so there had been no need to entertain this morning.

Christopher had expected to feel a touch relieved over the revelation; no doubt, from here on out, he and Fitzwilliam would be expected at every meal. But he hadn't. Christopher couldn't seem to get his mind to stay focused on the lighthearted conversation between Fitzwilliam and his grandmother.

Instead, his mind kept returning to the young woman he'd met in the tree not more than an hour ago. She'd been so polite, very nearly regal in her decorum and manner of speech, with a simple yet respectable attire and an elegant locket about her neck. And yet, she'd been dripping wet and up a tree. Her conduct and her situation were at such odds—one quite seemed to defy the other—that Christopher had to admit to being wholly diverted. She seemed a walking contradiction.

"I blame Dunn," Fitzwilliam said.

Christopher's focus returned to the conversation at hand. "Blame me?"

"Quite," Fitzwilliam said with a nod, turning back to his grandmother. "He was so far into his cups last night, it was all I could do to drag him into a bed at the nearest inn. Believe me, if I had been on my own, I would have gladly returned home before dinner."

Christopher huffed. Not that he actually worried the dowager would believe Fitzwilliam's bounder. The dowager doted on Fitzwilliam, but that didn't mean the man could mislead her as easily as all that.

"You drink far more than Dunn ever did," the dowager said, tsking. "Don't go blaming your sorry problems on him."

Far from looking repentant, Fitzwilliam only smiled all the more for having been caught.

"I think," the dowager said, turning toward Christopher, "he's hiding from my guests."

Christopher tipped his cup of coffee slightly toward her, a salute to her astute perception.

"I'm not hiding." Fitzwilliam scoffed. "I am a busy man with much on my mind."

"Such as what?" Christopher asked. Fitzwilliam's estate all but ran itself. The dowager had been most discerning when employing their solicitor, man of business, butler, housekeeper, and other important individuals. Neither she nor her grandson had much at all to worry over.

"Such as seeing to tenants and the staff. Curio Manor employs quite a large number of people, you know."

Christopher shook his head and took another sip of coffee. A large staff, yes. Individuals who needed Fitzwilliam's constant attention? Certainly not.

"Well, then," the dowager said. "If you aren't hiding from my guests, then you won't mind joining us this afternoon. Lady Blackmore has expressed a desire to see the gardens."

"The gardens?" Fitzwilliam whined like a five-year-old boy.

"Yes," the dowager pressed. "The gardens. And I am sure the young ladies Lady Blackmore has brought with her will have a desire to walk the path further than I can. Therefore, I shall need you there to see they are properly escorted and shown the best views."

"I do believe I have a meeting with my man of business this afternoon," Fitzwilliam quipped.

"You have not." The dowager shook her head.

Christopher finished his coffee and set the cup on the table. "Don't worry, Lady Fitzwilliam, he'll be there."

"You can't order me about." Fitzwilliam turned on Christopher. "I pay your salary. You do as I say."

"With all respect," Christopher said, leaning back in his seat. "You don't. Your grandmother does."

The dowager turned toward her grandson, nose held high and her smile confident. "That's right, I pay him out of my own pin money."

"Hang it all." Fitzwilliam slouched. "I forgot that part."

"If you *saw* the young ladies that Lady Blackmore brought with her, I doubt you'd find reason to hide," the dowager continued.

"I wouldn't be so sure," Christopher said. "I've seen him hide from any number of young ladies."

"Hide from a lady?" Fitzwilliam grumbled. "I would never do such a thing."

The dowager ignored his complaints. "There is one of the ladies, in particular, I wish you to meet."

"Oh?" Fitzwilliam returned to eating.

"Her name is Miss Rachel Chant. She is quiet and polite. Exactly the sort of woman you need."

Fitzwilliam seemed surprised. "How can you think that someone quiet and polite is right for me?"

Christopher wondered the same thing.

"She'll be the calming influence you need," the dowager said. "I know once you two are settled, you'll see I was right."

Settled? Christopher and Fitzwilliam shared a look.

"You don't mean I should *marry* the lady, do you?" Fitzwilliam said, his voice catching.

"Would you, please?" the dowager asked, quite as though she were asking him to pick her up another ribbon next time he was in Town. "I would so appreciate it if you proposed." She returned to her tea as though there was nothing more to say on the subject.

"I cannot propose," Fitzwilliam said. He glanced again at Christopher.

Oh no, Christopher wasn't about to be dragged into such a conversation as this. He held up his hands in surrender. Fitzwilliam was on his own.

"I don't even know the girl," Fitzwilliam continued.

"What is there to know? She's the ward of a Sir Mulgrave, a respectable man. She is unassuming and carries herself with great decorum." The dowager glanced up at her grandson. "Don't look at me like that. Surely by now you've realized you need to marry and produce an heir sooner or later."

"Yes, and I choose later."

Lady Fitzwilliam waved him off. "Pish-posh. You are back from your Grand Tour and 'later' is here."

"Dunn," Fitzwilliam said. "We're sailing back to Italy. I think my Grand Tour has just been extended for another five years at least."

"Silly boy," the dowager said with a light laugh. "I do thank you both for joining me this morning. I'm afraid this is the last breakfast we shall enjoy alone for some time. Starting tomorrow, I want you both in the breakfast room with my guests." Placing a hand heavily against the arm of her chair, the dowager pulled herself to her feet.

Christopher stood as well. "We'll be there." He bowed in her direction.

"I won't be." Fitzwilliam scoffed. "And sit back down. We're having this out right now. I'm not marrying any ward of a knight just because she's quiet and what have you."

Still, Christopher headed toward the door. "Either way, you'll have to excuse me. I *do* have some things to see to before this afternoon."

"Now see here," Fitzwilliam started even as Christopher opened the door and stepped out. He shut the door firmly, blocking out his friend's objections.

Two maids bustled down the corridor, quickly polishing the wall sconces and candlesticks sitting atop a side table before rushing off to finish cleaning other parts of the large manor. What was it the young lady he met in the tree did with herself all day? She'd worn an elegant enough dress that he didn't think she was a maid. Then again, it had been so wet, he could have been mistaken. Her manner of speech was refined, yet not as lofty or self-important as many ladies of the *ton* he'd met. No matter how he mulled over the encounter, he couldn't seem to make out where among society's many layers she fit.

Perhaps she was like him, shoved between one layer and another, not really fitting anywhere. Christopher's grandfather, Mr. Adolphus Dunn, had been a member of the landed gentry and quite a wealthy one at that. Or so Christopher had been told. Some years before he was born, Christopher's father and grandfather had a falling out—supposedly over Father's desire to compose music instead of acting like a "proper" gentleman, and his father had left home, refusing to speak to any of his family ever again.

He hadn't either, instead traveling the Continent, eventually marrying and having his own son. The few times Christopher had inquired after his history, Father had simply stated that he had been the second son, the spare, and quite unnecessary to anyone's happiness.

And so, Christopher had grown with never a word from his grandfather or uncle, the beloved heir. Life as the son of a musician had not been full of wealth or notoriety. But they'd gotten along well enough. His father had made enough to make sure Christopher was raised with a proper English education.

Christopher reached his own room and walked in. The Fitzwilliams were good to him; his room was large and comfortable. He had all he could ever ask for here. It was quite the best position he'd ever been blessed to have. Walking toward the chair closest to the hearth, he picked up the paper waiting for him. He skimmed over it. He'd had a good life. Only, now he didn't truly fit among the servants or tenants of Curio Manor, but neither was he a man of means or title, such as Fitzwilliam.

Certainly he had nothing that would recommend him to a lady. Not that he could ever make a remarkable impression with or without means. Why, only that morning, when he'd found the young lady in the tree and offered to walk her home, she'd refused him. He'd guessed she would say no, but oddly, he'd found he wanted to prolong their time together.

The paper grew slack in his hand, his fingers aching to dance across a set of ivory keys. It had been two days since last he played. No doubt, it was the single way in which he and his father were most alike—neither of them could go long without music. Christopher shook out the paper and lifted it higher. He needed to focus for the time being. Perhaps later there would be time for music. Now, though, he needed to secure himself a new position, and soon. More still, he needed to shake the image of the lovely young lady from his mind. No matter her pull on him, he was a man without a home or the possibility of stability and that wasn't about to change.

CHAPTER SIX

Rachel descended the stairs. She'd flatly refused to come out of her room after she and Dinah had slipped back into the manor that morning, regardless of Charlotte's insistence that she join them for breakfast. Rachel had endured enough humiliation for the day—for the next year—and she hadn't wanted to tempt fate by leaving her room again so soon.

Nonetheless, she had wanted to see the gardens, and if she'd remained in her room any longer, she feared the doctor would have been sent for. That would not do. Rachel reached the second floor and crossed toward the sitting room where they were all to meet.

Soft strains of a melody reached her. Rachel paused mid-step. Was that a pianoforte she was hearing? Rachel moved back toward the stairs and peered upward. When Lady Fitzwilliam gave them all a tour of the house, she'd mentioned that there was a music room with a very fine pianoforte on the fourth floor, in the wing opposite the guest bedchambers, but the elderly lady grew tired quickly and had been unable to actually show them the room. Rachel had been most anxious to see it.

However, the music did not seem to be coming from a floor above, but rather one below. Was there a second pianoforte, then?

Oh, to have the means necessary to own *two* such lovely instruments. Rachel glanced toward the sitting room door. It was open and she could hear voices coming from within, but if she were delayed a moment or two, surely that wouldn't put anyone out. Most likely, not all the party was gathered by now anyways. Rachel hurried down the stairs. The music grew more distinct as she descended, though never truly loud.

She reached the main entrance and turned about. Which direction now?

"Good afternoon, miss. It is I, Lorenzo the butler."

Rachel nodded; did he *always* introduce himself? She'd not seen him once since removing to Curio Manor when he had not. Sure enough, the orange cat stood nearby. "I was following the sound of the pianoforte."

"Ah yes, that would be his lordship's tutor, Mr. Dunn. He is the son of a musician, I understand, and plays exceptionally well."

How interesting. Was not Lord Fitzwilliam rather grown for a tutor? Most likely the man had been his lordship's tutor for many, many years and the family simply had not wanted to let him go. "Is he not playing in the music room Lady Fitzwilliam told us of?" Perhaps the elderly tutor wouldn't mind if Rachel sat and listened to him play now and then. Even better, perhaps he would let her play as well. Uncle Seth had bought a small pianoforte for her when she first came to live with him, Eliza, and Dinah. But they hadn't had one in London. Rachel's hand moved to the locket about her neck. Next to her mother, music was the thing she'd missed the most.

"No, miss. He plays in there but rarely. More often, he chooses to enjoy the pianoforte in the servants' quarters."

That could prove a bit of a problem. Guests were rarely permitted to enter that part of a house. Still . . .

"Might I persuade you," Rachel asked, turning her voice sweet, "to show me the way?"

"The pianoforte in the music room"—he motioned up the stairs —"is far superior."

"No doubt." But she'd wanted to meet the older man who played so well.

The music swelled from . . . the *back* of the house, Rachel would guess? It called to her. Beckoned her to come and find it.

"There you are," Charlotte called from the top of the stairs. "Rachel, dear, do hurry up. We are nearly all gathered and ready to start out."

She let out a sigh, glancing once more toward the siren call of the pianoforte, and then turned toward the stairs. Very well; she would have to meet Mr. Dunn and play the pianoforte another time. She slowly began to ascend the stairs. The music softened and soon it was lost to her completely.

Charlotte wrapped her arm through Rachel's the moment she reached the top of the stairs; either Charlotte was unusually excited to see her this afternoon, or Rachel had been making herself a bit too scarce as of late and Charlotte was worried she'd disappear again if not held tightly enough.

"I had rather expected you to be one of the first ones in the sitting room," Charlotte said as they moved that direction. "I know how keenly you enjoy gardens."

Rachel did love a proper English garden. Most likely, she would have been one of the first in the sitting room if not for the music that had called to her. "Are the gardens here extensive, then?" she asked, pushing aside the bubbling desire to make an excuse and find Lord Fitzwilliam's tutor instead.

"Yes, quite," Charlotte said. "I understand Lord Fitzwilliam's late father was quite the botanist and spent many long hours seeing that all was set just so."

They entered the sitting room to find Eliza and Dinah already seated comfortably by the hearth with Lady Fitzwilliam in a chair nearby. Dinah and the dowager were having a quiet conversation, one that seemed, based on the few words Rachel heard, to be about the latest fashion plates. Eliza, not surprisingly, was quiet, her hand absently running over the golden bracelet her betrothed had gifted her just before they'd left London. Eliza had not been long engaged, but never had Rachel known her to be happier.

The dowager noticed Rachel and Charlotte, and she smiled. "You have found her already?" Her eyes were bright, and though her face sported many wrinkles, there was something about her demeanor and manner of expression that almost put Rachel to mind of a young girl, one forever eager for life. Perhaps Lady Fitzwilliam was more accurately described as a youth who had refused to grow old, despite her human frame's best attempts to do so.

"You have quite bested me then," the dowager continued, "for I have yet to find my own grandson. Never fear, though. I sent Mrs. Crampton to Mr. Dunn. He always manages to get my grandson to do things he does not wish to do."

"Mr. Dunn?" Dinah asked as Rachel and Charlotte crossed the room to sit beside her. "I do not believe you have mentioned him to us before now."

"Have I not?" Lady Fitzwilliam looked about herself for a moment, clearly surprised. "Do forgive my addled brain. Mr. Dunn is Fitzwilliam's tutor and is a very fine man."

If that were true, then perhaps he and Rachel could find some time to enjoy music together. Though she had no desire to spend much time in the company of Lord Fitzwilliam, she could always find time for music.

"A fine man?" A masculine voice spoke from the doorway. "Is someone speaking of me again?"

Rachel turned. A man with shockingly light hair stood just inside the room. His smile was broad as he strode forward. He seemed vaguely familiar, and as his gaze turned from her cousins onto her, Rachel suddenly remembered where she'd seen him.

Earlier that morning—this was the very man who'd first thrown her boot up into the tree. It had been his friend that she had spoken to. Rachel turned toward the others once more, angling her back toward him a bit. Had his friend told him of her? Would he say anything?

Yes, she'd hoped her swimming would get back to Uncle Seth and he'd start to wonder if keeping her away from Mother for so long was such a good idea—but she didn't want to cause a huge scene right here in Lady Fitzwilliam's sitting room. Rachel caught Dinah's eye, but she either didn't know who they were speaking to, or she was a *much* better actress than Rachel had ever given her credit for.

"Good afternoon to you ladies," Lord Fitzwilliam began. His grandmother made the necessary introductions and soon they were moving toward the doors, readying themselves to go outside.

"Is Mr. Dunn not joining us, then?" Dinah asked.

"Sure he is," Lord Fitzwilliam said. "He only needed to grab a hat and walking stick first."

Yes, of course. Rachel was rather surprised that Lady Fitzwilliam had not brought a walking stick for herself as well. Though, it was possible that the tutor was even more advanced in years than she.

"Ah." Lord Fitzwilliam stopped the group just as they were about to step out of doors. "Here he is now."

Rachel looked back the way his lordship indicated but saw no elderly man. No stooped walk or shuffled step. Instead, she saw—

Oh, drat.

It was the very man she'd spoken with in the tree that morning.

Rachel hid her groan but stepped slightly to her right, placing herself a bit behind Eliza. Just how hard would it be to remain out of sight of this man for the duration of their garden tour?

Impossible, unfortunately.

He strode quickly toward the gathered party, an extremely tall hat in one hand and a most expensive-looking walking stick in the other. As he neared them, he tossed first one and then the other across the corridor and directly into Lord Fitzwilliam's waiting hands.

His lordship caught them easily and spun about on his heel, rather as though the force of catching the flying walking stick made him do it. He placed the hat atop his blond hair with a dramatic twirl and positioned the stick just so in front of him. "Rather completes the images, wouldn't you agree?" he asked them all, motioning toward his ensemble. Then he turned back toward the man Rachel was trying to avoid eye contact with. "Thank you, my good man. Ladies, may I introduce you to Mr. Dunn?" Once more, names, bows, and curtsies were exchanged.

When Lord Fitzwilliam introduced her, Rachel kept her eyes down for all but the briefest of glances up. It was enough, though, for her to see that Mr. Dunn clearly remembered her from that morning. Here she'd been so certain that she would never have to see him again. So much for that. Perhaps she best fake a headache from now until Uncle Seth finally saw fit to take them all away from this place.

With Lord Fitzwilliam and the two older ladies talking easily about the fine weather, and Eliza and Mr. Dunn falling into step behind them, Rachel took hold of Dinah's arm and held her back, seeing to it that they were the last two to exit the manor.

"I can't believe it's him," Rachel whispered once there was enough space between them and the others.

"Who?"

"Mr. Dunn," Rachel said. "That's the man who found me in the tree this morning."

"So?" Dinah truly seemed a bit puzzled as to why Rachel found such a thing so distressing.

"But he recognizes me, I am sure of it."

"Of course he does," Dinah said with a confused laugh. "You conversed face to face. How could he not?"

"Suppose he says something? I am certain he knew we were swimming."

"He knows *you* were swimming. He never saw me."

Rachel threw her cousin a sideways scowl. But it was true. Completely unhelpful for Dinah to bring up, but true all the same.

"I wouldn't fret if I were you," Dinah continued.

"That is easy to say for the one who wasn't caught."

Dinah pulled Rachel to a stop and faced her fully. "Why did you wish to swim this morning? I sincerely doubt it was because you were hot and needed a cooling dip."

At that time in the morning? Obviously not. It wasn't even June yet.

Dinah's lips pulled to the side. "Was it to get in my father's black books, perhaps?"

How had she guessed?

Rachel's consternation must have shown for Dinah only laughed. "You aren't the first one who's used mischief and carefully aimed scandal to get Father to do one's bidding." Dinah looped her arm around Rachel's, and they began walking once more. "Tell me this, then. If you did it *for* the scandal, then why are you hiding it?"

"I want Uncle Seth to allow me to return to Mother. I have no desire to become the laughingstock of all London."

For once, the laughter left Dinah's words. "You mean more than we already are?"

Rachel nodded. These past few months had been hard on them all. Uncle Seth had been knighted, but that didn't mean the upper echelon was willing to welcome his daughters and niece with open arms.

Mr. Dunn said something to Eliza, and she held out her wrist, showing off the bracelet.

Rachel set her jaw. "I think I need to speak with him."

Dinah lifted a single eyebrow. "First swimming and now seeking a gentleman out? Dear me, Father had best remove you back home and soon. Next, you'll be walking the ridgepole of a roof."

Just the thought made Rachel's stomach flip. "I think climbing trees is enough height for me, thank you."

Together they hurried forward, easily catching up to Eliza and Mr. Dunn. Several strides ahead of them, Lord Fitzwilliam led the way with his grandmother on one arm and Charlotte on the other.

"He is a most generous and kind man," Eliza was saying, pulling her arm back toward herself, brushing the tips of her fingers over the bracelet.

"It must be difficult being separated just now," Mr. Dunn said.

"Of course it is," Dinah said, breaking into the conversation as she moved up close to Eliza. Rachel, for her part, slipped up next to Mr. Dunn. "But then," Dinah continued, "Eliza is so very generous and kind herself, she knew this trip would mean much to Rachel and me and she didn't even consider standing in the way of it."

Eliza pinked. "We will be wed soon enough."

With the conversation coming to a natural end, Dinah took Eliza's arm and engaged her in a conversation just between them.

Rachel slowed her step a bit and, blessedly, Mr. Dunn seemed to realize she wished to have a word him with for he slowed as well. Soon, it was only the two of them with all the rest of the party quite a pace off.

"I see you did get home after all," Mr. Dunn began.

"Yes, thank you." Polite conversation wasn't going to get them anywhere. Rachel drew herself up, mentally preparing herself for what she had to say. "Actually, it is about this morning that I wish to speak with you."

"I guessed as much."

"You haven't, perchance, mentioned our earlier . . . conversation to his lordship or her ladyship, have you?"

"I have not."

"Oh, good." The words rushed from her, her relief overtly evident.

"Might I suggest, if you do not wish to be found out, that in the future you choose a watering hole not so close to the main road?"

"Yes, well, after all the anxiety I have experienced this morning alone, I may never try such a thing again."

He didn't laugh at her, thankfully. Neither did he judge or reprimand her. All of which would have been quite understandable. Especially considering what she now knew of him, that he was a tutor. Rachel looked him over out of the corner of her eye. Strange. She'd always assumed tutors were rather like governesses. And in her, granted, rather limited experience, governesses were nothing if not strict about rules and how one comports oneself.

In the silence that had fallen between them, he glanced her way and caught her looking at him.

"Forgive me," she rushed to say. "Only . . ."

"I do not look like a tutor?"

She shook her head. "Especially not when your pupil is at least five and twenty."

"Good guess. He will be six and twenty this fall. As will I, as it happens."

Her brow dropped. "Then how did you come to be in this situation?"

He shrugged. "My father was never content to remain in any one place for long. He, my mother, and I picked up and moved to some new country or another every couple of years. Then, after my mother passed, it was only the two of us. That is, until he joined her six years ago."

"I am sorry to hear of your loss."

"Thank you. When he died, I decided to return to England. I worked as tutor to two young boys at Woodside House, which is not far from here. But when I heard that Lord Fitzwilliam was wanting a Grand Tour and his own tutor was much too elderly to see him safely from country to country, I applied for the position."

Rachel watched the baron up ahead. He seemed to be forever motioning first one direction and then another, quite as though he couldn't tell the two women beside him about the garden fast enough. "Now that I have met his lordship, he strikes me as the sort of gentleman who would require a young tutor, no matter his own age."

Mr. Dunn laughed; it was a deep, engaging sound, one that made Rachel's stomach flip much as it had when Dinah had mentioned she walk the ridgepole. Only, it wasn't *exactly* the same; it was far more pleasant if upending, nonetheless.

"Yes, I think you have ascertained the very heart of it. But we had a glorious time."

"Do you like traveling, then?"

"Immensely. I think if I could establish a career out of taking young men on their Grand Tours, I should be quite content for the rest of my life."

"It is a shame, then, that so few young men actually do such a thing anymore." Though she'd understood it had been quite common a practice when Uncle Seth was that age.

"Too true. They have all gotten the rather silly notion that attending University is somehow more educational and are now preferring that to travel." Mr. Dunn scoffed.

Rachel smiled. "Nonsensical in the extreme."

A glimmer of light caught the corner of Rachel's eye. She turned her head; something was secreted halfway behind a well-groomed rose bush, but she couldn't quite make out what it was. She took a small step that direction. It was round and quite reflective.

"It's a glass ball," Mr. Dunn said, moving over to stand by her near the edge of the path. "Every baron has had at least a dozen commissioned and placed all throughout the gardens."

"You mean, gazing balls?"

"Not in the traditional sense." Mr. Dunn stepped around her and carefully pulled back a few branches of the rose bush so she might better see. As he had said, it was a glass ball, about the size of her own head, made of purple glass with many tiny bubbles inside, resting on the garden bed.

"The glass balls of this garden are all of various sizes and none rest on pedestals," Mr. Dunn said, slowly lowering the rose bush branches once more. "This one was placed by his lordship's father, I believe. That orange one over there"—he pointed off to their left—"was placed by his great-grandfather."

"And they're all throughout the garden?" she asked.

"Yes—partially hidden behind a bush or nestled between flowers in a bed."

Rachel studied the gardens in front of her. Now that she knew to look for them, she spotted several. "But . . . why?" She couldn't fathom why anyone would want to have glass made into balls and then placed on the dirt.

"I'm not sure how it all started," he said, "but I think at this point it's more about tradition than anything else. The current Lord Fitzwilliam had his placed just before we left for his Grand Tour."

Rachel looked over her shoulder and up the path. Up ahead, Lord Fitzwilliam helped first his grandmother and then Charlotte onto a bench. He gave them a bow and then began to retrace his steps. What sort of man was Lord Fitzwilliam? She'd heard rumors before they'd come to Curio Manor that the baron was just as peculiar as the rest of his home and family.

Lord Fitzwilliam said no more than a few words to Eliza and Dinah as he passed them before he continued on and reached Rachel and Mr. Dunn.

"Miss Chant," he said, not even bothering to acknowledge his tutor. "Might I have a word with you?"

Rachel glanced quickly over at Mr. Dunn. They had been having a nice conversation, and she was suddenly sad to see her time with him end. Nonetheless, she nodded. "If you wish it."

Mr. Dunn gave her a small bow and made to catch up to the others, but Lord Fitzwilliam stopped him with a hand on his shoulder. "You needn't go, Dunn. This isn't anything needing privacy or the like."

She would hope not; she'd only met the man a few minutes ago and this was the first time they'd ever spoken. Standing in the middle of the walk, Rachel turned toward Lord Fitzwilliam. "Was there something particular you wished to discuss?"

"Only this," his lordship said. "Miss Chant, will you marry me?"

The blood drained from Rachel's face. *Marry* him? That was the thing he wished to ask her that didn't need privacy? She was at a complete loss for words. His lordship only continued to watch her, silently awaiting her answer. Didn't a woman normally have more notice than this before being asked the single most important question of her life? Rachel glanced toward Mr. Dunn; was this some kind of joke? Surely this was a joke.

Far from looking surprised, and equally as far from looking diverted, Mr. Dunn scowled at Lord Fitzwilliam. "You cannot just walk up and ask a lady such a thing."

"Why not?" Lord Fitzwilliam replied. "Grandmother requested that I propose and now I have." His eyes turned back to Rachel. "Please do not hesitate to say no."

"No," Rachel blurted out.

Lord Fitzwilliam's smile turned brighter. "There. You see?" he said, speaking once more to Mr. Dunn. "Now I can tell Grandmother that I have done as she asked and am innocent of any negligence."

"I don't think I would consider your actions just now innocent," Mr. Dunn said.

"And why not?" his lordship pressed. "Miss Chant, you were sincere in rejecting my offer, were you not?"

"Most decisively."

"There. You see . . . wait." Lord Fitzwilliam swung back her way. "Most *decisively*? Why are you so certain you wouldn't care to marry me?"

Rachel felt trapped. Surely it wasn't a bad thing that she didn't care to fall at the feet of the first man who asked her. Especially considering that the man was one she'd never known before today. Still, she was his guest and didn't wish to offend.

"I only mean," she began slowly, "that I have no designs to marry *anyone* at the moment."

"Well, that is odd," Lord Fitzwilliam said, pulling back slightly. "I was under the impression that every lady who was out was most eager to make an advantageous connection."

Is that what he thought? Weeks of hearing her cousins and herself spoken ill of bubbled up inside Rachel. "Of course. A lady should gladly marry any fop or idiot who happens to pay her two moments' worth of attention. Is that it?"

Beside her, Mr. Dunn's eyes widened slightly. But she wasn't done. "Perhaps you feel I am too plain or too poor to ever attract another man's eye, and despite us being little more than strangers, I should absolutely accept you no matter that I know nothing of your character."

"Miss Chant," Lord Fitzwilliam said with a bow, "I meant no ill feelings."

At least he looked suitably humbled. "Very well," she said, suddenly feeling a bit foolish for her outburst. "It is only that I'm currently in the process of trying to convince my uncle to let me return home. I miss my mother something terrible and I feel she needs me just now." Indeed, the feeling was growing stronger with every day. Illogical though it was, somehow, deep inside her, Rachel knew her mother needed her. Everything else would have to wait until Rachel saw to her mother—until she learned for certain that Mother was healthy and would not die young as her parents had. Rachel was not so desperate to get married as all that, no matter that her uncle still insisted that all was well and that focusing on a match was for the best.

"I see," Lord Fitzwilliam said with a smile. "Then it is nothing personal for either of us."

"Apparently," Rachel said. What an unusual gentleman Lord Fitzwilliam was.

"In essence," he continued, his brow dropping, "you are saying I could not have proposed to you in *any* manner that would have convinced you to accept me?"

"None, whatsoever."

His eyes lit up and his smile suddenly grew bigger than Rachel had thought possible. "How very interesting."

"What are you planning, Fitzwilliam?" Mr. Dunn asked, apprehension evident in his tone.

"I may have just stumbled upon the most brilliant of all ideas."

"Ah, lud." Mr. Dunn cast his eyes heavenward and then leaned in toward Rachel. "Of all his ideas, his 'brilliant' ideas are the ones you must be most wary of." He shook his head and spoke to his lordship once more. "Very well. Out with it."

"No, I don't think I'll tell you both just now." Fitzwilliam looked back and forth between her and Mr. Dunn. "I need to think on this for a few days. But then, Miss Chant, we shall certainly speak again."

Lord Fitzwilliam tugged on the brim of his extravagantly tall hat and then turned and strode away. As he walked, he tossed the walking stick up into the air, catching it as it fell once more.

"Should we be afraid?" Rachel asked. Odd, his lordship clearly was. Dangerous? She didn't believe so. Then again, that glint in his eye had not portended a calm and easy stay in the country.

"Think of it this way," Mr. Dunn said, offering his arm to her. "You were looking for a good way to convince your uncle to leave, were you not?" He motioned toward his lordship who now spoke with Eliza and Dinah. "He may provide you everything you need and more."

Perhaps. But it was the *more* that worried her.

CHAPTER SEVEN

C hristopher felt a presence behind him, and he paused, his hands suspended above the keys of the pianoforte.

"Forgive me," a sweet feminine voice said. "I didn't mean to interrupt."

Christopher turned atop the bench to find Miss Chant watching him.

"I was only wanting a new book." She held up the one in her hands. "But then I heard your music, and I couldn't resist."

"I had rather believed I could not be heard back in this corner of the house." When he played in the music room several floors above him, it echoed about the whole of the manor, but down here in the servants' quarters, both the dowager and Fitzwilliam had insisted that he could not be heard.

Miss Chant smiled, tipping her head to the side, "Perhaps I was rather hoping to find my way to the pianoforte to begin with."

My, but she was charming when she smiled. "Do you play then?"

"A little." She took a few steps closer.

He stood and offered her the bench.

"I don't mean to force you to stop." Still, she took a seat.

"I would like to hear someone other than myself for a change," he said. Though, truth be told, it was more than that. He was quite curious to hear *her*. There was something about Miss Chant, and he found himself quite anxious to know her better.

"Do you have anything by Stamitz?" she asked.

Christopher turned toward the small shelf on which several sheets of handwritten music lay. "Not for the pianoforte, I'm afraid."

"What for then?"

"The violin." He flipped through a few of the sheets, hoping to find the right thing. But what would that be? He had no idea how accomplished she was or wasn't.

"Don't tell me you play that as well?"

He gave her a small smile over his shoulder. "My father was a musician." He returned to the sheets of paper, selecting an etude by Bach, a simple melody by Paganini, and the first movement of Beethoven's third symphony arranged for pianoforte. Standing, he offered her the three pieces.

He found her sitting very still and staring off, out the far window, her hand clasped around the locket at her throat.

"Miss Chant?" he asked. "Are you all right?"

She blinked, coming to herself once more. "Yes, sorry." She reached for the offered papers and began looking over them. Her lips pursed as she came to the Beethoven piece, and she pulled it out, placing it on the pianoforte.

"I'm not familiar with this one."

"It is fairly new," Christopher said. "I think you will find it quite revolutionary." Did his enthusiasm for the piece make him sound idiotic?

She lifted her hands, resting them easily on the keys, and began to play the first few measures. Her fingers moved over the notes with grace and confidence.

"This is quite different than his other pieces," she said after a minute.

"I thought so too." He moved over toward the stool that rested against the wall.

"My compliments to whoever wrote this out; they did a very fine job."

He picked up the stool, moving it closer to her. "Thank you. It took me quite a bit of time." He rested the stool next to the bench and sat atop it.

"You did this?" She glanced his way. "I should employ your help next time I wish some music written out rather than ask my cousins. I had Dinah help me once." The music slowed as she spoke, her attention divided between her words and her fingers. "I could barely make out anything she'd written. Then she got mad at me when I never played the piece she worked so hard on. But I couldn't enjoy it at all because it took far too much concentration to make out. We were at odds for two months straight over nothing more than a simple etude." She shook her head, her focus returning once more to the music.

"My father put me to work writing out music as soon as I was old enough to not spill ink all down myself." Only the wealthiest families frequently bought sheet music; most people Christopher knew copied the music of their friends then allowed other friends to copy the copied music. Even here at Curio Manor, most music was not original.

Miss Chant played for a bit and as she neared the edge of the page, Christopher stood and turned the pages so she might continue. He glanced down at her before sitting once more. She appeared focused, but her concentration was not intense. She seemed to absorb the music and lose herself in it, just as he did. After several more page turns, she neared the end of the first movement, and all too soon, the last notes rang through the air, leaving only silence behind.

"I hope to get my hands on the other two movements soon," Christopher said, sitting on the small stool once more.

"I'll help you copy them if you are able to find them while we are still here."

"I'd like that." Thanks to years of practice, he was quite fast at the task, but that didn't mean he wouldn't greatly appreciate the help.

Miss Chant turned back to the pianoforte, picking up the music and flipping through it. "If I'd known there would be a pianoforte here, I would have brought some of my favorite pieces."

"There's an even bigger selection in the music room upstairs should you wish to see what is available there."

"Thank you." She pulled out the Bach etude and placed it at the ready. "Did you write this one out as well?"

"Many times."

"Oh?" she shot him a quizzical glance before turning and beginning to play.

"My father insisted that I write out all of Bach's etudes over and over again. He believed the only way to truly play a piece was to understand it inside and out. That, he said, required writing it out multiple times."

Her fingers stilled over the keys, her lips turned down. One of her hands flitted to the locket around her neck. "My father always loved Bach."

She looked quite upset. Had he said something wrong? He couldn't imagine what. Eventually, her hands came together in her lap.

"Is something bothering you?" he asked.

She gave him an embarrassed smile. "I am quite well."

"Did I say anything unpleasing?"

She shook her head. "It is nothing, truly. It is . . . not something I speak of to most people."

Oh? "Whatever it is, you can tell me."

She ran a hand over her skirt. "It is not something I wish members of the *ton* to gossip about," she said in a whisper.

"Then tell me," Christopher said, leaning forward slightly. "I don't count."

"Whatever do you mean?"

He listed his head, giving her a small shrug. "As a tutor, I'm not a member of the *ton*. But I'm not exactly part of the household staff, either. I'm . . . in between. So you need not fear what you tell me will ever be spoken of to another."

Her expression softened, then she looked away, her eyes taking on a clouded look. "My father always called me his songbird. He tucked me in at night. He taught me my first song on the pianoforte. But when I was still far too young . . ." She paused for a moment, then drew herself up. "His store met with trouble. Shipments arrived late and goods rose in price." She shook her head. "Unbeknownst to me, my father went quite far into debt just to keep it open." She turned toward him suddenly. "I'll have you know none of it was his fault. He never gambled and he never overextended us." She looked away once more. "But all the entrenching in the world wasn't enough." Her last few words were quite soft. "He was taken to Marshalsea and died there shortly after."

"I am quite sorry to hear it." Indeed, Christopher had never heard such a mournful tale.

She smiled softly then shifted about on the bench, facing him more fully. "What was it like? Having a father around?" Her dark eyes watched him closely, her graceful figure not moving, not fidgeting. Whatever he said next was clearly of great importance to her.

"My experience was not typical, I believe."

"So that's why you can tolerate living in such a strange household?"

Christopher's lips ticked up. "Probably. It's certainly why I'm here, to begin with. As a musician, we traveled to wherever Father could find work. Sometimes Italy, sometimes Germany. I could hear him playing music, practicing music, or writing music nearly every minute of every day."

"Yes." Her voice turned almost eager. "But what was it like having *him* around?"

Her words seeped deep into him, and for a moment he could see both the beautiful woman she was today, but also the little girl she'd once been. A little girl who had just wanted her father to hug her again. "Have you no memories of him?"

"Only a few. He was . . . taken when I was still very young." Her gaze dropped. "I have tried to hold on to the few memories I have, but it seems time is even taking those away."

He knew a sudden urge to wrap her in his arms. He understood loss, and he wanted nothing more than to help lift the bone-deep ache that settled and seemed to never leave.

He didn't, however. She probably would not have welcomed such a display. Instead, he turned his mind to her question and the little comfort he might be able to provide. Christopher thought back over his life. How did one summarize years of experience in one conversation? How did one even begin to express the small, day-to-day differences a single, most important individual made in one's life? He looked up and found her watching him closely, her dark brown eyes pleading with him to help her understand.

"For me?"

She nodded.

"Like this," he said. Standing, he moved the stool over to her right and sat before the higher, lighter keys. "Go ahead and play."

She started again, the music dancing from her fingers. Christopher added his right hand to the keys, drawing out the interplay between notes by emphasizing certain ones, repeating others, and harmonizing with the ever-changing melody. He didn't elaborate much, but the few extra notes changed the piece, making it fuller and more engaging.

As they reached the end, their two parts blended, and they both lifted their hands off the keys as one.

"For me," Christopher said, sitting quite close to her now, "that's what having a father around was like."

"You two did that often?"

"Quite often."

"You must have had a very enjoyable childhood."

He had. "I was very fortunate to be his son."

They sat in silence for a minute and when Christopher glanced over her way, he found Miss Chant smiling once more.

She pulled the last piece to the front, the music by Paganini. "Shall we have another go at it?"

It had been ages since Christopher had shared his music with someone. He had performed many times, but he hadn't *shared*, not like this, for years.

"Lead on," he said.

Together, they placed their hands on the pianoforte and began to play.

CHAPTER EIGHT

W here was that man? Christopher reached a turn in the garden path and looked every which way. He'd had a bad feeling when Fitzwilliam had slipped away so quickly—and so quietly—after breakfast. It was the feeling Christopher always got when the man was up to no good.

He picked a direction and hurried down the path and—luck was with him—came upon Fitzwilliam with a pair of sheers in one hand and a large bouquet of recently cut flowers in the other.

"I hope those are for your grandmother," Christopher said.

Fitzwilliam didn't even so much as glance his way. "Guess again. They are for the lovely Miss Chant."

Christopher stilled. The *lovely* Miss Chant? "What are you up to?"

Fitzwilliam snipped a couple more brilliant flowers and added them to his collection.

"Can a man not grace a lovely lady with flowers simply because?"

"Not when I'm certain your motives are not pure," Christopher said, running a hand over his eyes. "I gather this is part of your *brilliant* plan I've been dreading hearing about?"

Fitzwilliam stood up straight. "I thought today was a perfect day for a second proposal."

Christopher's jaw dropped. "You thought what?"

Fitzwilliam shrugged and returned to his flower gathering. "I am going to propose to Miss Chant again."

"But . . ." Christopher could hardly believe what he was hearing. "You and I both know she has no desire to marry you and you have no desire to marry her." If Fitzwilliam truly loved Miss Chant, perhaps his actions would be somewhat understandable. But he'd seen them together several times these past few days, and he knew Fitzwilliam too well. His lordship held Miss Chant in no special regard.

"You're missing the point," Fitzwilliam said, pushing past him and moving further down the garden path. "It isn't to become engaged. It's to *practice*."

"Of all the nodcock notions."

"Come now, old man," Fitzwilliam said, turning back to him. "Someday, I shall be required to wed. It falls to me to see that the Fitzwilliam line continues, that there is an heir. When that time comes, a man needs to be certain he knows how to propose effectively."

"That's utter rubbish." Christopher shook his head.

"How can I turn down such a perfect opportunity?" Fitzwilliam continued, quite as though Christopher hadn't spoken at all. "Miss Chant has no inclination to say yes to me. She is not swayed by my wealth, my good standing in society"—he looked over his shoulder and grinned at Christopher—"or my good looks. It stands to reason her reactions to my proposals are based strictly on the proposal itself. I can, in essence, determine through trial and error the best way to propose without love or affection or concerns of that nature messing things up."

"You're treating this like a science experiment?" Of all the ridiculous things ever to be considered by an idiot.

"Here, help a man out." Fitzwilliam shoved the bouquet at him then bent to cut more flowers even as he spoke on. "Not many men get such an opportunity, and I intend not to waste mine."

Christopher clamped his jaw tight, turning the flowers over in his hand and looking them over. Fitzwilliam flirted with nearly every woman he met, but he never went so far as to put any of them in a compromising situation, never so much as danced too often with one lady in particular or was ever alone with another. For all his teasing and flirting, he was careful to never truly hurt anyone. But this? This seemed like it could go quite wrong quite fast.

"A man does not need to practice something like a marriage proposal," Christopher countered. "It is as you said. Someday you *will* fall in love and when that time comes, you will know what to do."

Fitzwilliam spoke over his shoulder. "I have no doubt that when I see the woman I am meant to marry, I'll know it."

Somehow Fitzwilliam's confidence didn't surprise Christopher. "Then trust that you'll know what to say to her as well."

"You mean leave it up to chance?" He paused. "Wait until the monumental, life-altering moment is here and pray I'll know what to do?"

"Yes," Christopher said emphatically.

Fitzwilliam shook his head, his lips pursed in disapproval. "Dunn, my friend, you are a fool."

"No more than you. Proposing multiple times to a lady of standing so that you might *practice*? What would your grandmother think?"

Fitzwilliam laughed out loud. "My good man, that's why she hired you. So when it comes to matters such as this, she never has to find out." With that, he stood and reached for the bouquet.

Christopher pulled it back out of his reach. "I cannot allow you to place Miss Chant in such an uncomfortable situation."

"I'll be careful no one sees us or overhears us. Trust me, I want to be forced into a marriage with her even less than she does with me."

Now he was just being belligerent and rude. "If you truly cared for Miss Chant's good name, you wouldn't even consider putting her in this position without at least asking her permission."

Fitzwilliam's expression fell. "*Ask* for permission to propose?"

But then he turned thoughtful. "Now that you mention it, I would rather appreciate her perspective."

"Most certainly you should. You cannot engage in such a foolhardy scheme without first—"

Fitzwilliam lunged forward, snatching the flowers from Christopher. He skipped back again before Christopher could so much as blink.

"You worry too much, old man," Fitzwilliam said, walking backward. "Trust me. I'll see to it no harm befalls Miss Chant." With that, Fitzwilliam turned around and hurried off, quickly disappearing among the trees.

Christopher shook his head at the man. There was nothing for it but to find Miss Chant first and warn her.

Rachel stepped out into the garden, humming the Paganini song she and Mr. Dunn had played together three days previously. Those moments with him had soothed her, granting a small moment of refuge from the guilt and uncertainty she forever felt. If only she could recapture such reprieve now.

Last night, she'd had a horrid dream. She couldn't remember the whole of it—partly because dreams were always hard for her to recall and partly because she couldn't bear to dwell on it for long. But she could remember snippets. There had been a storm. The waves she vividly recalled—they rose and fell in a turbulent swirl of constant change. Mother had been there. Then she hadn't. Then Uncle Seth was beside her. Then he, too, was gone. Eliza. Charlotte. A childhood friend whose name Rachel could no longer remember. The Dowager Fitzwilliam. Dinah. Mr. Dunn. So many people moved in and out, one moment there, the next gone, all without rhythm or reason.

She'd awoken nauseous and with a headache.

After calming her rapid heartbeat, Rachel had gotten up and written to Mother one more time.

Rachel turned a corner in the garden, the letter in her hand.

Writing felt like an exercise in futility. But what else was she to do? Beg to be allowed to return home? She'd done that last night. That Uncle Seth had told her was no surprise, but she hadn't been expecting the vehemence with which he'd denied her request. Even when she'd brazenly brought up the swimming. Uncle Seth was not a man prone to anger, but he could certainly be unmoving when he chose to be.

Rachel was at a complete loss as to what to try next. Perhaps after she asked Uncle to send her letter, she ought to stroll through the grounds. A turn about the garden might grant her some clarity of thought.

Or she could always return to the house. Would Mr. Dunn be at the pianoforte once more? She would very much appreciate playing with him again. It was rather a pity that asking him directly to sit with her would be considered far too forward. Just now, she needed the peace she only found in music.

"Adam sends his regards and hopes we are all well."

That was Eliza. Rachel hurried forward, coming to another turn in the path and looking down it, spotted Eliza with Uncle Seth.

"Is that all?" Uncle Seth asked, his voice as emotionless as usual.

Eliza blushed. She *did* turn pink frightfully easily.

"Never mind," Uncle Seth hurried on.

Rachel nearly smiled despite herself as she walked their way. For a man who'd raised three girls on his own, the poor man still struggled terribly with the expression of nearly any emotion.

"A letter from your betrothed?" Rachel asked once she was close.

Eliza nodded, and though she tried to keep her smile small, it seemed to shine out from her eyes all the brighter. "He is anxious for our return."

"We could cut our visit here short," Rachel offered, turning toward Uncle Seth.

"No, Rachel," he said evenly. "We could not. We have promised her ladyship two months and we won't be leaving before then no matter how often you ask us to."

Ah, well, she hadn't expected anything different. If only she could think up what to try next. Rachel extended the letter she'd written this morning.

"I know I have already sent her my letter this week," Rachel said, extending the letter to him. "But I wanted to ask if you wouldn't mind having this one sent as well."

"She already knows you are well," he said.

But Rachel didn't know if *she* was. "Please, sir?"

Uncle Seth took it, a small sigh of exasperation escaping him. "It is as I have told you before. My sister has more boarders this summer than ever. She has assured me that she will write if something goes amiss, but she simply does not have the time to write only to say all is well."

"Then perhaps an extra letter from me will help buoy her up during this time of additional stress and work." Though, truly, how hard would it be for Mother to pick up a slip of paper and simply pen, "I am well, healthy, and happy"? No—the more she thought on it, the more Rachel was certain Mother and Uncle Seth were hiding something from her. They probably still clung to the ridiculous idea that she would form an attachment more easily if she wasn't constantly thinking about her mother.

If only she could make them realize that by *not* telling her what was actually happening, they were driving Rachel to constant distraction.

"Do you trust me?" Uncle Seth suddenly asked.

Some of Rachel's emotions must have played out on her face plainly enough that even he could read them.

"Yes," Rachel said, drawing the word out. She did trust him. Truly, she did.

Only . . .

"In general," she amended.

His jaw tightened, and he gave her a small nod of understanding. "Very well. Then I shall simply say again that I know your mother is well. She has her hands full and hasn't time to write. She wishes you to enjoy your season and doesn't want to be a distraction." His voice softened. "Trust that I know such to be the case."

Rachel opened her mouth to counter, to press her cause. But the exhaustion from it all suddenly rushed over her, threatening to drown her. Exhaustion at waiting for the post every day only to be disappointed yet again, exhaustion at asking Uncle Seth over and over only to be denied. Her dream. The worry. The memory of standing before her grandparents' graves. She was so tired of pressing on. So tired of being told no.

Rachel shut her mouth and nodded. She would try to simply trust. Uncle Seth had never before let her down. She supposed she could at least try to believe him on this as well.

"Now," Uncle Seth said, "if you girls will excuse me, I believe I shall return to the house."

They bid him a good morning then turned and continued down the path, wordlessly moving away from the manor. Eliza didn't interrupt Rachel's thoughts and swirling emotions and Rachel was thankful for it. Sometimes, Rachel simply needed a moment to think, to work through her rushing emotions on her own.

"I must admit," Eliza said after several minutes of silence, "he and Charlotte are getting on far better than I'd expected."

Rachel's lips tugged upward. The other thing she needed in a moment like this was a change of topic. How blessed she was to have a cousin who understood her so well. Rachel set aside her heartache and overwhelming concerns and thought about Charlotte and Uncle Seth. She hadn't considered them in a romantic light before now, but her cousin made an excellent point. "For two people who were at loggerheads only a fortnight ago, they have taken to being in the same house quite well."

Eliza sighed, a ridiculously melancholy sound that Rachel had never heard from her before she'd become engaged. "Was it only two weeks ago that we left London?"

"My dear," Rachel said, bumping her shoulder into Eliza's, "I'm afraid you are hopelessly smitten."

Eliza's gaze moved up to the sky. "I am, and I can't even find it within myself to be ashamed."

"Well, stop trying. I think it's sweet." Perhaps, someday, she might even find herself in such a situation. The thought made her mood sour once again, the emptiness in her own chest only growing more noticeable. Someday she might find love, but certainly not now. Not when things were so uncertain regarding her mother. Not when she didn't know if Mother was working herself into an early grave or crumbling under the weight of her own loneliness.

Was her uncle correct in saying that Mother simply hadn't written because she was too busy?

Had not Rachel herself forgotten to write from time to time over the years? It wasn't hard to imagine her mother doing the same. With a house full of boarders and extra sewing and laundry, was it so very farfetched to conclude that Mother would work all day only to collapse at night from exhaustion?

Still, the niggling in Rachel's stomach that told her something was off would not go away.

No, a woman simply could not fall in love with such uncertainty hanging over her head.

Rachel didn't even care to try.

"You truly can trust Father," Eliza said softly.

"I know." Uncle Seth had never done or said anything that would cause a person to mistrust him. He was the most steady, level-headed, trustworthy man Rachel had ever known. "But I can't seem to stop worrying all the same." Until she saw for herself that Mother was well, Rachel's heart was simply too flooded with concern to make room for a gentleman, even one that made her smile as much as Lord Lambert made Eliza.

"Could it just be that the post has lost a letter or two and the rest are simply taking longer than we are used to in coming?"

Eliza asked an excellent question. It had only been three months since they had removed to Town and the letters from Mother had stopped coming. London, and now the countryside half a day's journey outside of London, was certainly farther away from Mother's home than she'd ever been. Rachel bit down on her lip. She supposed it *could* be nothing more serious than that.

"I am sure all will be well," Eliza continued, squeezing her hand.

"Then I shall have to rely on your confidence," Rachel said, hardly feeling like she could but wanting to reassure her cousin just the same.

Eliza pulled them to a stop. "You can, for I am certain in my feelings. Soon, all will be as it should be." She gave Rachel a soft smile. "If you don't mind, I would rather like to return to the house as well." She held up the letter she and Uncle Seth had been discussing before.

"Of course you want to pen a reply," Rachel said. "Don't concern yourself with me. I only need a little fresh air and will be set right fast enough."

Eliza pressed her cheek against Rachel's before hurrying back toward the manor, just as Uncle Seth had moments ago.

The moment she was alone, Rachel's shoulders sagged. *All will be as it should be*, Eliza had said.

Had not the neighbors said the very same thing when Father had left? Had she not heard those words whispered about at church when she'd first come to live with Uncle Seth, Eliza, and Dinah? Having things "as they should be" never seemed to mean having those one cared about nearby. Rachel had learned that time and time again. Change inevitably came, and it came only to take away those she loved. Was life taking away her mother now as well?

Rachel blinked and found she was near crying. Heavens, but sometimes the blue-devilment hit hard and beat against her, unrelenting. She blinked several more times; she had no desire to break down in tears just now, particularly when anyone might come across her at any moment.

But the concern—it was becoming almost more than she could bear.

How could she allow herself to feel happy, at peace even, while her mother was alone? Did not that make her the very worst sort of daughter? Dinah and Eliza would never truly understand. They had their family here with them. Uncle Seth, whose own sister was the very woman Rachel was concerned for, seemed to think that the money he regularly sent her was somehow enough.

She shook her head, walking further into the garden. He'd always been so very concerned for her mother's welfare. Why was he acting so unconcerned now? So confident that the only reason Mother had not written Rachel was that she was busy?

"Miss Chant." Lord Fitzwilliam stepped out from behind a large tree and stopped directly in front of her.

Rachel started, coming back to the garden once more. She'd quite lost track of where she was walking.

"How fortuitous it is that we have crossed paths," he said, pulling from behind his back the largest bouquet of flowers she'd ever seen. "Though, truthfully," he continued, dropping to one knee before her, "I have been searching the grounds these past two hours in the hopes of seeing your lovely face."

"What?" Rachel took a half step backward. Weren't they past this? He'd proposed only moments after meeting her, then they'd settled into an easy, if casual, acquaintance. And . . . now this?

"My dearest, most lovely Miss Chant. You are all that is good and beautiful. Say you will marry me. Say that I will never have to go without your smile."

CHAPTER NINE

Rachel placed a hand to her racing heart. She never had liked surprises, not even the pleasant kind which this certainly was not. "Lord Fitzwilliam, please stand."

"Will it make you more likely to accept my suit if I do?"

What on earth was he doing? When he'd proposed before, he'd been *pleased* she'd turned him down. Rachel grasped for something to say. "It's not that you aren't a very agreeable man. It's not that you aren't handsome."

"Go on," he said, leaning in closer.

"You are very . . ." She was running out of things to say, ways to let him down gently. "Very nice." And why in heaven's name was she needing to let him down at all? Hadn't they agreed that neither of them cared for a connection?

"If I'd known proposing was this entertaining, I'd partaken in the endeavor years ago."

She didn't doubt it; she could have sworn she saw his head grow with every compliment. "But I cannot accept you."

His face fell. "Was it the flowers?" He pulled the bouquet to the side and eyed it with serious misgiving. "I've always been led to believe most ladies enjoy flowers but perhaps I chose the wrong kind?"

"The flowers are lovely. Only, *as I explained before*, I cannot possibly accept your offer, or any man's."

"Fitzwilliam?" a voice called from around the way.

"Over here," Lord Fitzwilliam called back, still down on one knee, his voice as calm as ever.

The next minute, Mr. Dunn came into view. He took one look at Lord Fitzwilliam, flowers still extended to Rachel, and let out a sigh. "You didn't."

"Never fear, my good man," Lord Fitzwilliam said, pushing against his knee to stand. "She turned me down again."

"I'm sorry, Miss Chant," Mr. Dunn said, striding forward and scowling at his lordship. "My friend seems to have spent too many nights drinking himself into a stupor. I'm afraid his brain has been permanently addled."

Fitzwilliam only lifted his nose into the air. "Is that any way to speak to a man who is agreeable, handsome, and *very* nice? Because I am, you know. Miss Chant just said so."

She'd been right. They were paltry compliments and still his head was swollen because of them.

Mr. Dunn's expression did not lighten at his lordship's jest. "Did you at least explain to her first? Get her blessing to proceed with this ridiculous notion?"

"Explain to me what, exactly?" Rachel asked Mr. Dunn. She was certain she would more likely get the truth from him than from his lordship.

Lord Fitzwilliam waved his tutor's comments away. "I was just getting to that part. Miss Chant, when we were talking the other day, I realized that you have presented me with a most enviable opportunity, and I beg that you allow me to learn all I can."

Rachel leaned in slightly toward Mr. Dunn. "I have a growing inkling that I should just turn and walk away right now."

"I'd advise you follow that inkling."

Lord Fitzwilliam let out an offended grunt. "Wait until you hear the whole of my idea before you discount it."

Rachel pursed her lips. She supposed it would only be polite to hear what he had to say, though she didn't believe she was going to care for it. "Very well, then."

"Last time I proposed, you said that I could not convince you to marry me no matter the manner of my proposal. That got me thinking. Someday, I shall wish to propose in earnest, and I am not at all sure I shall know how to go about it. But . . . if someone who is uninterested in accepting my suit wouldn't mind me practicing a bit . . ." He let the sentence dangle.

Rachel wasn't sure she understood what he was saying.

She wasn't sure she *wanted* to understand.

"You mean to improve your method of proposal . . . by proposing to me?"

Lord Fitzwilliam gave her a firm nod. "Over and over again until you declare I have it right."

"If you wish him to leave off," Mr. Dunn said to her, "then just say the word and I will personally see that he does. I'll ply him with port until he's too drunk to know which way is up and personally cart him two counties away, if necessary."

She did find the sound of that more than a little pleasing.

"It's like this," Lord Fitzwilliam said. "You have no desire to find a husband."

"Correct," she responded.

"And I have no desire to find a wife."

"I'll take your word on that." It was probably more that he wasn't *grown up* enough to find a wife just yet.

"Now, correct me on this if I'm wrong, but despite our feelings on the matter, our families . . ."

Rachel knew immediately what he insinuated and she felt her face go hot.

"They have slightly different ideas," the baron finished.

"So it would seem." Gracious, if she'd known this conversation was going to suddenly turn so uncomfortable, she *would* have walked away before now.

Lord Fitzwilliam hurried on. "I propose we help one another. You allow me to practice my proposals on you—always away from others so no one's the wiser—and I will see to it that our families believe we are honestly trying to get to know one another but, isn't it a shame, we just don't seem to suit."

Rachel just stared. It was ludicrous. Utterly crazy.

But having his lordship on her side, helping her to convince Uncle Seth and Charlotte that they wouldn't suit . . . that certainly would help her get back to her mother sooner.

Mr. Dunn spoke in the silence. "My offer still stands."

An image of Lord Fitzwilliam passed out in the back of an old cart, sleeping atop a pile of apples, with a snore loud enough to chase away all the nearby geese, flashed through Rachel's mind and she found she couldn't stop the corner of her mouth from ticking upward.

Lord Fitzwilliam pushed Mr. Dunn aside and presented his bouquet once more. "As does mine. And my offer comes with flowers."

"You do realize," she said, still not accepting the flowers, "that if someone were to catch us, we might very well be forced to wed."

Lord Fitzwilliam placed a hand over his heart. "I am the very soul of discretion."

Mr. Dunn snorted.

This time, Rachel had to glance down to hide the smile pressing against her lips. She shouldn't be considering this. No sane person would. But could she truly pass up an opportunity to get Lord Fitzwilliam to help her?

"If I'm going to agree"—she couldn't believe she was saying the words out loud—"then, if the opportunity arises, you are to not only let both our families know we don't suit, but also casually mention to my uncle that you believe I *should* be allowed to return home to my mother as soon as possible."

Lord Fitzwilliam's shoulders bounced up and down. "Easy enough."

She pressed her hands together, placing both her pointer fingers against her lips. "It must sound natural. Not at all like I told you to tell him."

Lord Fitzwilliam cast his gaze heavenward. "You wound me with your lack of faith in my acting skills."

She looked from his lordship to Mr. Dunn.

He only shrugged as if to say this was her decision. She hadn't known Mr. Dunn long, but he had impressed her. Certainly if agreeing was a horrid idea, if Lord Fitzwilliam didn't know how to stay discrete or if his true intentions bent toward the cruel, she felt certain Mr. Dunn would tell her. But he seemed to believe his charge would stick to their agreement. So, she would as well.

For her mother.

"Very well. I accept your offer." She reached out and finally took the offered flowers, only then realizing that her words sounded very much as though she had just agreed to marry him. "That is," she said, eyes going wide, "I agree to *not* accept your proposal. I will allow you to propose to me multiple times if you help me convince my uncle to allow me to return home." Good heavens, but that sounded convoluted.

Lord Fitzwilliam chuckled. "Excellent."

"But I will ask one more thing of you," Rachel hurried on, then paused and waited until she was certain she had both men's attention. "No surprises."

Lord Fitzwilliam's face fell. "It won't be nearly so much fun for either of us if you make that a stipulation."

"In that, I must correct you," Rachel said adamantly. "It may not be as much fun for you, but *I* do not care for surprises of any kind." She hadn't since she was a young girl. She liked to know plans well in advance. She didn't even care for a present to be sprung upon her at birthdays or during Christmas. She'd made it quite clear to her uncle and cousins years ago that if they wished to give her something, they needed to tell her beforehand.

She continued, her voice firm so that he understood she was serious on this point. "You must tell me now when you plan to propose next. Say, in ten days from now, after dinner. Or Thursday next, just before teatime."

Lord Fitzwilliam shook his head. "I am certain most women do not have that kind of advance warning before receiving a true proposal. It will throw things off."

How could he approach a subject which was inherently so serious, so grave, and treat it as though it were no weightier than a feather? Rachel knew a brief moment of longing—a small part of her almost did wish she could see life as he did. As a game. As something that brought good and could be trusted.

Mr. Dunn spoke up. "What he means to say is that *he* never plans that far ahead."

Well, Rachel supposed she could compromise a small amount. "You must, at the very least, tell me the *day*. Say, twelve days from now? I will allow you to surprise me with the time and place."

Lord Fitzwilliam's lips pulled to the side. "I don't know . . ."

Rachel held out the bouquet. "Do you *want* your flowers back?"

"No." His lordship held up a hand. "I can work with that. We'll say two days from now.

"Two days?" She gasped. It would take her twice that long just to regain her equilibrium after this.

"You're only here for a few weeks and I never hesitate when facing a challenge."

"Make it five days and I'll tell you right now the biggest mistake you made both times you've proposed to me thus far."

His lordship gave her a firm nod. "Deal." He crossed his arms, a hand going to his chin. "So, tell me what I did wrong. Was it the flowers? Because I really wasn't sure if that was something *all* women like or just some."

He wasn't one to waste time, apparently. "The flowers *were* a nice touch. You were right in assuming that most women do care for them. However, finding a woman's *favorite* flower and gifting that would be a good idea in the future."

"Favorite flower." He tapped the side of his head. "Noted."

"But that wasn't the biggest error."

"Well?"

"You do realize," Rachel said, strangely enjoying dragging things out a moment longer. "I am in no way experienced in this matter."

"Inconsequential. What should I have done differently?"

She smiled. Though Lord Fitzwilliam was not a typical gentleman of the *ton*, Rachel suspected he might make a very entertaining friend. "I do believe a gentleman should use a woman's Christian name, at least once, while proposing."

Lord Fitzwilliam rocked back, smacking his forehead with the side of his fist and nearly sending his top hat flying off his head. "Of course. No one ever proposes without using their intended's Christian name. You are blessing my life already. Yes, most assuredly, I need to know your name."

A soft breeze lifted a few stray curls and brought the sweet scent of the flowers she was holding closer to her. "It's Rachel," she said.

"Rachel," Lord Fitzwilliam repeated. "Lovely. Is it not lovely, Dunn?"

"It most certainly is."

There was something in Mr. Dunn's tone that drew her eyes to him. He was smiling at her, a gentle, sincere smile. Rachel's stomach flipped and suddenly she couldn't stop smiling herself. She lifted the flowers closer to her nose, using the blooms to hide her very unexpected grin. Why his soft gaze had affected her so, she couldn't say. But neither could she seem to wipe it from her face. And the heat she suddenly felt spreading through her? Gracious, what had suddenly gotten into her?

Without another word to either of them, Lord Fitzwilliam spun about on the garden path and strode off the direction he'd come, muttering the name "Rachel" over and over again. Just before disappearing completely, he turned back. "You do promise to turn me down again next time, do you not?"

Oddly enough, Rachel felt herself ease a bit. "Most certainly."

Lord Fitzwilliam's smile grew bigger. "Capital." With that, he disappeared from view.

After a few moments of silence, Mr. Dunn spoke. "I am sorry, Miss Chant. I swear to you I did try to dissuade him."

"So long as he and I both understand that I will continue to reject him, and he does it where there are no witnesses, I suppose there is no harm done." Rachel breathed in the flowers yet again.

They were sweet with just the right hint of floral spice. "And I did get some beautiful flowers."

And who knew? Perhaps Lord Fitzwilliam's *casual* comments to her uncle that she ought to be allowed to return home might just be the solution she'd wandered the gardens in hopes of finding.

CHAPTER TEN

Rachel stood her ground. "But, sir, she is my mother. I do not understand why you are refusing to allow me to see her."

Uncle Seth grunted something unintelligible then lifted his head and faced her once more. "Because she is well, and you would be better off by applying yourself here."

"You mean, I'd be better off if I caught myself a baron for a husband." Rachel had never spoken so rudely before; she hadn't exactly intended to do so now. But the words were out, and there was no calling them back.

Uncle Seth's mouth pursed into a tight line. "He is a respectable man."

"Let me return home now, and I will turn my mind to finding a husband *after* I've seen for myself that Mother is well."

"He would provide for you every comfort, anything you ever desired." Uncle Seth lifted his gaze to the ceiling. "Why are you fighting me so hard on this?"

"Why can't I just go home?"

"Because you can't." The words were hard, final.

The bite of tears pricked Rachel's eyes. "I am not so desperate as you make me out to be." At least, she'd never considered herself so horrid a match as all that.

Uncle Seth let out a long, slow breath and then faced her once more. "It would be best if you secured your future before returning home."

Rachel's brow dropped. "What? Why?"

Uncle Seth shook his head. "It is your mother's wish. I promised her I would not say more than that."

Then he *was* keeping something from her. He and her mother both were.

"Is she truly well?" Rachel asked in a small voice.

"Her health is fine. There are no concerns there." He said it in a kind voice, but also one that sounded truthful. "The time to return home will come, but it hasn't come yet. Do as your mother wishes. Enjoy your season. See if you can't grow to care for his lordship, if possible. Imagine finding a home at Curio Manor. I think, when all is said and done, you will be glad you did."

"I don't want a new home," Rachel replied. "I already have one. I want to go back to it, not continually be replacing it."

Uncle Seth placed a hand on her shoulder. "Trust me a little longer on this."

What else could she do? Rachel nodded.

Without another word, he strode out of the parlor, leaving her alone in the room. Rachel watched him leave and then collapsed into a nearby chair. So much for standing her ground and making him see reason. She could argue all she wanted, but at the end of it all, Uncle Seth was the one who would be making the decisions, and she truly couldn't force him.

But, heavens, how she missed home.

And the thought of returning to London terrified her.

She'd always hated change. Visiting Mother once a month was nothing like actually living there. Why couldn't she just go back home and stay? Stay where things were comfortable, predictable. Where she knew she could look after Mother. She wouldn't have to forever be battling feelings of guilt over enjoying this outing or that peaceful afternoon while knowing Mother was probably struggling.

If Mother needed to take in extra boarders and more sewing and laundry just to get by, then surely having Rachel around would only be a help. She wasn't a little girl anymore, one who took time and energy. As a grown woman, now she could provide an extra set of hands. She could sew and do laundry and help with boarders. Together, they could make it work.

"What are you doing in here all alone?" Dinah's voice reached her, but Rachel didn't turn her way.

There was the soft pad of footfalls and Dinah sat in the chair across from her. "We ought to be getting dressed for dinner. It will be served soon."

Rachel only shrugged.

"Oh," Dinah said, her voice dropping. "You've been asking Father to take you back home again."

"He's never refused to allow me to visit her before. Why do you think he is now?" It was so out of character for him. He was emphatic that Rachel's mother was well, but he wouldn't elaborate. The more she thought on it, the more out of character it seemed. "What do you suppose he's hiding from me?"

Dinah's gaze shot to her and then immediately darted over toward the window.

Rachel sat up straighter. "Do you know something?"

Dinah composed herself. "Nothing I believe you wish to hear."

"Whatever it is, it cannot be worse than what Uncle Seth has already told me—that I cannot go back home to Mother."

Dinah pulled her lips to one side. "He's hoping you'll form an attachment with Lord Fitzwilliam."

Well, that was no surprise. "Is that all, though?" Rachel watched her cousin closely.

"As far as I know, it is." Dinah showed no sign of misgiving.

Then again, Rachel had known her to tell some very convincing bounders. But she didn't think Dinah would lie to her about this.

"Of a truth," Dinah pressed on, "why not consider a connection with the baron?"

"I feel no particular regard for the man, first of all."

"He is pleasing to look at, I suppose. And he is not vicious," Dinah countered.

"Oh, and that is all that is necessary to form an attachment?"

Dinah let out a dramatic sigh of impatience. "I suppose the real question is would he be more amenable to the idea of you visiting your mother than Uncle Seth is."

The idea somewhat shocked Rachel. "So now you are suggesting I marry a man simply so that I might circumvent Uncle's unwillingness to let me go where I choose?"

Dinah pursed her lips and listed her head. "I've heard of many wives who choose not to live in the same house as their husbands."

"You cannot be serious." The notion of marrying simply so she could live separate from her husband did not appeal to Rachel at all. This was the danger of moving on and simply believing the past would resolve itself—it led to the most convoluted and undesirable outcomes.

"It would garner you what you seek."

Rachel wasn't sure what to say. She *supposed* such might be true. "Lord Fitzwilliam would have to be very congenial if he would ever agree to such an arrangement."

"He seems to be."

Rachel shook her head. The notion was ridiculous. "Suppose he changed his mind after a time? Suppose he was even less willing to let me see Mother than my uncle?"

Dinah's brow creased. She looked quite as though she was seriously considering the notion. Rachel wasn't, though. The very idea of marrying someone simply so she could leave him was repulsive.

"I suppose," Dinah said slowly, "you would have to speak with his lordship about all this before the wedding. Perhaps even write up a contract."

"Dinah," Rachel said, not bothering to keep her disapproval out of her voice. "I will not use a man in such a way. Especially not one as good-natured as his lordship."

Dinah leaned forward. "So you do like him."

"Just because I can see that Lord Fitzwilliam is good-natured does not mean I wish to spend the rest of my life with him." Rachel placed a hand to her stomach. Indeed, the very idea made her feel a bit nauseated.

"Marriage is simply two people who need something from the other. In your case, you need a husband who will allow you to live with your mother. Or a husband who would allow her to live with you." Her face was emotionless, but there was a hardness in her eyes that Rachel could not remember ever seeing there before. "I suppose you could offer his lordship the choice—you both live with him or you both don't. I know the dowager would be thrilled he was wed, and you could be with your mother again. I am quite certain if you approached it in that light, you could come to an agreement."

"Well, I don't care," Rachel said. "*You* might have found pleasure in our new standing, in the new acquaintances and house parties and all the coming here and going there, but I certainly haven't." For Rachel, it was simply one more way that life forced her forward, forced her away from what was comfortable and loved. "If you are so anxious to make a connection perhaps you should *come to an agreement* with Lord Fitzwilliam yourself."

Dinah's jaw tightened, and she stood. "Forgive my intrusion," she said coldly. "You seem unwilling to move *forward* with life, so I was simply suggesting a way for you to permanently bury your head in the sand." She stormed toward the door.

Drat. Rachel hadn't meant to grow so frustrated, especially not with a beloved cousin. "Please," Rachel called after her, "don't leave mad."

Dinah paused with her hand on the doorknob. She stood there for several moments, then turned, placing her back against the door.

"You know," Dinah said, "when I first heard about Father's knighthood I was actually quite excited about it. I was overjoyed this exciting change was happening to me; I looked forward to the people I would meet and the places I could go." She laughed—a mirthless sound. "But don't you see? No matter what happens, I'll still be no more than than the youngest daughter. The last in the line. The one whose needs matter *last*."

"Oh, Dinah." Rachel stood and hurried over to her cousin. "I am sorry you've been made to feel that way." She wrapped her arms around Dinah and hugged her.

Dinah only sighed. "We stayed in London just long enough for Eliza to find her heart's desire. Now we're here, all waiting for you to fall in love." Her voice dropped to a whisper. "I'm not sure it will ever be my turn."

Rachel nearly said that Dinah was every bit as welcome to form an attachment at Curio Manor as herself. But she felt Dinah just needed to be heard right now, not contradicted.

Dinah pulled back. "I know your frustration is born out of a love for your mother. But do you not feel you could focus on both things at once? Returning to your mother *and* finding a gentleman you might love?"

Rachel's stomach twisted. "It's not that I don't want love, only . . ."

Dinah pressed her palms together, lifting her hands until the tips of her fingers brushed her lips. "Do you remember two summers ago, when that new family moved into the neighborhood, the one with a son you thought quite handsome? For weeks, you were so wrapped up over concerns about your looks and what he might overhear you saying that you not only neglected your flower garden to the point that nearly every bloom died, but you also were completely blind to the fact that the *younger* son of the very same family had eyes only for you."

"Are you saying I ought to go back and see if the younger son still cares for me?"

"Gracious, no," Dinah said. "What I'm saying is that you were so caught up in your worry that you completely missed something far more important."

Rachel didn't see it that way. "I never cared particularly for the younger brother, so what did it matter?"

"But might you have cared if you'd known him better?"

"What is your point?"

Dinah took Rachel's hands in hers. "I'm concerned you're doing the same thing again. You're so wrapped up in your worry that you aren't seeing what's right in front of you."

"What's right in front of me to see? A house full of the unusual and an uncle who won't allow me to go where I most want to go?"

Dinah quirked her mouth to the side. "Just try not to let your worry crowd out your ability to enjoy yourself while we're here."

"Very well," Rachel conceded, more to end the discussion than anything. "If I find myself falling for a man whose younger brother loves me, I'll be sure and let you know."

Dinah opened the door and they moved into the corridor together. "You know, someday you're going to look back and regret how you handled that whole situation two summers ago."

"I thought we agreed that neither man was right for me."

"Oh, no doubt there. But if it had been *me*, I'd have pitted the two brothers against one another and watched the fun."

"Dinah!" How could she say such a thing? Still, Rachel laughed. "Of all the wicked notions."

CHAPTER ELEVEN

Christopher looked up at Woodside House, his stomach feeling more and more sick the longer he stared at it. He'd avoided coming back here for as long as he dared. But he'd been back in England for nigh on six months and he wasn't getting anywhere in regard to finding a new position. Neither Fitzwilliam nor his grandmother had made any direct comments about his continual employment, but any clever cove could work out that his time at Curio Manor was limited. He needed to leave no stone unturned.

And that meant he needed to make this visit.

Still, he'd hoped that after being gone for so long, some of the dread this house brought might have faded.

"Mr. Dunn, is that you, sir?"

Christopher turned to find one of the groomsmen walking over.

"Stevens, how good to see you again." They shook hands. Not all his acquaintances here had been sickening. No, only the one.

"How was the continent?" Stevens asked.

"As breathtaking as the day I left."

Stevens reached for the reins of Christopher's horse. "Want me to rub him down?"

"No." It hadn't been that long of a ride over, and he didn't intend to stay half so long. "I only wanted to speak with Lord Keats for a moment."

"All right then, I'll just see this fine stallion gets to rest a spell."

"Thank you." Christopher waited until both his horse and the groomsman were out of sight. Then he turned back and faced the house once more. Lud, but he hated being here.

Well, there wasn't anything for it but to go in. He wasn't making any progress just standing there. He took the stairs slowly; once he reached the door, it was another three minutes before he lifted his hand and actually knocked.

It opened immediately. Mr. Hervey had probably seen him from a window and was simply waiting for him to gather his nerve.

"Mr. Dunn, it's a right pleasure to see you again."

"You as well, Mr. Hervey." Christopher entered, taking in the large entryway, a wary eye on the lookout. "Is Lord Keats home today?" Half of him wished he wouldn't be, and Christopher could make good his escape before being seen. The other half dreaded such a response; because if Lord Keats wasn't home today, he'd simply have to make the same ride over another time. Now that he was here, he'd much rather have done and return to Curio Manor knowing he'd tried every option.

"If you'll wait here a moment, sir, I shall see if he is home to visitors."

Christopher nodded his understanding and the man moved away. In his absence, Christopher took a moment to look about. He'd called this place home for the better part of two years. Not much had changed since he'd joined Fitzwilliam for a tour of the continent. Gads, but he'd been happy to leave this place.

"Mr. Dunn, is that you?"

Speak of the devil.

He slowly turned to find Lady Keats staring at him, eyes wide, her blonde hair pulled back in its usual coiffure, her attire more prudent than he'd remembered it.

"Lady Keats." Christopher bowed stiffly.

They stared at one another; she didn't say anything, and he

didn't care to. In his experience, the less said to Lady Keats the better.

"Sir." Mr. Hervey returned and, like he always had before, acted quite as though there was no tension between Christopher and Lady Keats. "His lordship will see you in his book room."

"Thank you, Mr. Hervey." Christopher offered a quick bow to her ladyship and hurried off, not needing anyone to show him the way.

He took the stairs quickly, turning down the wide hallway. At least Lady Keats hadn't called after him. She hadn't even batted her lashes or tried to sidle up close. Perhaps she'd changed these past few years? He did the math quickly in his head—it had been a full three since he'd left. Or at least, in that amount of time, she'd changed in her regard toward him? A man could only hope.

"Mr. Dunn," Lord Keats said cheerfully as he strode into the room.

"Good to see you again," Christopher said as they shook hands.

Christopher sat and for the next quarter of an hour, they discussed the continent and Parliament.

Lord Keats rested back in his seat. "I heard that in Germany, Fitzwilliam forced you to scale up the side of a building with him just so he might see the sunrise."

Christopher nodded. "He claimed there was no better place to watch the sun break across the fields."

"It is a wonder you've been able to tolerate living among such people for so long."

No, Christopher wouldn't have that. "The Fitzwilliams may have their own way of doing things, but they are good people." His voice deepened as he spoke. "They are truly some of the best people I have ever been privileged to know."

"Is that so?" Lord Keats muttered, clearly unconvinced.

Christopher glanced out the window along the wall just behind Lord Keats. The problem with those who cared too much about appearances is they often couldn't see past the clothes and manner-isms of their neighbors. But that was not a problem Christopher could fix right now. Right now, he needed a new position because no matter how thoroughly he'd enjoyed his time at Curio Manor, he could not impose much longer.

The silence that fell between himself and Lord Keats was as much of an opening as anything.

"My lord," Christopher began, "as much as I have enjoyed my time at Curio Manor, I am sure you realize it is time I found a new position."

"Ah, I had wondered if that wasn't why you'd come today."

"Please understand," Christopher hurried on, "I am not here expecting my old position back." In truth, he'd do nearly anything to avoid it. "I only wondered if you knew of a position somewhere and might be willing to give me a recommendation."

Lord Keats smiled. "Of course I'm happy to recommend you to anyone. Only . . ." He leaned forward, resting his arms against his legs. "I wouldn't be too quick to assume your old position isn't still open."

Christopher's back went rigid. "Surely you have not allowed your sons to go without a tutor for three years." Though it wasn't worry for his lordship's two sons that caused the tightness in his words. He'd always wondered how Lord Keats could be so entirely oblivious to his wife's actions while Christopher had been in his employ; either that or his lordship truly cared very little for his own wife.

Lord Keats laughed. "No, no. Quite the opposite. They've had no less than *seven* tutors since you left. Can't rightly understand it—everything went swimmingly while you were here. Then, the moment you took your leave and I secured a new man, my two sons could do naught but cause problems. Lady Keats is forever insisting a new tutor is what the house needs."

Oblivious. The man was certainly oblivious.

"Thank you, my lord," Christopher said, standing. "But I would not be pleased to be the reason another man was forced from his situation."

Lord Keats stood as well. "I'll most likely be letting him go, regardless. You could take up living here again with no pang of conscience."

Live here again? Christopher would sooner die a beggar on the streets of London.

"Thank you, but I think it is time I move on, all the same." Christopher bid the man a good day and left. His head swam as he made his way to the front door. Return to Woodside House permanently? No, that was not an option at all.

He got no further than the top of the stairs.

Lady Keats appeared, seemingly out of nowhere, and pressed herself up close to him.

"Why, Mr. Dunn, you were not leaving so soon, were you?"

She'd changed dresses in the past quarter of an hour. The one she wore now was *exactly* as he recalled—brightly colored and very low cut.

"Lady Keats, I am needed back at Curio Manor." It was a small lie—he certainly wasn't *needed* anywhere—but one he gladly told. "If you will excuse me." He tried to step to the side.

She matched his step, blocking off his exit. "Woodside House has not been the same since you left." She placed a finger atop his chest and slowly drew it down. "*I* have been so lonely."

He took hold of her hand and, as gently as he could, pushed it aside. "Then perhaps you ought to seek out the other ladies of the neighborhood." He moved quickly to the right and got around her. Without pausing, he hurried down the stairs and let himself out the front door. It banged shut behind him, no butler there to see it was closed gently.

Christopher lifted his eyes for a brief moment, breathing in the freshness of being out of doors. He should not have come. It was a dead-end, after all. Lord Keats had nothing for him, except a return to his own household, and Lady Keats had not changed regarding him in the least. Stevens appeared from around the corner of the house, leading his mount.

"He's been quite well looked after, Mr. Dunn," Stevens said, cheerful as always.

"Thank you." Christopher moved up to his horse, mounting easily. "Tell your wife I said hello."

"Will do, sir. Will do."

Christopher turned his horse away from Woodside House and rode quickly off. Truly, if it weren't for Lady Keats, Christopher would have gladly returned to his previous position. The staff here did not treat him like an interloper, as some households did. Lord Keats was not a hard man to please. More still, Christopher had grown quite fond of his lordship's two sons.

Slowing his horse, Christopher looked over his shoulder, eying the house. If it weren't for Lady Keats, returning to Woodside House would be an unexpected blessing. But no. Christopher shook his head at the very idea and urged his horse forward once more. He knew full well Lady Keats was not actually in love with him. She only sought him out because he was a nobody. A nobody who possessed polish and poise, perhaps, but a nobody all the same. To seek the attentions of a titled man, or landed gentry, would surely end in scandal. To seek the attention of a working hand probably made a woman like Lady Keats shutter. But Christopher, ah, Christopher had the unhappy situation of being in the middle. He'd been taught to speak and carry himself as though he *were* a gentleman, but he wasn't one.

He had no home.

He had no place to call his own. No refuge where he might settle down. Where he might have a family of his own. Such things hadn't bothered him so much before—he truly did enjoy traveling. But now it bit at him. Was this what he had to look forward to? Searching out new position after new position? Always wondering how the next household would treat him?

Though he despised the idea of returning to work in Woodside House, if something didn't turn up soon, he very well might be faced with either that option or wandering London's streets.

CHAPTER TWELVE

Rachel stood by the large window of the library, watching as the sun slowly sunk below the treetops. She loved this window, and with the summer sun setting quite late, she could enjoy the view it afforded no matter that dinner was already over and the day nearly done. This window was the reason she'd chosen to sit alone instead of with the rest of the family in the parlor. The view looked out over the front drive, out toward the road she would travel if ever she could convince Uncle Seth to allow her to return home.

Going for an unapproved swim had done nothing. All the begging and pleading since had not swayed his decision. Perhaps it was that swimming had not been upsetting enough? What else could she do? In a house filled with the nonsensical and outlandish, it seemed almost anything might be acceptable. Even now, she was counting down the hours until tomorrow—the time when her five days of proposal reprieve would be at an end. No doubt, Lord Fitzwilliam would have something planned for the next day.

Whatever it would be, she couldn't seem to care.

She wished she could ask him if he'd said anything yet to Uncle about allowing her to return home. But she was the one who had insisted he mention it casually, naturally. She supposed such things couldn't be rushed.

Rachel turned away from the window, looking over the grand room before her. The library here at Curio Manor was the most beautiful room she'd ever before seen. The ceiling stretched up far higher than any ceiling she'd ever seen, and bookshelves lined two of the four walls, so tall that there were stairs and a walkway halfway up. Books often provided her comfort when she was upset— it was the reason she'd retreated to this room after her most recent argument with her uncle. There was something calming about written words. Their order. Their neatness.

Suppose she wrote *Uncle* a letter? Yes, they spoke every day, but sometimes the written word could do more than the spoken. She looked about herself. Just to her right was a comfortable chair with a portable writing desk next to it. Rachel sat and pulled open the small drawer it contained. Blank paper rested inside. Perfect. She took a couple of sheets and then went searching for some ink and a quill. She found one in the larger desk off to her left. Sitting down, Rachel set her paper and ink where she liked them and thought over her first few words.

For the next couple of hours, she worked, penning first one line then another. Always careful to make each word count, to make each phrase emphasize how important it was that she be allowed to visit Mother. Without Father there for either of them, she and Mother needed to be together.

What she didn't add, for she didn't think Uncle Seth would understand, was that Rachel felt guilty being here, enjoying the country, while her mother was alone. It felt so wrong.

A gentle "ahem" at the library door brought Rachel out of her intense focus.

She turned in her seat and found a footman standing just inside the library.

"A letter's come for you, miss." The footman strode her way, a silver platter stretched out.

A letter? Rachel leapt to her feet, the heavy chair she'd been sitting in scratched loudly against the wooden floor. Rachel snatched up the letter. Could Mother have written her at last? Oh, after so many months of wondering, what a relief to have some words from her.

"Thank you," Rachel said, nodding that the footman could leave. She had no desire to have an audience when she finally gobbled up whatever Mother had finally deemed important enough to write. With the letter clutched tightly to her chest, she waited until he'd left and shut the door once more.

Rachel hurried over toward the cushioned seat nearest the window; the dwindling light lasted the longest in this seat. She sat hurriedly and tore the letter open while also being careful not to rip the parchment. It seemed very fine paper—where would Mother have gotten such a thing?

The letter was short.

Never mind though, it was a letter.

Mother had written her.

Rachel,

Loveliest of all ladies, wonderous of all women.

That didn't sound like Mother. Rachel was fairly certain "wonderous" wasn't even a word.

Her gaze jumped down to the signature at the bottom.

Lord Fitzwilliam

Disappointment rushed over her, drowning her in less time than it took for her to draw breath.

It wasn't from Mother.

It was nothing but a stupid note from that incorrigible Lord Fitzwilliam. Tears filled her eyes, blurring the sight of the paper and scrawled words. Hateful note—giving her hope when there was no reason. Rachel swiped a hand over her cheeks, but it did nothing to stop the tears that continued to fall. What a fool she'd been to think that Mother would *ever* write her. Letters had once come so frequently; every week she'd written Mother and every week, Mother had written back. But ever since they had removed to London—Rachel shook her head—well, she hadn't heard a thing.

She blinked several times, skimming over the rest of the note. There was much fluff and flattery, but the actual content was quite simple. He requested she meet him at the rotunda near the garden's edge. Rachel stood, folding the letter back up roughly. Heaven help him if he thought proposing a day early was charming.

Not caring that she stomped the entire way, Rachel walked out to the rotunda. Blessedly, she didn't see anyone along the path she took; she wasn't in the mood for company, nor did she care to explain away her red eyes and tear-stained cheeks.

"Lord Fitzwilliam?" she called as she marched up the few stairs and took in the sight before her. The entire rotunda had been covered in pink rose pedals. Candles shone from over a dozen candlesticks placed artfully all around, their gentle glow chasing away the beginnings of nightfall.

It was lovely.

It was romantic.

How *dare* he.

Rachel's lips pursed. "Lord Fitzwilliam!"

He strode up the steps of the rotunda across from her. The insipid man seemed to be humming. He veritably danced toward her, twirling once, and knelt before her as he did *four* days ago—four, not five.

"Radiant Rachel, light of my life."

"Stop with the alliteration or I'll depart directly."

"Dearest," he continued, not even fazed, "you must allow me to tell you of the deepest yearnings which have grown in my heart."

At least he'd stopped the alliteration. "I'm in no mood today, my lord."

"You are everything lovely and pure. I could not live another day without you."

"My five days are not up, need I remind you?" Why was he doing this to her? "You promised me more time."

"But I could not wait." His voice grew dramatic, as though he were on a stage instead of in a remote rotunda on his own property. "How could I when you are—"

"Livid," Rachel broke in, the tears starting once more. "I am livid, my lord, and so help me if you don't get up off your knee this instant . . ."

"Certainly you cannot mean—"

"Fitzwilliam," Mr. Dunn's voice called, deep and commanding from just beyond the rotunda. "Stand. Up."

Lord Fitzwilliam let out a loud sigh. "How can I properly woo a lady with you shouting at me from the sidelines?"

Mr. Dunn appeared from behind a few trees, striding up the steps and past Fitzwilliam until he stood beside Rachel. "Please forgive him; you know he meant no harm."

Embarrassment warred against the anger in her chest. She was completely overreacting. Who fell apart over something they knew to be only a jest? Still, the heartache at being so clearly reminded that her mother *would not* write to her wouldn't fade. "You want my suggestions on how to better propose?" She shook the note she still clutched in her hand in Lord Fitzwilliam's face. "Don't ever write to me again." She tossed it down.

The paper floated lightly, and most unsatisfactorily, toward the rotunda floor.

Both men watched her. All Rachel could manage was a tear-filled hiccup.

Unable to stand the silence, she turned on her heel and, picking up her skirts, rushed back toward the house.

She was an utter fool. A silly ninny.

"Rachel."

She ignored the masculine call and hurried yet onward. Lord Fitzwilliam could call until he was hoarse for all she cared. The only thing she wanted right now was her own room, a place to cry without witnesses and without pity.

"Rachel." Her name came again, from closer this time. It was deeper, too. So it wasn't Lord Fitzwilliam who'd chased after her, then.

She slowed her step and Mr. Dunn caught up to her.

"What is wrong?" His tone was soothing, calming.

She didn't dare look up. No doubt he would be repulsed by the evidence of unchecked weeping across her face. Instead, she kept her gaze on his dark boots.

"I only need a minute to collect myself. If you will excuse me, sir." She turned to leave him once more; at least this time she'd managed to speak without shouting or hiccupping.

He caught hold of her elbow. "Please, might I not help in some way?"

His blue eyes held hers, his expression full of concern. Rachel hesitated. If anyone could understand her frustrations right now, might it not be him?

"Mr. Dunn—"

"Christopher."

Her lips twitched upward of their own accord. "Christopher." Saying his name somehow made it easier to speak what was in her heart. Drawing herself up, she asked, "Do you ever get tired of your life not being your own? Of not being free to go where you want when you wish it?"

His brow creased. He dropped her elbow and moved up closer. "Is there somewhere you'd rather be?"

She nodded, the tears starting once more. "I want to go home."

Closing the small bit of distance between them, he encircled her in his arms. Rachel rested her head against his chest. The tears came faster, because somehow, she felt safe shedding them here, with him. It had been months since she'd allowed herself a good, hard cry. All the pent-up vexation rushed out, each sob shaking her entire frame.

She cried for her mother, she cried for the years they had spent apart, she cried out all the heaviness that had been dragging her down.

Christopher said nothing, he simply held her and let her cry. He would understand, at least on some level. He may not have a mother who suddenly, inexplicably, stopped writing him, but he was not free to live where he wished. He went where his position took him. Rachel needed someone who understood at least a little of what she was going through just now.

Finally, her crying eased, and she looked up to find it was fully dark now. Together, they walked back to the house. Christopher showed her the best way to get through the manor and up to her bedchamber without running across any of the family.

When they reached the door, he gave her hand a reassuring squeeze. "I would say things will look better in the morning, but I'm pretty sure you've heard that line before."

She wrinkled her nose. "It is what everyone tends to say, isn't it?"

"Then how about this instead? No matter what happens, I believe you will find happiness, regardless."

"Even if my mother is sick and alone? Even if she and I never . . ." Rachel took in a deep breath to calm herself; she'd cried enough tonight. She had no desire to start up once more.

"Oh, no." Christopher took a half step closer, taking her hands in his. "I mean you are creative and brave, and I have faith that you will find answers. You will make your life one you love."

That made no sense. "I feel guilty all the time," she whispered. "How can I enjoy my time here when I know she is alone?" In the past, Rachel had at least had frequent letters from Mother. Now, even that small tether was gone.

"She loves you; consequently, knowing you are happy will make her happy."

Rachel shook her head. "The opposite is more true. I love her; consequently, knowing she is alone means I cannot possibly be at peace away from her." Hang her uncle. He was keeping something from her, though he claimed it wasn't that her mother was in poor health. If only he'd come right out and *tell her*. But no matter what she tried, she hadn't been able to convince him to say more.

Christopher gave her arm a gentle squeeze. "Whichever it is, now I am going to say the commonplace you ought to sleep. It truly does help."

Very well. She could at least admit he was correct on that score. He stepped back a bit, turning to leave.

She watched him take those first few steps away and with each step she felt the distance growing most acutely. He'd been so very thoughtful tonight. Had he any idea how much his friendship meant to her? Was there not some way she could let him know?

She'd shown some bravery back when she went swimming, hadn't she? Summoning that elusive emotion once more, she hurried after him, stopping just in front of him and throwing her arms about him.

"Thank you for being a good friend when I needed it."

He froze for a moment, then slowly his arms come up around her waist. The feeling sent a thrill coursing straight to her heart. Though he'd held her not more than a quarter of an hour before, this felt different. This time it was less about supporting her and more . . . well, Rachel wasn't really sure what it was. And very probably, it wasn't half so significant to him.

Rachel pulled back, her hands sliding over his shoulders until they rested against his lapels. Looking up at him, his arms still around her, she was suddenly at a loss for words. His eyes held hers and a heated tingling spread through her.

"Everyone needs a good friend," Christopher said.

Friends. *Right.* Rachel blinked. Isn't that what she'd said just moments ago? Still, the way his hands pressed softly against her waist . . .

But no. Rachel pulled back and out of his arms completely. She couldn't even begin to think about being more than friends with *anyone.* Not until she knew for certain her mother was all right. Not while her heart was plagued with such a pervasive sense of foreboding.

"Thank you," she whispered again. "One really cannot emphasize too much the benefit of having a good *friend.*" She stressed the word more for her sake than his.

"Of course." His voice was upbeat. Perhaps too much so?

She was making up emotions on his part now, a fruitless attempt to make sense of just how much that hug had upended her.

Still, something inside her didn't quite feel ready to leave him. "Perhaps we could play the pianoforte again tomorrow?" she asked.

The corner of his mouth pulled to the side. "I'd like that. Good night, Rachel." He stepped around her and hurried down the corridor.

She watched him until he was around the corner and well out of sight. Stepping back, she rested against the wall and closed her eyes. Whatever had just happened, she could not allow it to happen again. Even if her heart suddenly found it could hold more than just worry over her mother, she was convinced her brain could not. Mother had to be her only priority. Convincing Uncle Seth to allow her to return would take all her focus. She drew in a deep breath and stood up straight, moving toward her bedchamber. Christopher was right; she best get right to sleep. As it was, sorting through the various, intense emotions she'd experienced these past few hours was going to take all night long and more.

CHAPTER THIRTEEN

"Perhaps I shall write a poem," Fitzwilliam said as he and Christopher watched the happenings inside the library from the open doorway. "Ladies always swoon when a man recites poetry."

A footman pulled two books off the shelf and Christopher felt his stomach tighten. "Only when they are well-written," he muttered. The footman reached for yet another book and Christopher caught a glance at the title: *Robinson Crusoe*. "Not that one," he called out.

The footman nodded his way, replaced the book, and then picked another. Christopher didn't see the title this time; he could only pray it was something uninspiring and easily replaceable.

Fitzwilliam chuckled softly to himself and elbowed Christopher a bit more roughly than necessary. "Stop scowling at my manservant and let us head to the drawing room. Grandmother's guests are waiting."

Christopher gave the footman one last stern glare and followed Fitzwilliam.

"Perhaps I ought not attend tonight," Christopher said. "Would not the dowager's guests think it odd a tutor is sitting down to dinner with them?"

Fitzwillam's expression only creased more. "Odd? Why ever so? Sir Mulgrave does not find it odd. Neither does Lady Blackmore, and if a marchioness finds nothing wrong with you joining us, I am sure the other people Grandmother has invited from the neighborhood will have nothing to say about it."

Still, Christopher hesitated.

"Are you certain you are all right?" Fitzwilliam pressed.

"Why wouldn't I be?" Besides having no future position lined up; besides his undesirable encounter with Lady Keats two days ago; besides knowing Fitzwilliam was, yet again, putting his best books at risk of being dirtied.

"Come now," Fitzwilliam said, clasping a hand on Christopher's shoulder and leading him toward the drawing room. "You celebrated the beginning of summer with us before, and you enjoyed yourself."

Is that how Fitzwilliam remembered it? Christopher had spent the entire night either avoiding Lady Keats, who had been invited to the celebratory dinner along with her husband, or cringing over the fine books that most certainly would not make it through the night. He'd been raised on a steady diet of music and math, literature and the sciences; it literally had hurt him to see books put in harm's way.

"I believe the ladies are already awaiting us in the drawing room along with most of the guests," Fitzwilliam said. "No doubt a bit of feminine company will cheer you up."

"I think you mean a bit of feminine company always cheers *you* up."

Fitzwilliam waggled his eyebrows. "Naturally."

Christopher laughed softly at his friend. It was going to be difficult to leave Curio Manor, most difficult indeed.

"If you are needing poetry," Christopher found himself saying, "I have a collection of very fine verses in my room."

Fitzwilliam turned, walking backward for a few strides. "Dunn, you are the best tutor a man could ask for." He play-punched Christopher in the shoulder.

Together, they moved toward the drawing room door and, as they approached, a footman opened the doors. Light conversation floated out to greet them. Fitzwilliam was correct when he'd said the women had already gathered.

"Good evening, ladies," Fitzwilliam announced to the room at large as he stepped in.

There was a murmur of welcomes. Christopher merely nodded his greeting. The room was quite full. Lady Blackmore sat beside Lady Fitzwilliam on a settee, Sir Mulgrave in the chair nearest them. His daughters, Miss Mulgrave and Miss Dinah Mulgrave were near a window speaking with a few of the guests Lady Fitzwilliam had invited. There were several people Christopher knew from the neighborhood, but more he didn't. Gratefully, he saw neither Lord or Lady Keats. He'd never uttered a single syllable regarding his previous interactions with Lady Keats to either Fitzwilliam or his grandmother, so they might still be coming. But, gads, he hoped not.

As he turned back toward the center of the room, his eyes landed on Miss Chant. His heart thudded as it seemed to always do whenever he saw her. In fact, that organ had taken to being quite nonsensical ever since he first lay eyes on Miss Chant, dripping wet and sitting quite demurely in that ridiculous tree.

She sat in a small chair near the empty hearth, it being far too warm a day for a room with so many westward facing windows to have a fire in it in the evening. She was facing Sir Mulgrave and the two matrons but seemed to only be smiling softly out of politeness, not out of a sincere interest in their conversation. Still, she looked absolutely angelic. She wore mint green, and while her dress was simple, devoid of the many ruffles, beads, and strands of lace that so many wore, the simplicity only made her appear all the more elegant. Her dark hair was done up, but a few curls still hung about her face, looking soft and oh, so touchable as they brushed against her cheeks. The light from a nearby candle danced across her lips and the turn of her neck. She glanced his way, and the polite smile melted away into one that was unmistakably sincere.

And, blessed day that it was, there was an empty chair beside her. Not caring where Fitzwilliam planned to take himself off to first, Christopher crossed the room and sat near Miss Chant—or rather, Rachel. He had no right to call her by her Christian name, but seeing her now, he found he couldn't think of her in such distant terms as "Miss Chant."

"Good evening," he said.

"Good evening to you, as well."

She looked even more beautiful when her dark eyes were on him. Though they'd conversed many times easily enough, Christopher was suddenly struggling to find a topic, struggling almost as hard as he was not to stare.

"How have you been occupying yourself today?" A lame question, but it was the best he could do, apparently.

Her smile grew, reaching her eyes and making them sparkle. "You mean since this afternoon?"

They'd spent a couple of hours earlier that day at the pianoforte. Since their first meeting many days previous, they'd "happened" upon one another many times in the small room in the servants' quarters.

"Yes, since this afternoon," Christopher said, forcing himself to rest against the back of the chair.

"Mostly getting ready for tonight. But I did have a few minutes to look over the music you suggested."

"What do you think of it so far?" When he'd found the piece by Haydn, he'd thought of her immediately.

"The second movement looks quite to my liking, though I suppose I won't know for sure until I can play it." Her lips tilted up on one side. "I fear I cannot *read* music and play it in my head so well as you."

"I wouldn't be too sure. But I do believe you will enjoy the piece. We can play it tomorrow if you like."

"That would be lovely. I must confess myself eager to hear it. The second movement seems . . . most lilting. The notes are simple, but I rather imagine them to prove quite dignified."

"You enjoy simplicity," Christopher stated, motioning toward her dress.

Rachel smoothed the mint green fabric over her lap. "Do you think it's too simple? My abigail was quite insistent that I wear something with ruffles, or at least a bit of lace." Her hand went to her throat where the locket she always wore rested against her ivory skin. "And then she tried to get me to wear several strands of pearls instead of my necklace. I refused all her suggestions, but I must say I feel a bit bland now." Her gaze left him, traveling over the other members of the gathering. Several of the women were dressed just as Rachel described—lace, ribbons, pearls, and ruffles. But those things weren't Rachel, and she didn't look any less charming for not wearing them.

"Simplicity carries its own sort of elegance," he said. What he truly meant but couldn't quite seem to say was that *she* was elegant. *She* needed none of the frippery or flounces. She was lovely just as she was.

"I am glad you think so." Rachel glanced back down at her dress, then up at him, her fingers playing gently with the chain at her throat.

"I don't think I've ever seen you without that necklace," Christopher said. She'd even been wearing it that fateful morning when they'd met near the lake.

She pulled it out, cupping the oval locket that hung there. She pressed against the clasp with her thumb, easily opening it, an action she'd clearly done many times before. Two very small miniatures were inside—a man and a woman. She angled the locket so he might see. Christopher had to lean in to make much out, the miniatures were so tiny. Sitting with his shoulder pressed just behind hers, their arms touching nearly the full length, he could smell the lavender soap she used. One of her curls brushed against his cheek, bringing with it the urge to take it between two of his fingers. He set his jaw. He was supposed to be focusing on the miniatures, not the lady sitting so close to him, captivating though she may be. Christopher gazed harder at the locket. The woman in the first image was not Rachel, but there were similarities. He could see similarities between her and the man as well.

"Your parents?" he asked.

She nodded, her dark curls brushing by him and filling the air with more lavender. "I try not to go anywhere without them."

"No matter how wet you foresee yourself becoming?"

She shut her mouth firmly, her eyes going a bit wide.

He should not be teasing her. Still, he turned his head, whispering in her ear. "Do you often take early morning swims?"

He was rewarded with a smile.

"Gracious, no. It was quite out of character for me, I assure you."

"Then why do it?"

Her gaze jumped back down to the locket. "For them. Mother, especially." She closed it up, letting it rest once more against her throat.

Sitting so close to her would cause tongues to wag, so no matter how much he regretted the necessity of it, Christopher angled in his chair, pulling away while also facing her more fully. "I am an excellent listener."

She looked up at him from beneath her lashes. "You will find me quite silly, I am sure."

"You have worried that before, and I haven't found you even remotely silly yet." What he did find her to be was unaffected by his nearness. How could he feel so much while she appeared to feel so little? Or perhaps she did feel something and was simply good at hiding it.

Rachel took a breath, fidgeting for a moment before she finally spoke. "I was hoping to cause enough of a scandal that my uncle would see the wisdom in allowing me to return home."

"He is not allowing it?" That surprised Christopher. His eyes moved toward where Sir Mulgrave still sat, listening to the older two women. Christopher had not had cause to speak much with Rachel's uncle, but he seemed a respectable man. Certainly no ogre, or one who demanded others be subservient.

"He only wishes for my happiness," Rachel continued. "And he feels I am more likely to find that here, or in London, rather than back home with Mother. It seems, ever since my father was taken away, everyone believes that I'll find happiness if I just keep moving." Her eyes glazed over as though she'd stopped seeing the room about them. She was probably seeing memories instead. "She hasn't written to me. Not once since I left for London. I haven't heard a word from her since, not there and not since arriving here. I used to receive letters once a week. For the life of me, I can't imagine why she suddenly stopped." She glanced his way, and he caught the shimmer of unshed tears along her lower lashes. "What if she is unwell? What if something has happened to her?"

He knew the pain of losing a parent; in that, he could relate. But while his father had been alive, they were always together. He couldn't imagine the ache that being separated from your last remaining parent would cause. It was likely even more troublesome because of Rachel's nature; she was a kind and considerate woman, one who cared deeply for others. He'd seen it in the way she interacted with her cousins, the other members of the household, even in how she responded to Fitzwilliam's *practicing*.

"I finally admitted to my uncle that I'd gone swimming and that I'd taken Dinah along with me," she continued. "I thought for sure he'd be furious."

Christopher did not like the idea of any man being furious at Rachel. "But he wasn't?"

"Far from it." She shook her head, her shoulders slumping a bit. "After I'd finished my story, he placed a hand on my shoulder and said, 'Nice try.' Then he walked away."

Christopher didn't know if he should laugh or not. "Nice try?"

"I think he must have pieced together *why* I'd gone swimming. I've spoken to him several times since. I even wrote an egregiously long letter explaining all the reasons why I ought to be allowed to return home. All to no avail." Her voice grew soft. "I'd happily steal a carriage and drive it myself if I could."

The thought brought with it a surge of protectiveness. Christopher almost reached for her hand but caught himself just in time. Instead, he said, "No matter what else has or hasn't happened, I am sure she knows how much you care."

Rachel blinked a few times, clearly trying to chase away the tears threatening to spill. How could Sir Mulgrave keep mother and daughter apart in such a way?

"Everyone seems to think I am foolish," she said. "But sometimes, the worry becomes so overwhelming. I know I ought to appreciate Uncle's good fortune and how it has blessed my life. But I cannot even begin to think about . . ." Her face grew pink and she looked away. "What I mean to say is I can't seem to find the focus to think about anything other than Mother. I just wish my family understood."

Christopher reached into his pocket and pulled out a handkerchief. As he held it out to her, dinner was announced and immediately the room sprang to life. Lady Fitzwilliam had chosen tonight would be a formal affair, so they would be entering the library-turned-dining-room by rank. Which meant Christopher would not be allowed to accompany Rachel in, or even choose to sit near her.

Rachel dabbed at her eyes. "Are we in for a most unusual meal, then? I've only heard bits and pieces of rumors from the maids. Are we really to eat in the library?"

Ah yes, the dreaded antics which might very well result in a casualty or two. "Yes, we are to eat in the library, where all those excellent books are within easy distance of gravy and any number of sauces."

"That's awful." Her sudden and sincere statement resonated with his own feelings on the topic.

"So long as no one grows overly excited or drunk, I think the library will fare the night tolerably well."

Rachel slowly shook her head, her expression of shock mixed with horror unyielding. "One can only hope. For the sake of the books, I shall try my best to keep the conversation boring."

Christopher chuckled. "My heart thanks you." Standing, he reached a hand out to her. The last of the gentlemen were finding their companions for the meal. Christopher himself should not have waited so long to do the same. As a lowly tutor, he would be walking in with Mrs. Lock, a lady's companion that had accompanied one of the guests. Even her standing was above his own; he was only in attendance because the Fitzwilliams's eccentricities extended so far as to invite him.

Still, he was quite reluctant to leave Rachel's side.

She, too, was watching as a couple more people left the room, a wisp of a smile returning to her lips. "I have all sorts of confessions for you tonight; in truth, I have another one already."

"I'm all yours." She, no doubt, was too concerned for her mother to understand just how true his statement was.

She leaned in and he smelled lavender once more. "I am not at all feeling up to this tonight. I don't know half the people present and feel certain I shall make a fool of myself."

"I am certain you shall do no less than captivate and enchant whichever gentleman you accompany." He wasn't sure where such brazen words had come from—he'd probably been spending too much time with Fitzwilliam. Nonetheless, part of him was glad she was so set against forming any attachments to the prim and proper gentlemen attending tonight, no matter that everyone knew her family wished she would.

Rachel smiled a reassured, flattered smile. His heart did a flip at the sight, especially knowing he was the cause of her pleasure. It was no doubt foolish to think, even after she'd discouraged every gentleman of her acquaintance, that, somehow, Rachel would come to favor him. But, hope, Christopher was learning, was rarely logical.

One of the gentlemen in attendance, one Christopher had never before met, caught sight of Rachel and headed their way.

Rachel tensed at his side. She placed a hand on his arm—the unexpected touch sending warmth through him.

"I'd feel a lot more comfortable if you were nearer me," she said.

Lud—the warmth he'd felt at her touch was nothing compared to that which he felt at her words.

"Any lady who can keep her composure while dripping wet in a tree can certainly charm any gentleman over dinner."

Her pink lips pursed. "What you must have thought of me."

Only that she was enchanting and quite intriguing. "And if you need a reminder," Christopher continued quickly, they only had seconds before the gentleman reached them, "look to me. I'll smile at you."

He didn't dare say more for fear of being overheard. The gentleman moved up, bowing before them both and extending his arm to Rachel. Apparently, unlike Christopher, they had already been introduced. With only a few words between them, the gentleman led Rachel away.

Christopher found his companion for dinner easily, as the room was nearly empty now. As she took his arm and they began their walk, Rachel turned around and caught his eye.

True to his word, Christopher smiled at her.

The effect was instantaneous and quite noticeable. At least to him it was. She stood a little straighter, smiled a little more authentically, and walked a little more confidently. She turned back to her own companion and said something. Christopher was too far away to hear what it was, but he could tell by both her and the gentleman's body language that they were talking.

One of the last to leave the drawing room, Christopher couldn't deny that Rachel looked quite at home on the arm of a titled gentleman. Part of him was glad she was too wrapped up in worry over her mother to even consider any of the men she met.

Was there some way he could be sure he was around when she finally found the reassurance she needed to see beyond her concern? How he wished he could. He was certain that waiting for someone like Rachel would not feel like a burden at all.

Just the same, when she did eventually find it in herself to care for more than just her mother, Christopher wouldn't have much to offer her. No home. No stability. No title or standing or even wealth.

He could wait for her; but he could not change who he was.

He could not make himself into the man she deserved.

CHAPTER FOURTEEN

Blessedly, Christopher was seated across the table and only down a little ways from Rachel. She couldn't speak to him, but at least she could look his way whenever her confidence started to wane. Seated beside Lord Nicholson, a man of far more wealth and standing than any man who'd ever walked her into dinner before, Rachel found she needed every smile she could garner.

Rachel glanced at Christopher. His eyes caught hers and his lips turned upward, as she knew they would. That simple gesture bolstered her up. He was right; she'd kept her composure in far worse situations, and she could do so again now.

It was strange sitting at such an elegantly set table while book-cases full of tomes and novels surrounded them. It was a lovely atmosphere. So long as no one drank so much as to become clumsy, she doubted any of the books were truly in danger.

"Do you find this part of England to your liking?" Lord Nicholson asked.

Her mind flew back to her idiotic dip in the lake not far away. "Yes, quite so. I do believe I prefer the country over Town."

Lord Nicholson nodded. "As do I."

He seemed a respectable gentleman. Rachel studied him out of the corner of her eye. He was certainly pleasing to look at with brown hair and a slender build. Though his hair didn't sport any hint of red and his shoulders didn't fill his jacket half so well as Christopher's. No matter how good-looking he was, or how pleasing she might find his company, Rachel meant what she'd said earlier. She couldn't even begin to think of making a match just now, not when she was so wrapped up in concern over her mother. Why Uncle Seth believed this was her last and only chance to secure her future, she couldn't say. Perhaps it was because he was a man and when he focused on something, nothing else mattered. Now was the time to marry his girls off. Nothing else would stand in the way. Or . . . a new thought snuck into her mind. Suppose whatever it was that he was keeping from her would *prevent* her from forming an attachment in the future? A chill ran down her spine.

If that was so, then what Uncle was keeping from her was very bad, indeed.

Rachel set her jaw. It didn't matter. Regardless of what Uncle was or was not hiding, Rachel wasn't forming an attachment to anyone just now. She'd set her mind. She was determined.

She glanced over at the man beside her. Still, she could not be rude. For now, she needed to at least draw her mind away from its wanderings long enough to not appear completely dismissive.

"Is your estate far from here?" she asked.

"About two hours on horseback."

"My, that is far to come for a simple dinner invitation."

"What? And miss an opportunity to partake in one of the infamous Curio Manor celebrations?" There was something to his tone that made Rachel feel he wasn't here so much to enjoy the experience as he was to look down on other attendees. "I'd have gladly traveled twice the distance."

Rachel's guard went up. He hadn't exactly stated that he saw himself as superior when compared to his hostess, but he certainly gave her that impression. Any inclination Rachel may have been feeling toward the man quickly faded.

A long line of footmen entered the library. Each brought with him a plate piled high with food, and every plate rested atop a book.

The aroma of fine food filled the room, mingling with the gentle scent of old books. It was a strange combination, one Rachel had never smelled before and one she wasn't sure she particularly cared for.

The footmen lined up behind each of the guests. Surely they'd remove the plates from the books before placing them down on the table? But they didn't. Instead, in perfect unison, the footmen reached around the individuals seated at the table and placed the food-laden books at each place setting. Rachel's gaze flitted to Mr. Dunn. Surely they weren't going to *eat* with their plates atop books? If they did, more than one book would not survive the night.

Mr. Dunn shot her a glance that showed he clearly understood her distress. Did the Fitzwilliams not care for their books at all? Silly and a bit outlandish, Rachel could handle. But this was nothing short of dangerous.

"Served on books. While we sit in the library," Lord Nicholson said with a snort. "How childish."

Rachel's brow creased. She didn't like the idea of so many fine books on the table with so much food, but neither did she like the idea of a gentleman criticizing their host. To disagree was one thing. To be outright rude was another thing entirely. Though she still felt apprehension for the books whose lovely pages were now at stake, she simultaneously couldn't countenance anyone speaking ill of the dowager in her presence.

"I find it delightful," Rachel said. It was stretching the truth a bit, but that was far preferable to agreeing with him.

"But of course," he said with the most condescending smile Rachel had ever been privileged to receive.

Rachel turned back to her food. The sooner she could end her time with Lord Nicholson, the better. She picked up a bit of cooked carrot with her fork. It dripped a sweet-smelling sauce. Her stomach growled at the promise of delicious food, but her heart could not quite feel at ease. She resisted the temptation to lift her plate and see exactly which beloved book she was putting in harm's way. But, as no one else was lifting their plates, Rachel knew she couldn't lift hers without causing a bit of a scene. Instead, she allowed her fingers to slip beneath the plate and run across the spine of the book. The cover was soft to the touch, and she could feel the indentations where the title was printed. Unfortunately, she couldn't make out the name just by touch.

Her eyes, almost of their own accord, found Mr. Dunn's again.

Careful, he mouthed.

Calm, she mouthed back.

Together, they both lifted their forks to their mouths, taking a bite in unison.

The meal continued, ending only after no fewer than five courses, each of which put yet another long array of books at risk. Though Rachel had started the meal content to converse with Lord Nicholson, by the end, she was more than ready to be done. When Lady Fitzwilliam stood and suggested the ladies withdraw, Rachel was right behind her.

She, Eliza, Dinah, and one of the matrons invited to dinner that night all sat down to a game of whist. They were still in the middle of it when the gentlemen arrived. Rachel's eyes found Christopher and they shared a smile before she looked back at her cards while he found a seat not far away from Charlotte, Lady Fitzwilliam, and Uncle Seth.

What was it Christopher had said the other night? He believed she could find happiness regardless. Watching him over the top of her cards, a peace filled Rachel's chest. Perhaps she truly could. Perhaps, since it was clearly her mother's wish they not communicate, she should come to terms with that and move on.

"Your turn, Rachel," Eliza said from across the table.

"Yes, sorry." Rachel glanced down at her hand. "What was trump, again?"

Eliza gave her a slightly worried glance. "Spades."

"Of course." She had no spades, however. Grabbing a nine of diamonds, she placed it with the other cards in the center of the table. Dinah played a higher card, however, and took the hand.

Rachel's gaze moved back to Christopher. But was letting her mother go truly what she wanted? The idea of finding happiness was enticing; how could it not be? And she couldn't disagree that she was happy now. But at what cost? Had she not determined when first coming to Curio Manor that nothing would stop her from reconnecting with her mother?

"Rachel?" Eliza's voice brought her back to the game. Rachel's gaze snapped back to her cousin, and she offered an apologetic smile. "It is your turn again."

"Sorry." She grabbed a card and tossed it onto the table.

Christopher caught her eye once more, but this time he didn't smile. What were her uncle, Charlotte and Lady Fitzwilliam discussing? Whatever it was, it seemed not to be much to his liking.

"Rachel." Dinah's sharp tone brought her back to the table once again.

"Is it my turn?" Rachel asked, her eyes moving to the cards in her hand. There was only one left, so she tossed it into the center.

Dinah shook her head, clearly frustrated, and gathered the cards back up.

"Are you quite all right?" Eliza asked.

"Yes," Rachel said quickly. "Why wouldn't I be?"

Eliza looked over her shoulder toward the rest of the room. Had it been obvious Rachel's gaze continually found Christopher? Even if Eliza had noticed, it wasn't as though that would be enough for Eliza to piece together the heavy thoughts weighing on Rachel's heart.

Still, she would be wise to apply herself to the matter at hand for the rest of the night. Blessedly, the beginning of summer celebration ended early. As the guests were being handed their wraps, hats, and bonnets, Rachel noticed Christopher slip down the corridor toward the back of the house.

A quick glance about her proved that no one was watching her either, so she followed. A few minutes of conversation with Christopher would set her to rights. The ideas and thoughts she'd been mulling over during whist had yet to truly settle in her mind. She felt unsure of her next move but knew speaking with Christopher would help to shed some light on her situation.

She caught sight of him just as he pushed open the kitchen door and moved inside. That was strange. She'd half wondered if he hadn't been heading toward the pianoforte in the servants' quarters, but that would have necessitated him turning right and heading down the hall, not directly into the kitchen.

Rachel pulled the door open and peered inside. It was far larger a kitchen than any she'd ever seen before. A giant hearth rested against the far wall; the biggest collection of pots and pans hung to her left; in the center was a massive work table with several maids and footmen bustling about it, carrying recently cleaned plates and the like away to where they would be stored for use again in the future. Along the wall directly to her right was a smaller worktable, but still a very long one. Christopher stood beside it, piles and piles of books stacked up before him.

"'N that's the last of them," a large woman said, dropping a final stack onto the table. "We've cleaned them the best we could. But I figured you'd want to once-over them before we put them all back."

"Yes," Christopher said, picking up one of the books. "Thank you."

The woman bobbed her head and strode back into the heart of the kitchen, calling out to one of the footmen as she walked off.

Rachel slipped into the room and up close to Christopher. "Making an account of today's casualties?"

He glanced her way and his lips pulled up on the side. But it wasn't a smile, not a full one.

Rachel knew a moment of disappointment but brushed it quickly aside. "May I help?" She picked up the top book of one of the stacks and slowly turned it over. There was a bit of a gravy stain on the back side. Her heart felt sad for the little tome.

"You can use this." Christopher handed her a damp cloth.

Rachel took it but didn't miss that Christopher barely glanced at her and had yet to start up any kind of conversation. Silently, she began scrubbing at the stain. It was clear it had already been scrubbed once, but, hopefully, a second time would improve the cover. Rachel worked for several minutes before coming to the realization that little more could be done at this point, and she set the book aside.

Picking up the next one, she looked Christopher over. He appeared to be focused on the book in his hand, carefully opening the cover and inspecting the inside, even going so far as to flip through the pages.

"Is everything well?" she asked. He wasn't acting his normal happy self. Christopher had never been as exuberant as Lord Fitzwilliam or as light in spirit as the dowager, but he was still a consistently happy person, if a bit less extravagant about it.

"I just don't like seeing so many books soiled," he said.

No—there was something more than that. He'd been quite fine before dinner and even seemed fine during dinner. After dinner, however, when he was sitting with Uncle Seth, Charlotte, and Lady Fitzwilliam, he'd lost his smile.

"Did you find enjoyable conversation after dinner?" she asked.

"It was agreeable, I suppose." His voice tightened slightly.

So *that* was the problem. "What did my uncle, Charlotte, and Lady Fitzwilliam have to say?"

His eyes shot toward her and back to the books again. "Nothing of much consequence."

"Christopher," she said firmly.

He sighed, placing the book he'd been inspecting down. He turned and rested a hip against the long work table, folding his arms. "They spoke of you."

Oh. Rachel's hands paused. Drawing in a breath, she placed aside the book she'd been looking over and took hold of another. "And what did they have to say?" She chose to look at the book in her hands instead of at him.

"Lady Blackmore started by saying she'd hoped Lord Fitzwilliam's jovial spirit would be the perfect complement to your . . . subdued nature."

"Well." Rachel still couldn't meet his gaze; she only hoped her embarrassment wasn't turning her face a motley shade of red. "That is understandable, isn't it? Opposites attract and all that. And he and I have become something of friends. Though his constant proposing has put a bit of a damper on the acquaintance." She laughed lightly, but it fell flat.

Her shoulders dropped; why was she trying to pretend around Christopher? He'd always understood her. Lips pulled to the side, she placed her inspected book down with the other ones and looked up at him.

Christopher's expression told her that he hadn't yet told her all.

"What else?" she asked. She had to know, even if part of her didn't want to.

"Your uncle spoke up."

"Drat," she whispered.

"He said he still sincerely hoped that you and Lord Fitzwilliam would make a match of it so that you would stop . . . pining after the things you left behind."

Her jaw tightened. "He means my mother."

Christopher nodded, his voice soft. "I know."

So now Uncle had taken to telling others how Rachel "pined away," how she ought to be setting her cap at Lord Fitzwilliam. How ironic; if only Uncle knew she'd already turned down his lordship three times. She blew out a harsh breath. It was unfair.

"I knew he felt that way," Rachel said. Still, it stung to know he was speaking of her so. "And what of the dowager?"

"She spoke rather long regarding how she would love to have you for a granddaughter."

"Heaven help me."

Christopher gave her a sympathetic smile. "I think she just wants to see her grandson married and settled."

"Well, I don't care to marry him," she said through gritted teeth. "And he doesn't care to marry me. Why can't they see that and let me *go home*?" With the last two words, she slammed an open palm down on the work table. It hit with a low *smack*.

"Come now." Christopher took her hands in his. "You know he only wishes for your happiness."

She scowled at him. "Don't take his side." Maybe tomorrow or the next day when she wasn't so angry she could handle Christopher speaking up for Uncle Seth, but just now, she was furious and didn't care to be anything else. "If they'd all stop talking *about* me and start talking *to* me, then we might actually be able to find a solution I can live with. But all this shoving me and his lordship together"—she let out something between a groan and a sigh—"it has to stop."

He gave her hands a gentle squeeze and despite the frustration bubbling inside her, it did feel calming. "I know you and Fitzwilliam are not suited to be any more than friends."

"At least someone here can see reason," she muttered.

His lips ticked upward at the words. But then he grew serious once more. "However . . ."

Her scowl deepened; if he thought he was going to get her to change her mind, he was sorely wrong.

"If there were someone . . . someone quite suited to you . . . might you . . . reconsider?"

Her heart did a strange flip, one that sent tingles coursing through her, leaving her lightheaded, her stomach giddy.

But reality returned with a peace-crushing weight. "I can't give up on Mother."

"It's not as though once a woman marries she is forbidden to see her mother thereafter."

Strange. She could have sworn he'd just agreed that she and his lordship would not suit. Rachel picked up the book she'd been cleaning. "Then perhaps I ought to say yes next time Lord Fitzwilliam proposes. We'll be married, and I'll promptly drive him to Bedlam, and then he'll be more than willing to allow me to return to my mother. Would that please you?"

He tossed her a scowl. "No, it most certainly would not."

His denial came across a bit stronger than she'd anticipated. She paused in her scrubbing even as he placed both hands on the worktable and leaned against it.

"Do you believe you will," he said slowly, "perhaps, after you have seen that your mother is well, return to London for the season?"

He appeared as though the answer was quite important to him, though Rachel wasn't sure why. "It depends on when Uncle Seth finally allows me to go see her, and if she truly is all right when I get there." Not that she believed such was likely. Every day, that niggling

—the one in her stomach that whispered something was certainly wrong—seemed to grow stronger.

"Just for a moment, imagine that you will see her again and when you do, you see that she's just as well off as your uncle has said. What then?"

Rachel closed her eyes and tried to imagine exactly that. Suppose all was well when she saw her mother again. What would she do after that? Try as she might, something in her heart said that wasn't what she would find, and she couldn't picture herself past the moment when she first laid eyes on her mother. She tried to reply—she truly did—but no words came.

Finally, she opened her eyes and shook her head. "I know everyone thinks I should be overjoyed at my uncle's change in station. He's titled now, and I should just happily find a new life among the *ton*."

"Understandably so. If there's one constant among the *ton*, it is that they are very strict about who they allow into their ranks."

Rachel froze, his words hitting her like a pound of rocks. "What did you say?"

Christopher's brow creased. "That the *ton* are strict?"

"About who joins their ranks." Oh, gracious. "Do you think that's it? Do you suppose that's why Mother has stopped writing and Uncle won't let me visit her? Because she wouldn't be welcome among the *ton*?" Why had she not seen it before? "That has to be it. Mother is distancing herself from me on purpose. Not so much in the hopes that she won't be a distraction, but because she doesn't want to be the reason none of the gentlemen come up to scratch." It made more sense than anything, not unless her mother had fallen gravely ill, which Uncle repeatedly claimed wasn't the case. It would also account for Uncle Seth's uncharacteristic behavior, for his insistence that Rachel make a match *before* she visit her mother again.

Christopher didn't seem convinced. "Surely they know you would never attach yourself to a man who wished to ignore your mother."

"We are both smart enough to know that. At the same time, I can honestly think of at least a dozen gentlemen who would indeed prefer to pretend I don't have so lowly a connection as they'd certainly see my mother." She very well may have just stumbled upon what Uncle and Mother had been hiding. After all, if they had simply come out and told her their fears, she would certainly have dismissed them. In all honesty, if they had been honest with her, she very well may have responded by making her mother's current situation *more* well-known just to prove to all that Rachel didn't care. She knew a moment of chagrin. Uncle and Mother probably believed they were protecting her from herself.

Rachel wasn't at all sure they weren't in the right on that score.

"All that being said, I would guess . . ." Christopher spoke slowly as he straightened and returned his gaze to his book, "that you *will* want to make a connection someday."

"I suppose." It was hard to even consider with her heart so heavy. "With someone who *loves* my mother, regardless of whether or not she has boarders or makes a little extra by sewing and doing laundry."

"Granted. But aside from that, what sort of man do you see yourself forming an attachment to?"

What an unexpected question. Christopher was deliberately not making eye contact, no matter that she didn't respond right away. Eventually, she said, "One who lets me visit my mother as often as I desire."

He let out a small chuckle. "What else?"

"I don't know." She shrugged. Why was he pressing this point? She gave him a stern glare. "Did Charlotte put you up to this? Did she tell you I'm not seeing the wonderful opportunities right before me just because I'm too worried for my mother? Or perhaps it was Dinah?"

"Not at all." He didn't look her way as he spoke. "Just consider me a curious friend."

She didn't believe that was all it was for a minute.

"Fine. I want a husband who doesn't make me change homes every few years. Who doesn't require that I give up what I have come to love on the feeble promise that somewhere out there, there is something *else* I might love even more. Why go searching for something new when I already know what I want and where it is?"

Christopher was very still.

"I see," he said at length.

But he didn't at all sound as though he agreed.

She wished he, of all people, would understand. "You said you believed I could make myself a life where I am happy, and I've thought much on that since. I know most people"—she glanced up at him, for he was included in that statement—"believe that means I should move forward, that I should embrace a future and stop *pining* for the past. But I disagree. I would rather return to my mother than forever chase some new supposed happiness."

"Don't," Christopher said. "Don't close your heart off."

"I'm not closing it off so much as I'm closing *her* inside."

"The result is the same."

"Perhaps. But I have lost so much already; I can't lose her, too."

"Rachel, please—"

"No." She drew herself up. She'd made up her mind, and she wasn't about to waver. "On this, you will find I am quite determined."

Leaving Christopher with his books and damp rags, Rachel turned on her heel and hurried out of the kitchen.

CHAPTER FIFTEEN

Rachel paced the length of her bedchamber for nearly an hour. The words she and Christopher had shared swirled inside her, drowning out any other thought, emotion, or awareness. How could he—her friend who'd understood everything else—not see that she couldn't simply walk away from her mother? Rachel couldn't give up now. She couldn't build a future and shrug off her past. Even if making known her connection to her mother materially hurt her chances of securing a desirable match, what did that matter? Certainly it wasn't more important to her than her mother's health and happiness. It wasn't more important to Rachel than her relationship with her mother.

How could Uncle Seth have voiced such thoughts aloud, even if it were only to Charlotte and Lady Fitzwilliam? It was humiliating. It was also quite unfair. Her uncle knew she didn't wish to make a connection until she could rebuild what she once had with her own mother. If Mother had continued to write her back even after they'd gone to London, perhaps Rachel would feel differently. Even better, if only Mother had agreed to come to London with them. Regardless, ever since that last visit to Mother before the season began, Rachel had not been able to feel at ease.

It always came back to Uncle. As her guardian and the one who legally could tell her where to go and where to be, her life—her future—was in his hands.

Coming to stand before the window, peering up into the night sky, Rachel had to be honest with herself. She had always been loved. Uncle Seth had always acted in her best interests.

Why couldn't he do so now?

Only he could answer such a question.

Turning away from the window, Rachel quickly re-dressed herself in her simplest morning dress. It didn't take her long. She hadn't always had a lady's maid at the ready and had much practice seeing to her own toilet. Once she was again presentable, Rachel slipped out of her bedchamber. It was well past midnight, but this couldn't wait. Not any longer.

Rachel strode down the corridor, the light from a moving candle catching her eye. From around the corner strode Lorenzo. Rachel half-smiled to herself; how the man forever knew when he was needed, she would probably never know.

"It is only me," he said with a bow, "Lorenzo the butler."

"Yes, I know." His odd way of always introducing himself had long since endeared him to her.

"Is there anything I might do for you, miss?"

"Actually, there is. I wish to see my uncle in the library."

"I believe he is already abed."

Rachel was sure of it. He'd never been one to stay up late, not when, for decades, he'd always had much work waiting for him the next morning. Even now, when he could boast a title and connections with many of the *haut ton*, he wasn't ready to give up most of his habits.

"Nonetheless," Rachel persisted, "please let him know it is urgent, and I wish to see him now."

"Of course, miss." Lorenzo bowed again.

Rachel hurried toward the library. It would be some time before her uncle arrived, but she wanted to be prepared for when he did.

Christopher stared up at the ceiling. Normally, he was asleep within minutes of lying down in his bed, but not tonight.

Tonight, there was far too much he was trying to sort through for his brain to calm down and find sleep.

There was a sound from the floor below—probably someone up and walking about. Rachel, perhaps? It would stand to reason since the guest wing was directly below the family wing, which is where Fitzwilliam had graciously granted Christopher a room.

In all respects, while here at Curio Manor, Christopher had been treated like one of the family. He was given a room next to Fitzwilliam's. He was always welcome, even expected, at dinner parties and afternoon teas. He'd been granted an excellent wage, a mount to ride whenever he wished it, all that was comfortable.

And what had all that done to him?

It had gone to his head. Made him start to believe that he might actually *be* a man who was free to choose a path, a man free to dream of a home, a man free to fall in love.

But he wasn't. He didn't truly have any of those privileges. He was here only because Lady Fitzwilliam was too considerate to insist he leave. He was still fully dependent on Curio Manor for his horse, his bed, his food, his everything. He had nothing to offer Rachel. No home, no security. Nothing a woman depended upon her husband for. Devil take him, if her mother was truly ill, which Rachel seemed to half-believe, he wouldn't even have the means to see her taken care of. He could provide neither woman a home in which they would be warm and comfortable.

Lord Fitzwilliam could. He could provide both women those things ten times over. It made perfect, logical, reasonable sense that Rachel and Fitzwilliam should make a match.

Blast.

Rolling over, he kicked at the blankets, sending them down toward his feet and off the bed completely. He sat up and looked over his room. No—not *his* room. The room he'd been allowed use of. The room he would have to leave soon. Perhaps if he found a new position? If he was hired on to a fine household with one or more young boys, he could reasonably expect to stay there for many years. He'd saved nearly every bit of money he'd received from Lady Fitzwilliam; he'd had no reason to spend it. Would it perhaps be enough to secure a small house? Would it be enough to convince Rachel to step into a largely unknown future with him?

With a loud groan, he flopped back onto the bed. What kind of security was that?

Excuse me, Rachel, but despite the fact that I can offer you no house, no promise of food in the winter, no guarantee we won't find ourselves in worse straights in only a few years, do you think my love for you enough reason to consider marrying me?

What kind of proposal would that be? It made even the worst of Fitzwilliam's ideas appear like brilliant offers. His friend wanted to "practice" proposing so that he might find the best way to do it. Perhaps Christopher should have offered to do all the proposing. His pitiful offering would have made it much easier to judge the proposals on merit alone.

Christopher shut his eyes, slowly rocking his head back and forth. Fitzwilliam's proposals had been lavish and what he had to offer was almost exorbitant. But he'd never offered love. That much Christopher *could* offer. When he had fallen in love exactly, he wasn't sure. Honestly, it might have been that first moment he'd looked over the hill and seen Rachel stepping out of the carriage. He'd been too far away to truly see her, and yet he'd felt something. Unknown to him though she was, his heart had known she was the woman he would someday want.

And then when they'd met in the tree? Lud, but who wouldn't have been drawn in by the sight?

But no matter how compelling those first few meetings had been, it truly was because of the many hours, many days they'd spent together. Walking the gardens. Trying to deal with Fitzwilliam's ridiculous proposals. Playing the pianoforte together.

He'd started to wonder if she felt the same way. He'd hoped that she did.

Tonight ended that hope. No matter what she did or didn't feel for him, she wasn't interested in pursuing things further. Rachel only wanted one thing and that was to return to her mother. How could a man fault her for such a desire? She wanted it, he knew, less for her own happiness and more because she was deeply worried that her mother was not well, either in spirit, body, or mind. For months now, ever since her family first brought her to London and later here to Curio Manor, Rachel had only wanted to know her mother was all right.

She wanted it more than her own happiness. She certainly wanted it more than she wanted him.

Rachel was determined; that was the word she had used. And during all these weeks together, if there was one thing Christopher had learned, and loved, about Rachel, it was that when she was determined, she didn't let anything stop her.

Rachel sat near a low-burning candle in the library. After waking her uncle's valet, Lorenzo the butler had come to the library and lit several candles and stoked up the fire. Having had a chance to calm down a bit, Rachel felt a bit foolish for causing so many people to remain awake. Still, perhaps this was just what Uncle Seth needed to realize he wasn't going to wear her down; she wasn't going to look upon a man one day and suddenly change her mind. She wasn't going to stop.

The door opened and Rachel sat up straighter.

Uncle Seth walked in. He was dressed properly, but his hair was still mussed from sleep and his scowl made it appear as though he wasn't fully awake. "Rachel, what's wrong?"

She sorted through many phrases. Picking the right words was paramount. "I wished to speak to you, again, about returning home to see my mother."

"Oh." Seth dropped into the chair across from her. "So now you've taken to waking me up in the middle of the night?"

"If that's what is required of me."

"Interestingly enough," he said, "Lord Fitzwilliam brought this very topic up in conversation with me earlier today."

Had he? Well, good. That was part of their deal, after all. Still, all Rachel said was, "Oh?"

Uncle eyed her closely. "I found it interesting that a man whom you claim to have no interest in is very concerned that you are granted the single thing you most want."

Rachel struggled to appear innocent. "If he does, then it is because he's a good man who's taken the time to listen."

Uncle Seth watched her for a minute, but then seemed to decide it wasn't worth pursuing why Lord Fitzwilliam was taking her side. He shook his head and settled further into the large chair. "Very well; have your say."

Clearly, he had already decided on his own response, all before she'd even begun. It was a battle she'd already lost. He wasn't even considering *re-considering* his stance.

"Sir," Rachel began, "I don't think you understand just how important this is to me."

"Your love for your mother is admirable," Uncle Seth said. "It does you great credit."

She opened her mouth, ready with all the same accusations, same pleadings, same arguments she'd used dozens of times already. But they died before she could speak them. They hadn't worked before; they weren't going to work this time. Lord Fitzwilliam at least had the wisdom to realize that if you asked a question over and over again, the least you could do was change up *how* you asked.

"Do you dislike your sister?" Rachel tried.

Uncle Seth's brow lifted. "Dislike Grace? Goodness, no. That's ridiculous. No sister could ever be a better, kinder soul."

"Do you believe if my connection to her is made known by society, I won't ever find a man willing to take me?"

Uncle Seth leaned forward, placing an elbow on his knee. "Where are these questions coming from?"

He didn't deny it. It was almost an agreement. The feeling that she may have just uncovered the truth spurred her on. "Then you admit it? You and Mother have determined that for me to have a life among the *ton*, she can no longer be a part of it?"

"We have determined nothing of the kind."

"Then why does she never write me?"

"She is unable to at this time." His words were not placating like an excuse might be, but sounded quite factual.

Rachel's brow creased. "How do you know that?"

He glanced away.

"Have *you* received word from my mother?" Rachel asked, scooting forward in her seat.

He didn't respond right away.

"She wrote to you?" How could Mother have written her uncle, but not *her*? She hadn't even sent a letter to Rachel *with* her letter to Uncle Seth?

"Grace and I both felt it was better if we didn't tell you," he began.

Rachel returned her gaze to him, willing him to speak faster, terrified of what she might hear.

"Perhaps we were wrong," he continued, his words painfully slow.

"Is she ill?"

"No, your mother is in fine health."

"Then you are worried that my connection to her would be looked down on."

"Your connection to her would be found out, regardless."

So she had been wrong in that line of thinking. It was nearly as frustrating as it was relieving to learn as much. Rachel shifted about. "If not that, then why?"

"She has not written because she is . . . otherwise engaged."

Otherwise engaged? What did he mean by that? "You're still trying to tell me that she hasn't written—for months now—because she is simply *busy*?"

He nodded. "Something like that." He obviously knew more than he was saying.

"Too busy to write her own daughter?" Rachel pressed. "While *not* being too busy to write her brother?"

"You mustn't be hurt; I only received the one letter. Trust me when I say she loves you, she is well, and she will write you when she has something worth writing about."

His words struck her as odd. Rachel wasn't expecting Mother to only write when something miraculous had happened. They'd always found everyday life worthy of discussion in their weekly letters. But Uncle Seth was a man, so perhaps he only saw communication as something one did when one could not avoid it any longer.

"Well," Rachel said. She wasn't about to give up. "If you are so certain she is well, then why not allow me to see her for myself?"

"Because she wishes you to find a husband," Uncle Seth blurted out. "She wants to know you are settled and happy; we both do."

And they were back to this. Back to the argument that taking time away from her London Season would damage her chances of meeting the right man. More specifically, it would damage her opportunity to secure his lordship. Well, perhaps Uncle needed to be set clear on that point.

"You know," Rachel said. "I have had plenty of time to get to know Lord Fitzwilliam. I realize that you and Charlotte had high hopes that we would . . . temper one another. But I can say with complete certainty that we would not suit."

"We have seen you together quite often," he countered. Rachel could only guess that when he said 'we,' he meant himself and Charlotte. "And you two always appear to rub together well."

"We are good friends." And they would be better friends once Lord Fitzwilliam took off proposing to her every few days. "But that is all. I do not care to marry him, and he does not care to marry me."

"Are you certain?"

"Quite." Of few things had she ever been *more* certain. Perhaps if Uncle understood the depth to which she was certain she and his lordship would not suit, he would rethink taking her home.

Uncle Seth let out a long sigh and let his head rest against the chair. "Here I was hoping we could forestall returning to London at least another month."

Rachel cast her gaze heavenward. Of all the various reasons she'd dreamed up why Uncle Seth was unwilling to return her home to her mother, she never once, even for a moment, wondered if it was because *he* was enjoying the London Season. No one who truly knew him would ever make such a monumental mistake.

"Uncle, I cannot for the life of me understand why you simply will not allow me a visit home."

"Because you are better off staying here and finding a match."

His immediate and wholly unenlightening reply made Rachel purse her lips in anger. "Are you sure that's it? Or perhaps it is that you have stopped caring for *me*? Is that why you have ignored my request all these times? Now that you have a title, you must focus on seeing your two daughters wed, no matter what your ward asks of you?"

"You know that isn't true." His voice grew in intensity. "You are every bit as much one of my daughters as either Eliza or Dinah."

"Unlike them, though," Rachel's deep need swelled up and she nearly shouted, "*my* mother *isn't* dead."

Uncle Seth only stared at her, his face an unreadable blank slate.

"I can't allow Mother to work herself into an early grave like your mother did. Or be consumed by loneliness like your father. Or die from lack of proper treatment like your wife."

Her words, harsh and unfeeling, seemed to echo about the library well after the sound of them died. She'd never seen Uncle Seth look so overwrought.

Rachel knew a moment of guilt. She shouldn't have mentioned his wife; she knew full well he carried a heavy shame that he'd not had the resources to see she get better treatment when she'd grown ill.

"My mother is still alive," Rachel said, "and I cannot leave her behind while I move forward into a new life."

"You wouldn't be leaving her behind," he finally said, sitting back once more, but his tone was hollow.

"Wouldn't I? It is as you said. Society will find out that she's been forced to take in boarders. That she takes in sewing and laundry just to put food on her table. They struggle to accept *us* even with your title; they will never accept her."

He didn't say anything, and his silence seemed to pull yet more truth from her. "You are asking me to give up my mother. To replace her with a husband."

He said nothing after that; he only stared into the fire.

Rachel's guilt returned. It seemed her comment about his wife had cut deep.

"I am sorry, Uncle," she said in a soft voice. "I know no man could have done more for your wife than you did."

He didn't so much as blink. Indeed, he remained so motionless, if his eyes had been shut she would have been convinced he was sleeping. Only, instead of sitting in a calm relaxed pose, he was tense all over.

Rachel had no desire to make an enemy of this man, this man who'd taken her in and raised her as one of his own. This man who frequently sent her mother money and had, up until recently, allowed them the freedom to write one another, paying the expense for both letters sent and letters received without so much as a grumble.

No, she had no desire for a wedge to come between them. Perhaps if they could only compromise?

Rachel's brow lifted, an idea striking her.

"What if we made a bargain?"

His gaze shot to her and then returned to the fire. He was listening, at least.

"Let us stay at Curio Manor for one more month. I will do my utmost to meet any gentleman who crosses my path and get to know him sincerely and fully. In essence, I will do my best to find my 'perfect match.'" Uncle Seth's head slowly turned toward her. Rachel hurried on before he could interject. "However, if, in a month's time, I have yet to find someone who turns my head, you promise to return me home to my mother before continuing on to London with Eliza and Dinah."

"You would sacrifice your entire future only to see your mother a half-year earlier?"

Though the words were different, his tone and the spirit of the question put Rachel in mind of Christopher's statement earlier that night. *Don't close your heart off.*

Tears unexpectedly bit against her eyes. Drat, but she cried so much these days. Rachel dropped her gaze to her lap, blinking furiously in the hope that Uncle Seth had not seen how close she suddenly was to tears.

Uncle's voice was soft when he spoke. "You very well may never have another opportunity such as this."

"Then I waste it fully aware of the consequences."

Uncle Seth leaned forward. "Rachel, there are matters at work here that you do not understand. If you go home now, you may never have such an opportunity again. I ask you once more, are you *certain* you wish to throw away your best shot at a secure and happy future?"

"Yes, sir." She kept her words short and firm. He was giving. She could feel it as one feels the sand slipping away beneath one's feet as it yielded to the water's current.

"Even though I sit here now, telling you your mother is fine and all will be well?"

Rachel gave him a nod.

He watched her silently for several moments, then his shoulders slumped, and his eyes turned sad.

"Think carefully, Rachel. This decision will impact the rest of your life."

"I have thought it over," she stated. "I have thought of little else these past several months."

He watched her for a long moment, the only sound the soft crackle of the low fire. She held his gaze.

Finally, he looked away. "Very well. We have a deal."

CHAPTER SIXTEEN

C hristopher stood rooted in the doorway. The soft strains of Rachel at the pianoforte called to him, but he couldn't seem to make his feet move. She was nearing the end of the movement, the part that always drew her concentration in, and he'd hate to disturb that. At least, that's the lie he told himself. Truly, he was plain scared to walk in and hand her the bunch of flowers he'd purchased for her.

Silly, really. But here he was.

Would she take them well? Fitzwilliam's proposals—of which there had been *many*—nearly always included flowers. Gads, but if he was turning to Fitzwilliam for ideas then Christopher was in sorry shape for sure.

But what else could he do? It had been nearly a full week since the dinner party in the library. The very next morning, with a bright smile and more optimism than he could ever remember seeing from her, Rachel had informed him of her deal with her uncle. All she had to do now, she'd cheerfully explained, was continue on as she had been—not becoming attached to anyone—and in a month, she would have her heart's greatest desire.

Surely, she had no notion what it had done to him. In essence, she'd left him with two choices: Christopher could admit his feelings for her, court her and try to show her how happy they would be together only to admit that he had nothing more to offer her than poverty and uncertainty, or he could remain silent, continue on as her friend, and watch her walk out of his life forever.

Neither option sat well with him. Neither seemed the right choice. For the past many days, he'd chosen the latter; he hadn't reached for her hand again, he hadn't held her or comforted her. Then again, since making the deal with her uncle, she hadn't needed him to. Perhaps being with her mother once more truly was all she needed in life.

But blast it all, he needed *her*.

He supposed he could suggest they move in with her mother. The three of them could at least try to eke out an existence together. Devil take him if that wasn't the most pathetic offer a man could ever give a woman.

Nonetheless, that morning, when out on a ride through town and hoping to find a better option than the two she'd given him, he'd ended up riding past a hot house. The colorful flowers seemed to call to him. He'd bought this bouquet, hoping he'd think of what to say by the time he'd arrived back at Curio Manor. He was back now, but nothing was coming to mind.

So he stood.

Listening to breathtaking music.

Holding flowers meant for her.

But not giving them.

All the while, Rachel was unaware for her back was to him and her focus entirely elsewhere.

It was like a poetic symbol for his life. A symbol for his *miserable* life.

Well, there was no returning the flowers. Sitting back saying nothing hadn't worked; maybe this little nudge in the opposite direction would prove beneficial? Or prove catastrophic. There was really no way to know. It was do it or turn tail and run.

Christopher drew in a deep breath and forced himself into the room. Rachel ended the piece and slowly lifted her hands from the keys.

"That was beautiful," Christopher said.

"Thank you." She said it casually, as though they'd shared the compliment so many times between them it had stopped meaning anything. No matter what she may think, he never had meant the compliment casually. He had never heard anything as provoking as Rachel playing the pianoforte.

Christopher held out the bouquet.

Far from smiling, however, Rachel only pursed her lips and shook her head. "Is Lord Fitzwilliam wanting to propose again already? He proposed yesterday." Still, she took the flowers and held them close to her nose. For all her complaining, Rachel couldn't deny her love of flowers.

"No," Christopher said, his stomach pathetically tight, "actually those . . ."

"What? Don't tell me they're his way of saying he's finally crying off?"

"Oh no, I don't think he has any intentions of ceasing the proposals."

Her expression softened, the flowers still covering most of her mouth as she spoke. "Can I tell you a secret?"

"After all this time, you still have to ask?"

She scooted over on the bench, making space for him. "Ever since Uncle Seth and I came to an understanding, I have felt freer, more at peace."

Christopher nodded as he took the offered seat. It placed him close enough to her that their shoulders touched, and their knees bumped against one another. It was incredibly distracting. A distraction he wished he could enjoy for years to come.

"Knowing that I will see my mother again in a month's time," she continued, "I have found I am at more liberty to enjoy the *now*. And in so doing, I have discovered something that has quite shocked me." She paused long enough to take a deep breath of the flowers.

"Don't tell me you have decided to accept Lord Fitzwilliam,"

Christopher said with a laugh—a tight laugh because that was all he could manage.

"Oh, gracious no." Rachel laughed as well, but hers sounded light, airy, and sincere. Christopher found himself breathe out in relief.

"No, he and I will only ever be friends." Rachel spoke on, seemingly unaware of how her actions and words were quite upending him. "But, I have found I actually . . . kind of . . . enjoy his proposals."

"Truly?" Again, his stomach clenched; normally when a woman was pleased to be proposed to, it implied she meant to accept. But she had just said they would only ever be friends.

"Not that I plan to ever accept him," she said with a firm look his way. "But it is a sort of silly diversion. If you'd asked me two months ago if I could ever enjoy such a thing, I would have said never. Nonetheless, here I am, holding these flowers and knowing that, if he were to burst in here any minute now, singing and using all that silly alliteration, I shouldn't really mind. I guess what I am saying is, I have always hated change of any kind. It has never been good to me. However, this one small piece of change has not been too bad."

"Life can be unexpected," Christopher agreed. "You know, if you want to learn from those who have faced challenges and made a happy life for themselves regardless of their struggles, this house is full of them."

"Is that so?" Rachel asked, turning toward him.

"I'm sure it has not gone without notice that Fitzwilliam and his grandmother are all the family either of them has."

"Well, yes . . ." She seemed to consider his words for a moment. "I know both his parents have passed on. I guess I just never thought of it in those terms."

"There are many stories here at Curio Manor. Most are silly, nonsensical."

"Such as eating dinner in the library."

"The very same. However," Christopher's voice dropped, "some are truly sad. And knowing those puts the silly nonsense in a different light, I think."

She was silent for a moment, her gaze somewhere past him. "I think I should like to hear some of those stories."

"You ought to ask Lady Fitzwilliam then. I believe she quite likes you and just might be willing to share."

"I think I shall." Her smile slowly returned, growing to be as big as it had been before. "And don't tell me that even his lordship is more than foppish proposals?"

"Just don't tell Fitzwilliam I said as much. It'll all go straight to his head."

Rachel laughed again and bent down, resting the flowers on the floor beside her. "Before I go break his heart yet again, pick a duet for us to play."

Christopher glanced down at the flowers. It wasn't exactly what he'd hoped would happen when he gave them to her; still, she was smiling, laughing even. She was, for the first time ever, truly seeing how change and the future wasn't always about losing people.

He reached to the small shelf of sheet music and pulled out a piece by Beethoven. "How about this one?"

"Oh, I love this one." As she helped him set the papers on the pianoforte, their arms brushed, their fingers meeting once or twice. For her, it seemed this was just another song they would play, just another afternoon whiled away with music.

But for him, this was all he ever wanted; sadly, like the house he lived in and the food he ate, it was only temporary. He would have to move on one day and so would she. He couldn't stay here forever, and she didn't want to. Yet, it was only here, at Curio Manor that their paths crossed. And all too soon, he knew, those paths would take them both away. Even as she was opening her eyes up to better things, all *his* joy was coming to an end.

For this happiness—this moment of laughter, smiles, and music —was not within his power to keep.

CHAPTER SEVENTEEN

Lorenzo the butler said Rachel could find Lady Fitzwilliam in the drawing room. She walked quietly down the corridor in that direction. She could only hope that Charlotte was still out shopping with Dinah and Eliza and that Uncle Seth wouldn't care to spend an afternoon alone with their host. The two of them—Uncle Seth and Lady Fitzwilliam—were always polite and kind, even friendly with one another. But that didn't mean they wished for their own little tete-a-tete. The stern, often emotionless Sir Mulgrave huddled over a tea cup whispering to the giggling Lady Fitzwilliam? The very idea made Rachel smile.

She reached the drawing room and peered inside. Just as Lorenzo had said, there Lady Fitzwilliam sat, her white lace cap pulled down low over her eyes and her breathing deep. Rachel pulled her lips to the side in disappointment. She had rather been wanting to *talk* to the elderly woman, not sit with her while she napped. It had been three days since Christopher had suggested she speak to her host. His lordship had never actually proposed that day even after Christopher had brought her his flowers. But he had proposed the day after, and again yesterday. Between two proposals and the usual afternoon teas, dinners with everyone present and listening in, Rachel hadn't had time to pull Lady Fitzwilliam aside and ask about his lordship's parents. She'd been so hopeful when Charlotte suggested they all drive into the small town nearby to do a little shopping. It left Rachel with the perfect opportunity on her hands. But now she'd have to find another time.

Rachel turned to leave, but a floorboard creaked under her weight. In the wholly silent house, it moaned like a great giant giving up its last breath. Rachel froze, slowly turning to look over her shoulder.

Lady Fitzwilliam sputtered and pushed the cup back up off her face. "Rachel, dear, is that you?"

So much for not disturbing her host. Rachel walked fully into the room. "I am so sorry, Lady Fitzwilliam. I didn't mean to wake you."

"I'm glad you did. Honestly, if I take more than a five-minute nap in the afternoon, I'm up half the night." She patted the seat beside her on the settee. "Please join me and keep me awake if you wouldn't mind."

"Not at all." Rachel sat facing Lady Fitzwilliam.

"Tell me, dear, have you been enjoying your stay here at Curio Manor?" Lady Fitzwilliam ran a finger beneath either eye. She seemed to still be wiping away the last traces of sleep.

It would probably be best to let her wake up a bit before Rachel asked for stories of the woman's past. "Yes, very much so."

"My grandson seems to be quite pleased you and your family are here."

No doubt; her presence gave him something with which to occupy his time.

"He and Mr. Dunn," Lady Fitzwilliam continued, "talk of you constantly."

Oh dear, she hoped neither man was giving Lady Fitzwilliam the wrong impression. "We are good friends, my lady. But that is all."

"Is it?" The older woman seemed fully awake now and was not at all too sleepy to pin Rachel with a most intense look.

—"Quite so." Rachel looked away, shifting a bit under the dowager's stare. "Actually, I come into the drawing room in search of you, specifically."

"Was there something particular you wished to speak to me about?"

"There is." Though how Rachel was to bring it up, she still was unsure.

"Splendid," the elderly woman said while standing. "Now I feel less guilty asking you to stay. I'll just ring for some tea and we'll have a right little gossip, you and I."

A footman showed up only seconds after Lady Fitzwilliam rang and soon tea was sitting before them.

Rachel sipped slowly while Lady Fitzwilliam spoke on about how she'd enjoyed the roast beef at dinner last night and how Mr. Dunn *still* insisted on nothing more than a cup of coffee every morning, despite Cook providing the best spread of breakfast foods anywhere in the country.

When Rachel had mentioned she'd wanted to speak with Lady Fitzwilliam in particular, what was or wasn't served wasn't what she'd had in mind. "Does your grandson enjoy a full breakfast then?" she asked. Perhaps if she could steer the conversation toward his lordship, that would help.

"Oh my, yes. Ever since he was a little boy. Now, though, he eats fewer biscuits and jam and more meat. But, other than that, he is very much the same little knave he's always been."

"Did you come to live with him while he was quite young, then?"

"Interested in his past, are you?" Lady Fitzwilliam lifted a brow, knowingly.

"No," Rachel quickly said. Perhaps a bit too quickly, for the woman's raised brow morphed into a triumphant smile. Drat—now *she* was giving Lady Fitzwilliam the wrong impression. That would never do. "May I speak frankly, my lady?"

"I certainly hope you will."

Rachel nodded, placing her tea cup back on the table. "I have been struggling to come to terms with certain events in my life. I was speaking with Mr. Dunn the other day and he mentioned that if

I ever wanted a good example of someone who accepted the . . . less pleasant aspects of life and made something joyful out of it, I ought not look further than Curio Manor."

As Rachel spoke, Lady Fitzwilliam stilled, her gaze dropping to her own tea cup. "I see."

It was the shortest sentence Rachel had ever heard the woman say.

"If you don't mind," Rachel pressed on, "I wondered if you might tell me of when his lordship's parents passed. I am sure, whatever the particulars, they were most heartbreaking. Yet, to come here, one would never know that you both faced any adversity. Why, the whole of the house is forever optimistic."

"Yes, well, you are right in assuming it didn't just happen that way without any effort." Lady Fitzwilliam rested her teacup on her lap, her eyes roving over the room but never landing on Rachel. "It was a boating accident that took the life of my son and his beautiful wife. They were quite young themselves. They left behind so much. A new dress for the ball that night. Contracts for a farmer and his family, recently come from Scotland. And a little boy asleep in the nursery." She blinked and shook her head. "I was visiting a friend up North when I received the news. I left that very day to come here. Fitzwilliam was so young, I think he struggled to understand what had happened. He cried himself to sleep, asking for his Mama, every night for months. I would just hold him and rock him and sing to him until finally, we both drifted off."

Rachel teared up just hearing of it. "I am so sorry."

Lady Fitzwilliam glanced at Rachel briefly before her eyes flitted away. A sad smile graced her lips. "Those first few years were very hard, indeed."

"And yet," Rachel said, "you managed to find happiness again."

"Like I said before, it wasn't without a great deal of effort. Fitzwilliam and I were all the family either of us had after that. My husband, rest his soul, and I were only blessed with one son, no daughters. He had passed on well before that time, regardless. So Fitzwilliam and I depended upon one another. That's the reason I never sent him away to school or to University but chose to employ various tutors instead. I couldn't bear to be parted from him; and, between you and me, I sincerely believe it wouldn't have been good for him to be parted from me either."

"May I ask *how* you found happiness again?"

Lady Fitzwilliam picked up her tea and sipped a bit. "I think it started the moment I accepted—truly deep down accepted—that I couldn't bring my son and his wife back. I *could* make sure the one boy who was most important to them was loved and cherished just as much as though they'd lived. Grieving takes its own time and its own space, but as much as I could, I focused on Fitzwilliam. I focused on helping *him* be happy, and my own happiness eventually followed."

"And you are happy now?"

Her smile returned, radiant and sincere. "Yes, my dear, I most certainly am."

For a moment, they sat in silence, both preoccupied with their own thoughts. Eventually, an easier conversation started up, one regarding what they supposed Dinah, Eliza, and Charlotte might find at the shops that morning. As they spoke, Rachel held closely to the words Lady Fitzwilliam had spoken. She'd talked of grief and heartbreak, but also of changing what *could* be changed and of moving forward instead of pushing to go back.

For the first time ever, Rachel wondered if perhaps Charlotte and Dinah hadn't been right all along. Had they not been encouraging her to look forward more? To focus on what could change and what could be? Knowing that she would see her mother again soon put her heart at ease. And with the weight of concern lifted, Rachel could more easily see how she'd blinded herself to every opportunity, every joy for months now.

She had no desire to marry a man who would force her to choose between his world and Mother; if he did, she would choose Mother every time. No, instead she would do as Lady Fitzwilliam suggested and accept that she was not meant for high society. Rachel could enjoy these last few weeks at Curio Manor, and then she would return to her mother, never to be seen among the *ton* again. The idea brought peace to her heart. She was happy for Eliza and Dinah, but she wouldn't be sharing in their good fortune. She'd much rather have a simple life that her mother could be a part of.

And what of Christopher? A small part of her brain wouldn't leave the question alone.

Or, more truthfully, not a small part of her brain, but a small part of her heart.

In that moment, she could no longer deny that her feelings toward him were far more than just cordial. Suppose she did as Dinah had encouraged so many weeks ago, and not only found a way to see Mother again but also fell in love?

Rachel was in no way certain she knew Christopher's feelings, but he did seem partial to her company.

Could she imagine it? What would a life with Christopher be like? Excitement rushed through her at the thought. But it was immediately replaced with uncertainty. As the wife of a tutor, they'd never have a home—not one that was theirs to keep until they wished it otherwise. Much like growing up, she'd be forced to move and to give up the places she'd come to love. Christopher had said multiple times that he rather liked the uncertainty of his chosen career. He enjoyed change.

But sitting with Lady Fitzwilliam, sipping tea and speaking of inconsequential things, Rachel couldn't find it in herself to feel as Christopher did. He would never ask her to give up her connection with her mother because of Mother's need to work. But if they were forever moving across all of England, she might not see Mother any more frequently than if he had. No, life with him would mean constant upheaval. Constant change.

Constantly leaving behind the people she'd grown to care for.

Constantly wondering if and when they'd have to uproot their lives and start over somewhere new.

He may like the adventure of it all, but Rachel had known too much separation to see anything but heartbreak in such a life. Indeed, she wasn't at all sure she could be brave enough to do it, even if it meant being with him.

CHAPTER EIGHTEEN

Rachel continued to turn over Lady Fitzwilliam's words in her mind for the next few days. She thought on them as she played the pianoforte with Christopher. She thought on them even while Fitzwilliam proposed yet again—this time in verse. She thought on them at breakfast and while walking the gardens and while dressing for dinner.

Tonight, she'd had a particularly hard time thinking of anything else. Lord Fitzwilliam and his grandmother's happiness had been more apparent than usual while, as a group, they'd all played charades after dinner. Truly, she struggled to think of two happier people. Yet, neither could she deny the intense sorrow they must have known when Fitzwilliam's parents died unexpectedly.

Rachel rolled over in her bed, sleep as elusive as a skittering rabbit. As much as she respected Lady Fitzwilliam for bringing happiness back to Curio Manor, Rachel also knew their situations were not the same. Lady Fitzwilliam could not reverse death; however, Rachel *could* return home to Mother. She could go home and see that the woman who meant the most to her didn't die young from overexertion or loneliness as her grandparents had.

A loud bang came from the corridor just outside her bedchamber. It sounded like something falling over—not the sound of something shattering, but rather of something hitting the floor with a thud. Rachel pushed up onto one elbow, but no other sounds reached her. Strange. Whatever the sound, no doubt Lorenzo the butler was not far away and would see to it. Rachel rolled onto her back and returned to staring up at the ceiling.

Lady Fitzwilliam had found happiness in moving forward, and Rachel could now accept that it was a virtue she needed to better emulate. But she couldn't quite figure out *how*. She wasn't willing to forget about her mother, but she couldn't continue to push away all of life simply because she couldn't see Mother *right now*. There had to be a middle ground. A way of both loving her mother as a good daughter ought, while also looking after her own future.

In theory, it sounded almost noble.

In practice, Rachel felt wholly lost.

She'd never before thought of it this way. Never before tried—

Her door opened with a bang. Rachel bolted upright in her bed.

Lord Fitzwilliam staggered inside. His cravat was completely untied, the ends hanging like two dead fish about his neck. He reached for one of the chairs by the hearth, missing it the first time but finding hold of it the second. Singing horribly off-key and in far too muddled a tone for Rachel to make anything out, he turned about and slammed the door shut once more.

"Lord Fitzwilliam?" Rachel sputtered. "What on earth are you doing in here?" She was in no more than her shift. Proposing multiple times was one thing but barging into her room in the middle of the night was another thing altogether.

He took two steps toward her and threw himself onto the bed beside her. Rachel scrambled to kick off the blankets and get off the bed before he rolled over closer. She did not, however, escape before smelling the port which hung heavily about him.

"Is that you, Rachel?" he asked, rolling onto the spot she'd just vacated. "What are you doing in my bedchamber?"

Standing by the edge of the bed, peering down at a man resting against her own pillows and on top of her own blankets was not at all a situation Rachel felt confident in dealing with.

"Lord Fitzwilliam." She tried to keep her voice calm, but her insides were all upended. "This is *my* bedchamber and I demand you leave at once."

"No, it's not," he said with a saucy smile, even as his eyes closed. "Are *you* trying to propose to *me* now?"

Rachel grabbed her robe which was draped over a chair and pulled it on, securing it tightly around her waist and throat. "You, sir, are drunk."

"Only a little. And besides," his eyes opened suddenly, and he pushed himself onto an elbow and leaned toward her. "Why should I have all the fun?"

Rachel took half a step back.

"Go ahead," he said. "Propose to me. I promise to turn you down." He gave her a firm nod, one which almost sent him face-first onto the mattress. He pulled back just in time, but in doing so, he overcompensated and fell back onto the pillows.

"Oh, drat," Rachel muttered to herself as she rounded the foot of the bed, walking over toward the side Fitzwilliam rested on. She took hold of his arm and tugged. "Time to stand back up, my lord. You need sleep and you need to do it in your *own* bedchamber."

"But this *is* my bedchamber," he countered, not in the least bit willing to rise. "Why would you propose to me in *your* bedchamber?"

"I'm not proposing at all," Rachel said, teeth grinding as she gave his arm a final, forceful tug. It did no good, however, and he remained flat on his back in *her* bed. "You stumbled in here in your foolish, drunken stupor and if anyone finds you in here we *will* have to marry."

They'd gotten away with all his many outlandish proposals; if him drinking to excess one night was what finally ruined life for the both of them, Rachel would be a most peevish new bride.

She rounded the bed once more. Kneeling beside Fitzwilliam, Rachel placed her hands against his chest and shoved. He slipped toward the far end of the bed. Rachel drew in a deep breath and pushed with all her might one more time, finally slipping him off the edge where he landed hard on his backside.

"Rum bugger," he all but shouted.

"Quiet!" Rachel hissed. She would have felt more sorry for him, but right now she was too busy making sure neither of them had to spend the rest of their lives together. It was a fate she knew he would wish to avoid as eagerly as she—at least he would if he wasn't two sheets to the wind.

Footsteps echoed down the corridor, coming closer and closer until they stopped by her door.

Someone knocked.

"Now you've done it," Rachel whispered. Hopping up, she pushed a chair in front of where Lord Fitzwilliam sat like a lump on the floor.

"Not a word," she warned. Then she pulled a few blankets off the bed, draping them over the top of him.

The knock came again.

Rachel walked toward her door, turning back to quickly inspect how well his lordship was hidden. The room was dark, with only embers in the hearth to provide any light. From here, it was hard to see the white linens behind the chair. And even when one did stop to look at them, they appeared to be no more than a pile of blankets.

Hopefully, it would be enough. If not, whoever stood on the other side—be it Lorenzo, her abigail, or some other footman or maid of the house—could very easily ruin everything.

Rachel pulled the door open, but only a few inches.

"Rachel, is everything all right in there?"

Christopher. With a rush of relief, she took hold of his arm and pulled him inside before shutting the door behind him.

"Some tutor you turned out to be," she said, walking back toward where Lord Fitzwilliam was still sitting on the floor, remaining dutifully silent.

"Excuse me?" Christopher said, shifting about and glancing over the room.

Well, if he was uncomfortable being in her bedchamber at night, it was nothing compared to what she'd just been through. Rachel shoved the chair out of the way and, taking a handful of linen, tugged the blankets off his lordship.

"Surprise!" Lord Fitzwilliam shouted.

"Hush!" Rachel said, very nearly kicking him in her frustration.

He only laughed, his head rocking from side to side as his back rested more fully against the bed. "Look, Dunn, Rachel's proposing to me."

"I am doing nothing of the sort," she said, turning back to Christopher. "I am *trying* to get him out of here."

Christopher spoke to his lordship. "I warned you tonight's port was rather more forward than usual." Lord Fitzwilliam's smile only grew, however, and Christopher let out a sigh, turning toward Rachel. "I told him not to drink so much."

"Let me guess," Rachel said. "He took it as a challenge?"

"Quite so." Christopher rubbed the back of his neck. "I shouldn't have left him. I only did so for a minute to speak with Lorenzo. When I came back and he was gone, I was worried he would end up somewhere he shouldn't be."

"But why did he have to end up in here?" Of all the rooms he could have stumbled into.

"His room is directly above yours," Christopher explained, stepping up closer to his lordship. "He must have miscalculated by one flight while climbing the stairs." Squatting down, Christopher pulled one of Lord Fitzwilliam's arms over his own shoulders. "I suppose this wasn't too far off, considering the state he's in. I had rather worried he'd made his way outside."

"From where I'm standing," Rachel said, "that would have been preferable."

Christopher glanced at her, his lips tilting up. "Don't worry. I'll get him out of here without anyone being the wiser." He slowly hauled Lord Fitzwilliam up until they both stood. His lordship was a few inches taller than Christopher and clearly wasn't easy to keep standing.

Rachel walked up to Lord Fitzwilliam's other side, pulling his free arm over her shoulders.

"No need. I can handle him," Christopher said, though his tone belied his words.

"You'll get him to his room faster with my help," she countered.

Rachel began pulling Lord Fitzwilliam toward the door, Christopher following suit. In only the space between the bed and the door, they nearly tripped over the blankets, bumped into two chairs, and toppled a small table.

"You two aren't very good at this," Lord Fitzwilliam said as they finally arrived at the bedchamber door.

Neither she nor Christopher replied. Rachel slowly twisted the door handle and let the door swing silently open.

"Careful," Christopher whispered low, "you best check the corridor first."

Rachel nodded, passing more of Lord Fitzwilliam's weight on to Christopher as she leaned out the doorway and peered either direction.

"It's empty," she said. Rachel moved through the doorway first, pulling Lord Fitzwilliam along with her. Christopher was the last to step out, and he noiselessly shut the door.

"Let's take him up the back steps," Christopher said, nodding behind them.

"Aren't most the servants still up, though?" Rachel asked. She was certain they used the back steps quite often.

Christopher's lips pursed as he thought. "I hate the idea of going up the main steps; it's too easy to be seen from there."

"So long as no one sees my face, you can claim you had a maid help you get his lordship upstairs."

"I asked a maid, in her night robe, to assist me in getting Fitzwilliam to his bedchamber?"

Suddenly fully aware of her state of undress, Rachel cleared her throat. "I couldn't very well pass for a footman in this, now could I?" At least the corridor was dark enough he wouldn't see her blush.

Christopher nodded. "Main stairs it is then."

<hr />

Christopher stared up the foreboding length of stairs. "This isn't going to be easy," he said to Rachel. It had taken them a frightfully long time just to get here. And though both he and Rachel were trying to walk quietly, Fitzwilliam had made enough noise for an entire royal court. It was a wonder they hadn't been spotted already.

"Lucky you asked such a strong maid to help you then," she quipped back.

Christopher chuckled softly. He knew she was frustrated and quite on edge about being found in such a compromising situation, yet she still hadn't kicked the two of them out of her bedchamber and slammed the door shut behind them. No matter what problems Rachel faced, she always did it with dignity and kindness. Did she have any idea how inspiring it was to know her?

Pulling Fitzwilliam—now forever to be known as The Idiot—closer to himself to better support his weight, Christopher moved them toward the stairs. Rachel's hand was wrapped around Fitzwilliam's torso, which meant the back of it pressed against Christopher's waist. The touch—one that was unavoidable and not purposeful in the least—still made him wholly aware of every inch of himself. Aware of himself, and of Rachel. They made it up a few more steps and Christopher's gaze flitted to Rachel as it had been every few minutes since he'd first knocked on her door. She looked quite angelic all in white, her hair in a loose braid down her back. At least he'd had the good sense to button his jacket and re-tie his cravat after hearing a noise coming from her room.

His eyes caught sight of her bare feet. Heat, along with a heady desire, stole up his neck. Christopher forced his eyes forward once more. They reached the top of the stairs and turned to the right.

"Mr. Dunn, sir, is that you?"

Without needing to tell the other, he and Rachel forced Lord Fitzwilliam up against the wall and just out of sight.

"Lorenzo," Christopher whispered softly to Rachel.

She nodded and gave him a small push. "Go."

His brow creased. He hated the idea of leaving her with Fitzwilliam, alone, supporting all his weight. If the three of them were found together, it was far more likely they could explain away what was happening. If Rachel was found alone with Fitzwilliam, veritably in his arms, things would not go so smoothly.

"Mr. Dunn?" Lorenzo called again from around the corner and down the corridor.

Rachel gave him a firm shove. "Get rid of him."

Christopher relinquished his hold of Fitzwilliam, tugged on the sleeves of his jacket, and turned the corner. "Good evening, Lorenzo," he said, quite as though nothing were amiss.

—"I thought it was you," Lorenzo said with a bow. "Is there anything you are in need of?"

"No, thank you." Hopefully, the man would leave, and they could get Fitzwilliam to his room without any more trouble.

"Are you sure?" Lorenzo pressed. "This is quite late for you to be out of your room, is it not?"

Yes . . . but Christopher wasn't about to explain the whole of it. "I needed a bit of air, that is all."

Lorenzo, astute man that he was, didn't appear very convinced.

"I am quite fine; a walk around the house was all I needed," Christopher continued. He motioned toward the back stairway. "Please, don't let me keep you up any longer. I am sure you've had an exhausting day."

Lorenzo watched him, wordless, for several seconds before bowing once more. "Very well, sir. I will bid you a good night."

"Good night, Lorenzo." Christopher waited as the butler strode off. Once he was certainly gone, Christopher hurried back toward the main stairs. As he reached the corner, he could hear Fitzwilliam's voice.

"I like you, Rachel, did you know that?"

Christopher's step slowed.

Rachel said something, but he couldn't make it out.

"Dunn likes you, too," Fitzwilliam said next. "He likes your hair. He likes your smile. He likes it when you play the pianoforte together most of all."

Christopher felt his face heat. The Idiot was at it again. If they weren't such great friends—and if Christopher wasn't actually employed by his grandmother as Fitzwilliam's tutor—he would have been sorely tempted to leave the man in a heap on the floor there at the top of the stairs and let him awake to a painfully stiff back in the morning.

He heard no more from either Rachel or Fitzwilliam, so drawing himself up and choosing to act as though he hadn't heard anything at all, Christopher turned the corner. The sight was rather comical. Fitzwilliam, far taller than Rachel, was placing nearly all his weight on her, leaning over her to the point that his head rested atop hers. She seemed very nearly squished between his great, lumbering form.

Christopher moved up and took hold of Fitzwilliam's other arm.

Rachel's nose was scrunched up. "If a man wishes to imbibe, why can't he imbibe on something that smells a bit better?"

"One of the great conundrums of life," Christopher sympathized.

Together, they hobbled down the corridor and made it to Lord Fitzwilliam's door.

Rachel pulled back slightly. "You'll have to take it from here; I'm not about to further endanger myself by going in there."

He didn't blame her. She'd shown quite a bit of courage already in helping him get Fitzwilliam this far. "Just hold the door open if you would."

Rachel nodded, slipping out from under Fitzwilliam's arm. As she moved toward the door handle, it brought her closer to Christopher. She smelled of lavender, as she always did. It was a scent that was now so ingrained in his memory, he doubted he could ever smell lavender again and not think of her. Fitzwilliam had been right; he did very much love her hair and her smile, and he did, indeed, love it when they sat down to play the pianoforte together best of all. His gift of flowers the other day had not gone the way he'd hoped, but perhaps in another time and another setting, things might go better? Say, in the middle of the night when they just happened to find themselves together? A man could only try.

"Thank you, Rachel," he said as she twisted the knob and pushed the door open. "And you were right about not using the back stairs."

She turned his way and gave him a smile. "I hope you give him a stern talking to in the morning for this."

"Don't you worry," he said, hauling Fitzwilliam past her and into the bedchamber. "I'll make sure it's a lesson he doesn't soon forget."

"I guess that's what tutors are for."

He all but dragged Fitzwilliam, who was growing less and less aware by the minute, toward the bed. "That is what I'm paid to do."

He heard the door slowly shut just as he got Fitzwilliam to the bed. With a grunt, he angled his friend around and let him collapse onto his own blankets and pillows. Not bothering to help him remove his boots or settle better onto the bed, Christopher hurried back toward the bedchamber door. Perhaps he would start by telling her how beautiful she was with her hair down. Or, maybe he would tell her how impressed he always was with how she handled the unexpected. He smoothed his hands over his jacket as he opened the bedchamber door and stepped out.

But the corridor was empty. His hands fell limp to his sides. He wouldn't need to think up the right thing to say after all.

Rachel had already gone.

CHAPTER NINETEEN

Rachel walked directly up to the large tree and stared up at its hundreds of branches. To think, it had nearly been two months since that fateful morning she'd foolishly decided to go swimming. Two months since she'd sat atop one of the tree's thick branches while meeting Christopher for the first time. La, but she'd been so humiliated—she'd wanted nothing more than to never see the handsome man with a bit of red in his hair ever again. Rachel's mouth quirked up to one side. Who would have guessed then that he'd become one of her dearest friends? One of her closest confidants?

Which was why she was so eager to see him today. After last night's nearly disastrous debacle, she'd awoken to a startling revelation—and she couldn't wait to tell Christopher. She turned away from the tree, her gaze moving to the lake instead. She'd been rather disheartened that he hadn't been at breakfast. Hopefully, this afternoon she might find him.

Rachel closed her eyes and tipped her head up toward the sun, feeling its bright warmth against her nose and cheeks. It was a good day for a revelation. It was a good day to realize the future might not be so bleak as she had originally assumed.

"There you are, Rachel."

Christopher's voice made her stomach leap, and she turned around. He was walking toward her, his hand firmly gripped about Lord Fitzwilliam's arm. In truth, Christopher seemed to be dragging his lordship her way.

"Here I have one gentleman," Christopher said, pushing Lord Fitzwilliam ahead of himself and toward her, "ready to make a full apology."

"A short one," Lord Fitzwilliam moaned, his hand heavily shading his eyes. "And then please take me back to bed."

Rachel had rather spoken to Christopher alone, but she didn't mind terribly if his lordship was present. It wasn't as though what she had to say was private, only very important. At least it was to her. As the two men neared, Rachel looked Lord Fitzwilliam over more carefully. He did look dreadful. His face was drawn, and his shoulders stooped. He must have had a massive headache upon waking up.

The two men stopped before her. Christopher patted his friend heartily on the chest. "Well, on with you now, and don't shorten any of it. You put Rachel in a terrible position last night and you owe her the most heartfelt of apologies."

"I'm sorry, Miss Chant," Fitzwilliam mumbled, his eyes never leaving her slippers.

Christopher looked to her. "Did that feel heartfelt to you?"

"Hardly." Lord Fitzwilliam seemed far too wrapped up in his own suffering to care one whit about the situation he'd put her in last night.

"That's all I got," his lordship said, turning about as though he were headed back toward the house.

Christopher stopped his progress. "Too bad. Rachel deserves better."

His words made her heart flutter strangely in her chest—she could not deny that a woman would be hard-pressed to find a better looking or more sincere friend than Christopher.

"Actually," Rachel said, an idea striking her—one that should help his lordship understand the serious nature of what he'd done.

"Lord Fitzwilliam, when you and I were speaking last night, you promised me another proposal first thing this morning. You have not proposed these past two days and I am beginning to wonder if you truly value our friendship."

Lord Fitzwilliam reached out an unsteady hand and plopped it down on her arm. "I value our friendship." He turned to Christopher. "Please, can I go back to bed now?"

"Nothing doing." Christopher stayed rooted to the spot. "You promised this respectable woman a proposal, and as your tutor, I'm going to see that you do it."

Lord Fitzwilliam muttered something under his breath that sounded a lot like a "very well" mixed with a few words Rachel was certain should not be uttered within the presence of a lady. If he was annoyed, well, all the better. He needed to see that he'd taken their lighthearted joke far enough, it could have ruined both their lives.

"Rachel," Lord Fitzwilliam said, his brow creased and his mouth in a firm line. "Will you please marry me?"

"Yes," she said with a small curtsy. "Thank you for your offer."

"What?" Lord Fitzwilliam's head snapped up, his eyes finally meeting hers. The next second though, he shut them tightly against the bright sunlight and cupped a hand over them, but not before Rachel had time to see how horribly red they were.

"I said yes." Rachel spoke lightly, quite as though she were only discussing their view of the lake. "I believe we *should* get married. After all, you have a very fine house and loads of money. Between you and me, I have grown tired of having no one to boss around. Eliza will soon be married, and Dinah never listens to a word I say."

Lord Fitzwilliam groaned even as Christopher smiled.

Rachel gave Christopher another wink—she was feeling quite brazen after her revelation that morning—and continued on. "We shall have the bans read this Sunday. We can be married in only a few weeks and then I shall be sure that you dress the way I wish, that you come and go as I see fit, and that every meal suits my taste." She placed a hand against his, the one covering his face, and pulled it out of the way. "Isn't that what you wanted? After last night's visit, I can assume you desire nothing else."

"You just took all the fun out of proposing," Lord Fitzwilliam said, his words heavy. "Just put me back in bed. I promise I'll never touch another bottle of port ever again."

Rachel placed his hand back over his face and turned her smile toward Christopher. "I think he's learned his lesson."

"I think you'd have made a fine tutor," Christopher said with an approving nod.

"She's tougher than you are," Lord Fitzwilliam said, lifting his hand only long enough to send a scowl Christopher's way.

"If I'm such a softy," Christopher said, turning him and his lordship back toward the road, "then how about I see you back to Curio Manor?"

Lord Fitzwilliam sighed with relief. "I take back every unkind thing I ever said about you, Dunn."

Rachel hurried forward—now wasn't the time to speak to Christopher, most unfortunately, but at the very least she could make sure they could speak later. She stopped Christopher with a hand on his arm. "Might we meet up and play the pianoforte later?" she asked.

His eyes held hers and her stomach did that strange flip again. "I'd like that very much." All she could do was nod. She let go of his arm and took a small step back, allowing him to continue on. Gracious, she must be more excited to tell him her thoughts than she'd realized; it was making her quite addle-brained.

Christopher pushed Lord Fitzwilliam up the small incline and toward the road that would take them back to the house. "While we walk," Christopher's voice floated back to Rachel as they moved away, "you can apologize to me, too."

"So long as you don't accept when I propose," Lord Fitzwilliam said.

Rachel smirked. There went two very fine men.

She would most certainly miss them when she left to return home next week.

Christopher did, in fact, have a little nursemaid tenderness tucked away somewhere in his heart. For not only did he see Fitzwilliam all the way back to his bed, he also made sure The Idiot had plenty of water nearby and the drapes were pulled tightly closed. After all that, he hurried down to the pianoforte. Rachel was not there yet, however. He knew a pang of disappointment but pushed it aside. She had seemed quite eager that they meet today, so no doubt she'd be here soon enough.

He moved over to the small shelf and began fingering through the various sheets of music. They met here nearly every day, so the fact that she had felt compelled to *ask* him to join her surely meant there was something particular she wanted to speak to him about. He wasn't sure if he felt excited or nervous. It was getting harder and harder to be near her. Harder and harder not to reach for her hand, not to admit how he truly felt, not to kiss her soundly.

Blast, he wanted so desperately to kiss her.

Christopher grabbed the next bit of music he came to and pulled it off the shelf. Whatever it was, it had to be better than standing here, dreaming about a moment that might never be. He placed the music on the pianoforte and sat himself on the bench.

His fingers followed the notes without thought. After so many years of musical training, it was unfortunately easy to play and think on other things at the same time. Was it possible that what she wished to see him about today related to her feelings for him? He knew she cared for him as a good friend, but he hadn't been able to tell if her feelings went deeper than that or not. She clearly enjoyed his company—she wouldn't spend day after day with him at the pianoforte if she didn't.

Then again, she did love her music. So, did she just put up with him so that she might play?

No, that didn't ring true. They got along; truly, he'd never gotten along with anyone better. But did that mean she felt the same?

He hit a sour note and his mind reverted back to the notes on the page. He'd completely missed the key change. Christopher shook his head, going back a few measures and starting the musical phrase over again.

Most likely, whatever Rachel wished to say to him had nothing to do with the single thing Christopher wanted most—her, and him, and a future together. His fingers slowed, then went limp atop the keys. He hadn't exactly been able to tell her how he felt. She was probably completely unaware of how much she mattered to him. Perhaps he should say something today?

Lud, but the thought was intimidating.

Christopher drew in a breath, lifted his hands up, and once more resumed the music. After only a few measures more, he suddenly became acutely aware that Rachel had walked into the room. How he knew, he wasn't sure; sitting at the pianoforte, his back was toward the door. But he knew all the same. She walked wordlessly up to him. Without needing to look up to know it was her, Christopher scooted over on the bench, making a space for her.

Rachel sat beside him, her hands comfortably resting against the bench to either side of her. As he played, the fingers of her left hand, the hand that was directly beside him, began to move. It was as though she were playing along with him, at least in her own mind, and her fingers were responding of their own accord. They brushed once, twice, multiple times against his thigh.

He glanced at her quickly, needing to return his gaze to the music almost immediately. She watched the music with him, following his progress across the page. The music swelled louder, more broad, and her fingers seemed to replicate the action. Pounding against the bench with more strength, moving across his thigh faster. The touch was distracting in the extreme. He only managed to continue playing because he knew if he stopped, so would she.

Heat started where her fingers brushed against him, moving throughout him until he could barely think past the desire to take her hand in his, turn her toward him, and kiss her pink lips.

The music came to an end. He could always repeat the last few pages, keep her fingers moving close to him. But no, it would be unwise. Her touch was tempting enough already, and the feeling had only grown the longer it had lasted. He let the music die off.

As expected, the moment he was done, Rachel lifted her hands, clapping softly for him.

"That was lovely," she said. "You play with such feeling."

Such feeling? How could he not? With her beside him, he'd had so much 'feeling' coursing through him, he couldn't have stopped it overflowing out and into the music if he had tried.

"Were you able to sleep well after . . . everything last night?" he asked. He needed something mundane to converse about and hopefully, in a few minutes, he'd have his head back on straight.

"I did," Rachel said, but instead of standing and searching out more music as he expected, she twisted a bit on the bench, pressing her knees against his leg and facing him. "But it was actually what happened this morning that I wanted to tell you about."

She seemed quite excited; in truth, she seemed happier and more vibrant than he'd ever seen her before. His heart gave a small jolt—*could* this possibly be about them? No, he clamped down hard on the arrant thought. He gave her a smile, one he hoped showed he was a supportive friend who *wasn't* jumping to outlandish conclusions. "You mean when I forced Fitzwilliam to apologize to you?"

"No, before that." She placed a hand behind herself on the bench and leaned in. Lavender enveloped him. "I had a *revelation*." She gave him a pointed look.

"Oh?" Just a friend—one with no outlandish *revelations*.

"Yes. It's like this. If, some months ago, anyone had told me what was going to happen to me here at Curio Manor—especially in regard to last night—I would have flatly refused to ever come."

Well, that put a damper on the outlandish revelations he was trying hard not to hope for.

"What woman would? To find oneself the recipient of multiple fake proposals? To have a man, a *drunk* man, stagger into one's bedchamber in the middle of the night? I would say it is reprehensible and should be avoided at all costs."

When she put it that way, he could see why she was desperate to leave—and that was before adding her concerns over her mother into the mix. "I am sorry your stay has been so miserable." More sorry than he could say.

"But that's just it," she said, putting a hand on his arm. She really needed to stop touching him if she didn't want to be very soundly kissed. "I'm *not* miserable here."

All right, that was a bit more promising.

"That's the revelation I had this morning." She pulled back a bit, her gaze leaving him and roving over the room. "Things I didn't want to have happen *did* happen and you know what? I'm fine. I know that sounds childish." She scrunched her nose and shook her head; had she any idea how charming she was when she did that? "It's only that, I've spent so much of my life scared of bad things happening. And this morning, I realized, that even when bad things happen, it doesn't mean . . ." Her hands opened and closed a few times, as though she were searching for the right words. "It doesn't mean they have to *stay* bad. Does that make sense?"

"Things may happen to you, but you don't have to sit back and do nothing about it."

"Yes!" Her eyes lit up. "That's exactly it. I don't have to just sit there and accept it and do nothing. Take last night, for example. I'd have to say, scared though I was we'd be caught, it was also a little fun."

Christopher smiled. "Yes, it was."

"That's what I realized this morning. I've had some bad things happen in my life." Her voice softened. "But I don't always have to be scared that the bad things that happen in the future will ruin my happiness."

She truly was an inspiration. Christopher took her hand in his. "You are a very wise woman, Miss Rachel Chant."

Her smile turned bashful. "Oh, please, it was only something small that most people learn when they are far younger than me."

"But you've had a harder hand dealt to you than most. We all learn life's lessons on our own schedule."

"Yes," she said softly, leaning in so that their heads were nearly touching. "And though I would only say this to you, I am very happy to have finally learned it." She was so close. Her hand fit so perfectly when held by his. Would her lips?

She smiled up at him. "I have never felt so ready to return home than I do now."

His breath froze in his chest, his thoughts coming to a heart-wrenching halt.

"I have worried and fretted over what condition I might find Mother in when I arrive," Rachel continued. "But now I feel, no matter what awaits me, I can face it." Her tone grew confident. "Coming here to Curio Manor has taught me much, not the least of which is how to better handle unexpected situations." She laughed softly. "You and his lordship have given me plenty of those."

Christopher tried to laugh along, but he couldn't find it in himself. She was still going? She was still planning to pack up and leave just as soon as her month was up?

He looked away, forcing his eyes to stay on the music still resting atop the pianoforte. Of course she was still going. Of course her deep-rooted need to see her mother again hadn't changed. He had been a fool, caught up in the moment and the look in her eyes, to think otherwise.

But that didn't mean she had to go without knowing how he felt. If she knew, might that change her mind? He had no desire to keep her away from her mother, but did it have to be either him or her? Might they not find a way to both be in Rachel's life?

Christopher sat up straighter and took both Rachel's hands in his. "Speaking of futures."

"Yes?" She looked at him most unassumingly. Quite as though she expected nothing extraordinary to come from him. He really had been a fool, not allowing more of his true feelings to show before now.

"I was thinking—"

The door opened and Lorenzo hurried into the room, a letter atop a silver platter in his hand. "Mr. Dunn," he said, his words rushed. "This just came for you. The boy who delivered it said it was quite urgent and you were to read it at once. No delays."

Ah, blast. Christopher let go of Rachel's hands and reached for the letter. "Thank you, Lorenzo."

The butler bowed and then, turning on his heel, hurried out of the room.

Christopher turned the letter over; his name was scrawled across the front in a masculine handwriting. He didn't recognize the hand, so it wasn't Fitzwilliam or any other member of this house. Who would be writing him? And it had been brought here by a boy, not by the post. So it had to be someone in the neighborhood.

"Well?" Rachel asked, her gaze also on the letter. "Aren't you the least bit curious?"

No, he wasn't. He was too put out by the untimely manner of the missive to be curious. Slowly, he flipped it over so that the sealed side faced up.

"I can leave if you wish it," Rachel said, standing.

"No need." He wasn't done speaking to her just yet. "I'm sure this will only take a moment." He broke the seal and started to unfold the letter.

Rachel took up a bit of music and sat back on the bench. She slid fully over, bumping forcibly into him. "Then the least you can do is move so that one of us might play."

Christopher smiled—he always did so more when Rachel was around—and stood, giving her full range of the instrument and the bench. With a gentle shake, Christopher opened the letter completely. The sounds of Rachel's music filled the small room and for a moment he couldn't read, so caught up was he in the sound.

With a few blinks, he brought his mind back to the present.

Mr. Dunn, the letter began.

You must come at once. There is a man here who needs to speak with you. I hope you haven't found a new position as of yet, for after this meeting you might not need one. Not now, not ever.

A blessing of this size could not have come to a better man.

Hurry over,

Lord Keats

Christopher read the letter a second time, then a third. There was hardly any information there, yet what it hinted at . . .

Never need another position again? The only way that would happen was if . . . well, he wasn't even sure he dared *think* what that might mean. His gaze lifted above the letter and landed on Rachel. If he never needed to find a new position, it means something *permanent*. And permanent meant he could make plans. Real plans. Plans that included a woman he desperately loved.

But the letter said he had to go see Lord Keats right away. Christopher quickly folded up the letter.

"A previous employer wishes to see me at once," he told her.

Rachel paused in the music, her gaze moving to him. "Right now?"

"Immediately." He took hold of her hand and kissed it lightly. "May we continue our conversation when I get back?"

Her brow creased for a moment, but she didn't stop smiling. "I'm afraid I have told you all I had to tell."

"Yes, but when I return, I may have something to tell you."

CHAPTER TWENTY

C hristopher arrived at Woodside House not half an hour after receiving the letter from Lord Keats. Along the way, his doubts had repeatedly tried to take hold and oust his optimism. In the end, he'd chosen to shelve both his hopes and his concerns and simply hear what the man visiting Lord Keats had to say and then figure out which response was most appropriate.

No matter how he'd debated the issue within himself, Christopher couldn't really figure what the man might have to say. He'd never heard of a tutor post that was permanent. Not truly. Perhaps Lord Keats, in his excitement, had simply exaggerated. This was most likely a position that appeared, for now, to be many, many years long. But nothing more than that.

His nerves somewhat subdued, he knocked on the door. It opened immediately.

"Lord Keats is in his book room," the butler said with a bow. Apparently, he'd been made aware of Christopher's imminent arrival.

"Thank you, Mr. Hervey." He hurried past the man and toward the large staircase.

"Pardon me, sir," Mr. Hervey called after him, "but would you like me to take your hat and gloves?"

Christopher paused, one foot hovering above the first stair. Mr. Hervey had never offered to take his hat and gloves before. He was only a tutor, after all. A working man, not far above Mr. Hervey himself. Still, as Christopher turned, he found Mr. Hervey waiting patiently to be handed the items.

"Very well," Christopher said, slowly peeling his gloves off and then removing his hat. He handed them to Mr. Hervey before hurrying up the stairs. He shook his head as he neared the study. That had been strange. Christopher knocked on the door and, after hearing Lord Keats's deep voice bid him enter, he pushed open the door and stepped inside.

Lord Keats was sitting at his desk, as Christopher knew he would be. Across from him, in the very chair Christopher himself had sat in last time he'd been here, was another man who stood as Christopher walked further into the room. He was not a tall man, and his clothes denoted he was a man of work, not a man of leisure.

"Mr. Andrews," Lord Keats said with a wave, "this is Mr. Christopher Dunn, the man you have been searching for."

"Let us not jump to conclusions," Mr. Andrews said as he eyed Christopher up and down.

"You have been looking for me?" Christopher asked the man. Why the blazes would *anyone* be looking for him?

"Tell me, Mr. Dunn." Mr. Andrews didn't stop looking him up and down as he spoke. "Who was your father?"

"Mr. Richard Dunn."

"And your father's father?"

"Mr. Aldophus Dunn. Pardon me, sir, but may I ask where all these inquiries lead?"

"An inheritance," Lord Keats said, standing as well and moving around his desk. "Just wait until you hear."

"An inheritance?" Christopher echoed. He'd believed he was coming about a desirable position. But an inheritance? He hadn't put any emotions on the shelf that seemed to fit that declaration.

"If you are indeed the grandson of Mr. Adolphus Dunn then I am here to see that you receive what is now rightfully yours."

"I don't have an inheritance." Christopher, in part, didn't want to believe it. It was too outlandish, too perfect. If he believed it and then all was shown to be a joke or a misunderstanding, it would be no small blow.

After all, an inheritance might mean a house—a home—a place he could bring a wife.

"Mr. Adolphus Dunn had two sons," Mr. Andrews began, clasping his hands in front of himself, clearly settling in for a bit of a history lesson. "Your father—the second son—disappeared without word of where he'd gone."

"I have been told as much," Christopher stated.

The man gave him a polite nod. "What you might not have been told, indeed what I believe your father never knew, was that shortly after his leaving, Mr. Adolphus Dunn's elder son passed away from a dreadful illness."

His grandfather had been left without either of his two sons? How awful. The few times Father had talked of Grandfather, it was always to say that at least Grandfather had his heir—the 'more perfect, more loved' son. But all these years, that hadn't been true. Though Christopher never knew either his grandfather or his uncle, he couldn't help but feel quite sad for them.

"With no heir, and under the mistaken belief that your father must have also died," Mr. Andrews continued, "Mr. Adolphus Dunn made some unwise business decisions. Soon it became clear, no matter how much he retrenched, he could not avoid the inevitable. In a last effort to save something of his wealth, he sold everything here in England and moved to the East Indies. It was there I came to be under his employ. I am proud to say that I, along with his business partner, took his small sum and grew it into a large wealth once more." Mr. Andrews ended with a puffed-out chest and a firm nod. Clearly, the man took great pride in all he'd helped Christopher's grandfather accomplish.

"Why have you come in search of me now?" Christopher asked, certain he knew the answer already.

"Two years ago, your grandfather passed away." At least Mr. Andrews had the common sense to look mournful over the passing of a client. "It was his dying wish that you inherit his half of the business."

"But you just said he was under the mistaken notion that my father had passed on well before the time I could have been born." Christopher crossed his arms over his chest. "How did my grandfather even know I existed?" Father had told him of many years traveling about the continent before meeting his mother.

"Yes," Lord Keats came to stand beside Christopher. "How did either of you know Mr. Richard Dunn had had a son?"

Mr. Andrews pulled a letter out from his jacket pocket. It was well-creased and very yellow. Quite old, if Christopher wasn't mistaken. Mr. Andrews held it out to him. "Your father sent this letter to your grandfather twenty years ago, after the elder Mr. Dunn had already removed himself to the East Indies."

Christopher took the letter gently; it appeared ready to fall apart at the slightest touch.

He unfolded it, reading over the contents quickly.

It was, indeed, a letter from his father. It had been years since the man had lived, but Christopher still had many sheets of music his father had written out, and the handwriting was not foreign to him. In the letter, Father told the recipient that he'd gotten married and had a child—a son. He spoke of how proud he was of his own little boy, and of how someday, he hoped his son would grow into a fine man, someone his own grandfather would be proud of. The end of the letter was a clear, if subtle, request to come for a visit.

Father had wanted Christopher to meet his grandfather. Had wanted to mend bridges.

"Did my grandfather ever reply to this letter?" Christopher asked. He didn't remember his father ever mentioning the man or the letter.

"I am not sure," Mr. Andrews said, his gaze dropping. "But I believe he did not."

Gads. Christopher ran a hand through his hair. In addition to feeling sorry for his grandfather, now he couldn't help but feel a touch upset as well. What man turns his own son and *grandson* away? Refuses to see them? To even let them come for a visit?

"If I am not mistaken," Mr. Andrews continued, his gaze finding Christopher once more, "not responding to that letter was his biggest regret. It was what he spoke of with his last breath—that letter, how sorry he was he never made amends with his son, and his desire that you were found so that you might inherit his estate."

Christopher didn't know what to think. Or feel. Or say.

Yes, he'd wondered at his father's and grandfather's relationship, especially once he'd grown old enough to understand that most children were not completely separated from their extended families. Still, he'd never had so many emotions warring inside him over the grandfather he'd never known.

"Are there any stipulations?" Christopher asked.

"Stipulations?" Mr. Andrews asked. "Such as what?"

"Such as, does it matter who my mother was?" The frustration he felt for his grandfather was quickly turning to anger. "I am sure a man who went so far as to ignore such a letter as this would not have accepted a boy born to the daughter of a farmer." Though his father had been born into a gentry family, his mother had not been. But his parents had loved each other—Christopher had never had wondered about that. He learned from his father at a very young age that love was infinitely more important than wealth or situation.

"No. No stipulations. His last wish was that you be found; he even allocated enough of his own funds so that I might travel to find you. I was given twenty-four months."

Christopher twisted his mouth to the side. "Twenty-four months to find a lost heir is hardly long." Did Grandfather truly want him found? Or simply wanted to placate his own conscience?

"No it is not, sir," Mr. Andrews said, his words lengthening out even as he looked Christopher directly in the eye. "The time frame was not based on his desire to have you inherit. It was based on his lack of certainty that you had lived to adulthood."

Far too many children never made it to adulthood; it was a valid point. Christopher could grant his grandfather that much. A bit of his anger eased. "Is there anything I must do to prove who I am?"

"Goodness, no," Mr. Andrews said, sitting back down at last. "I have searched plenty long enough. I'd almost given up hope two months ago when I finally heard rumor of a Mr. Dunn who'd been employed by Lord Keats and was well known for his impressive pianoforte performances. I figured you had to be the man I was seeking."

Lord Keats pulled a couple more seats over and the three of them sat in a small circle in front of the desk.

"Then there must be much you have to tell me," Christopher said, his displeasure over his grandfather's neglect slowly easing.

For the next half hour, Mr. Andrews went into great detail regarding the massive Dunn estate in the East Indies. It seemed when Mr. Andrews had said they'd grown his grandfather's wealth back up to sizable proportions, he hadn't been exaggerating.

All Christopher could hear, however, was that he now had a home. He now had the wealth necessary to set himself up for good. He wouldn't have to work. He wouldn't have to be at the mercy of whoever employed him.

He could ask Rachel to marry him after all.

He could do it knowing full well he could provide for her. He had a home to give her.

"There is a ship leaving for the East Indies in two weeks' time," Mr. Andrews said, coming to the end of his speech. "I will see we both have passage aboard it."

"Excuse me?" Christopher asked.

"We must head back as soon as possible." Mr. Andrews looked at him as though he was daft to think otherwise. "I've been away far too long as it is, and you are no doubt anxious to take possession."

Of course he was; the sooner he had a home to offer Rachel the better. But he couldn't ask her to go to the East Indies. She had hardly tolerated being away from her mother for a few months—this would be asking her to leave her mother forever.

A new feeling—a sickly one that bit hard—settled in his stomach. "I cannot leave for the East Indies," he said.

"Sir." Mr. Andrews's voice turned hard. "If you do not return by the time the twenty-four months stipulated are up, all your inheritance reverts to your grandfather's business partner."

Christopher went cold. He'd known there had to be a catch somewhere. "You cannot be serious."

"I assure you I am."

"So if I do not accompany you in two weeks' time . . ."

"There won't be another ship that gets you back in time to claim what is your right. Your grandfather's business partner will take ownership of the entire business and your grandfather's entire fortune will go to him."

"I'll be left exactly as I am now." Christopher's brow creased, aware that Lord Keats was watching him and Mr. Andrews like an old hen waiting for gossip. "When *exactly* did my grandfather pass away?"

"Twenty-two months ago, three weeks, and . . ." He seemed to be running calculations in his head. "Six days ago."

Christopher leaned back. Everything he wanted—a home, security, a future he could count on—and it was slipping from his hands. "Even if we board the ship next week we won't arrive before the twenty-four months are up."

"No, but we will arrive not *too* long after. Your grandfather's business partner is eager to continue growing the business, which requires your new funds, but if we leave immediately I am certain we can arrive in time to make him see reason."

This could not be. "And you arriving as soon as possible and me coming later?"

"Would not work, I'm afraid. The heir needs to be at the estate to claim what is rightfully his."

There was no way out. He either left England—left Rachel—and laid claim to his inheritance, or he stayed and lost his one chance of being able to settle down and provide a home for the woman he loved. Lud, a year ago the decision would have been easy. He would have gone to the East Indies without looking back. But a year ago, he was abroad with Fitzwilliam. No wonder Mr. Andrews had struggled to find him before now.

Several minutes of silence stretched out until finally Mr.

Andrews stood and held out a card. "I'm staying at the Brown Duck. I'll be there for a couple more days and then I'll have to leave so as to make the ship back to the East Indies. Let me know what you decide before then."

Christopher took the offered card. "Certainly." He only had a few days to decide on the best path, then. It seemed a terribly short amount of time for a terribly big decision.

CHAPTER TWENTY-ONE

Christopher sat for some time in Lord Keats's study. The gentleman seemed to understand that Christopher needed to simply sit and think and had left him alone. Eventually, as the sun slipped closer toward the tree tops, Christopher stood and made his way to the front door. Mr. Hervey met him there, handing him his hat and gloves. The manservant must have caught wind of some of Christopher's good fortune; why else had he offered to take his hat and gloves, as he would only do for a man of status?

Christopher didn't say much to the butler as he moved out into the evening air.

What was he to do? He couldn't leave Rachel, and he was certain she wouldn't come with him. Would she? If he asked, if he told her how he felt, would she come? They could certainly return to England in a couple of years once the estate was all sold off. Still, he found he couldn't imagine her agreeing to leave England for so long.

He walked toward his horse but paused just before mounting. Someone stood just on the other side of his horse. Someone in a skirt.

Lud, he didn't have the time or energy for Lady Keats just now.

Sure enough, she walked around the front of the horse, smiling coquettishly all the while. "Why, Mr. Dunn, how good of you to visit me again."

He kept his eyes off her, focusing instead on seeing that his saddle was properly secure. "I have not come to visit you." As she well knew. "I came to see your *husband* and a man of business from the East Indies."

She slipped up between him and the horse. "Oh? How intriguing."

"If you don't mind, I am needed back at Curio Manor."

She laced her hands around his neck. "Not nearly as much as you are needed here."

Christopher took hold of her wrists, untangling her hands from him, and placed them down at her side. "You have a husband, Lady Keats, and I think you would do well to remember it."

She scowled and her cheeks turned pink. "If it is no matter to me, then it should be nothing to you."

Christopher picked up the horse's reins, then turned back toward her. "Why are you so anxious to leave him?"

"Leave him?" Her brow dropped. "I am imprisoned here. There is no *leaving;* not for me, at any rate."

Christopher drew in a breath and asked the heavens for patience. "Believe me, I fully understand you do not wish to leave Woodside House." She would have sought out a wealthier, more influential lover than himself otherwise. "But why are you so willing to betray your husband? You cannot lie to me and say he is vicious or unkind."

"Is that all a woman should expect? A bore for a husband and enough responsibilities to drive her mad?"

"The man has provided you with a home, security. How can you be so ready to turn your back on all of that?"

Lady Keats drew herself up. "Perhaps he has, but I asked for none of it. It wasn't my idea that we wed. He set the whole thing up with my father." She crossed her arms, glaring up at Christopher. "All our marriage has ever been was a business transaction. Well, I gave him an heir and a spare besides—our agreement is fulfilled as far as I'm concerned."

He only stared at her. He had no notion how cold and unfeeling she truly was.

Christopher couldn't understand. "Your husband has provided you anything a woman could ever want."

Her lips pursed and she raised an eyebrow. "There are some things I will never be granted so long as I live in this stone prison."

"But is the passion you seek truly worth the risk?" Christopher knew Lord Keats well enough, but not so well as to guess what the man might do if his wife was unfaithful.

She took a step toward him, but this time as she drew near there was a different air about her. A desire to be closer to him that seemed to come not from a desire to manipulate, but a desire to be understood. "I want more than just passion, Mr. Dunn. I want a *choice*," she said, her tone softer than before. "I just want it to be my turn; a turn for *my* needs to be heard, a turn for *my* decisions to matter."

Christopher shook his head. "Are you not mistress of all Woodside House? Surely that requires dozens of decisions a day."

She scoffed. "Of course—I choose which plates to use when guests come, I decide what meals are served, and sometimes even which jewelry to wear." Her jaw tightened. "But nothing important. Never anything of consequence." Her eyes flitted back toward the house. "Lord Keats chooses when we reside here and when we travel to London. *He* decides my pin money, who I might invite, where I might go. I may be mistress, but I am not free."

Christopher had never seen her like this. So open, so obviously hurting. He'd known he was only meant to be a distraction in her life, but he'd never guessed that her need for a distraction was born from such pain.

She turned back to him. "I know you have found my actions in the past appalling. I guess I have grown rather desperate." A tear ran unchecked down her cheek. "I just *need* for someone to hear me, to see me. To care about what *I* want. I need to make a decision, all on my own. A big one, a decision that means something. I don't even care if it is a good decision or a bad one, I simply need to feel like I have a say in what happens to me." She shut her eyes and her hands came up, clutching either side of her face. "I can't live like this any longer. I feel so trapped—so overlooked all the time."

Christopher reached out and placed a hand on her arm. It was the first time he'd ever initiated any physical touch between them, but he couldn't leave her in her agony. It was true, he had been adamantly set against Lady Keats and her machinations, but that didn't mean he couldn't understand what being overlooked felt like.

"You need to tell your husband," he said in a low voice.

Lady Keats didn't drop her hands, neither did she open her eyes even as she shook her head. "He wouldn't listen. He wouldn't understand."

"Then keep telling him until he does."

She peeked one eye open just long enough to glare at him.

"If you employed even half as much energy toward convincing your husband that things need to change as you did in . . ." There really was no way to explain it and still keep his language suitable for a lady.

"In chasing you?" she supplied for him.

Christopher nodded. "Lord Keats wouldn't be able to say no to you for long, of that I'm certain."

Her scowl morphed into the coquettish smile she usually bore. "Are you flattering me, Mr. Dunn?"

Christopher took a small step back. "I'm saying you know how to be persistent."

Lady Keats's smile dropped as her gaze shot toward the house. "What you suggest would take a great deal of persistence, indeed."

She stepped forward, placed a kiss on Christopher's cheek, and quickly moved back again. The whole thing happened so fast, he didn't even have time to react before she was once more standing a pace away.

"I knew you were the man I needed," she said. "I just didn't realize that what I needed most from you was friendship. Thank you for being a friend to me today."

Whirling around, she hurried back into the house before he could say anything.

Christopher stood, stunned, for several minutes as she made her way in, and the door was shut behind her. He mounted his horse, putting little thought into directing the stallion back toward Curio Manor. Gads, but nothing today had gone the way he'd expected.

Riding slowly, Christopher couldn't help but acknowledge to himself that he'd always seen Lady Keats one way—as a flirt and an unfaithful wife. Someone who cared little for others. But what she'd said before? She'd just wanted it to be her turn. He saw her differently now. Suppose she hadn't always been a woman willing to break vows just to feel loved. He turned in his saddle for a moment and looked back the way he'd come. What kind of loneliness must she have endured before reaching a point low enough that she was willing to corner Christopher just for a little attention?

It all came from decisions made *for* her. She'd said she hadn't wanted to marry Lord Keats, and that little of the life she now led was of her own making. If left to heed her own heart when she was younger, what might her life look like now?

Christopher faced forward once more, taking a firmer hold on the reins and directing his horse to go a bit faster. Though he did not believe Rachel was anything like Lady Keats, he couldn't help but wonder. If Rachel were forced into a future she didn't want, what would become of her? How long could she endure putting aside her need to see her mother well and happy? How long could she be apart from those she loved and cared for?

How could he ask that of her?

Drawing near the house, he caught sight of her between a few of the rose bushes, several small glass balls catching the last of the evening light beside her. Her dark hair was pulled high atop her head, and as she bent down to smell the roses, several curls fell in front of her face. She was wearing her simple purple dress. She looked so beautiful.

What would she say when he told her he had to leave?

Rachel breathed in deeply, enjoying the sweet scent of the yellow roses. Soon it would grow too hot, and the rose bushes would be nothing more than leaves and thorns, colorless until autumn came again. But, until then, she would enjoy every last breath of the floral aroma. The soft crunch of boots against gravel brought her head up.

Christopher strode her way. Behind him, and closer to the front of the house, a groomsman led his horse toward the stables. He must have only just returned from whatever errand the unexpected letter had sent him on that afternoon. Rachel smiled as he drew near, and though he smiled back, it wasn't his usual confident, sincere smile. She looked deeper into his eyes. There was something troubling him.

"Is everything all right?" she asked once he was near enough.

He stopped an arm's length away. "Rachel, there's something I have to tell you."

That did sound like trouble. "Then perhaps we ought to walk." She motioned toward the garden path, and they fell into step beside one another.

Christopher was silent for several minutes. Rachel tried to be patient; she managed not to insist he speak, but she couldn't stop herself from glancing at him from around her bonnet every few minutes. His brow was low, and his step was heavy.

Finally, she could stand it no longer. "Is it the letter you received this morning?" He hadn't seemed upset when he'd first read it. In truth, he'd seemed rather excited. She'd assumed it had been good news.

"Yes." He drew the single word out ever so long. "I suppose I ought to start there. The letter this morning informed me that there was a Mr. Andrews looking for me and that he was currently at Lord Keats's house."

"I do not know a Mr. Andrews."

"He's a man of business." His voice dropped low. "From the East Indies."

"He came all that way to speak with you?"

Christopher nodded, but his head looked twice as heavy as usual with the way he moved it. "As it turns out, my grandfather moved there some years ago. He had a grand estate and a thriving business —all his wealth is out there now."

"Had?"

"He passed away two years ago."

"Christopher." She placed a hand on his arm. "I'm so sorry."

He only shrugged. "I never knew the man, though I did learn today that he'd flatly refused to forgive my father leaving like he had, despite my father writing and wishing to make amends."

Truthfully? "Well, if I hadn't been raised to speak well of the dead, I'd have a few things to say right about now. Regardless of the fact that your father was not the heir, he should have been willing to make amends."

Christopher gave her a sad sort of smile. "Interesting you should mention my grandfather's heir."

Rachel stopped her step, turning to face Christopher slowly. "You said your father was the second son."

He paused beside her. "I also learned today that my uncle passed away some years ago before I was even born."

Rachel's eyes widened. "You're the heir?"

He nodded again. "With the way my father described things between him and my grandfather, I always just assumed I'd never hear from my family and that would be that. Until today, I wasn't even sure if they knew I existed." Christopher took in a long breath. "The problem is . . . this means I have to go."

"You're leaving? For London? Or . . ."

"The East Indies."

Rachel's heart dropped into her stomach. He wasn't just leaving, he was saying goodbye.

Christopher took half a step closer, but then seemed to rethink it and stepped back again. "Part of the reason I was so long at Woodside House is I was debating with Mr. Andrews all the reasons for me to stay in England. But there is no other way for me to secure my inheritance. I have to go."

Christopher was leaving. Not that it should matter. She would be leaving soon herself. Only, she always envisioned waving to him as the carriage pulled away from Curio Manor, always envisioned knowing he was here. Her chest felt tight, and she struggled to find breath. He was going away. He wouldn't be here if she ever came back.

And she had wanted to come back.

Since learning that she would be returning to see her mother, Rachel had begun thinking forward. She'd begun to envision what would happen *after* seeing her mother was well-situated. The image of her future was not yet clear, but Christopher had always been in it. She hadn't realized it until now but seeing that part of the image suddenly stripped away, she knew deep down that he was a most vital part of the happiness she desired for herself.

Was that even possible now?

"How soon?" she asked, her voice broken.

"A couple of days."

"What?" That was not nearly enough time. She couldn't let her best friend, the man she most cared for, go in only a couple of days.

"I have to be on the next boat sailing for the East Indies if I am to secure the estate in time."

The world felt like it was spinning, and she still could not catch her breath. Rachel placed a hand to her forehead and looked about the garden, at the flowers and the glass balls, the sunset and the tree-tops. This was where Christopher belonged, here, at Curio Manor, or at the very least, here in England. Anyplace where she could return to him when the time was right. But that moment that she'd imagined where she was free to open her heart to him and he was standing beside her ready to fill her days with music and laughter . . . that moment would never happen.

He took her hand. "Suppose . . . you came with me?"

She looked back at him. He seemed hesitant in his question. "What? To the East Indies?"

"We could . . ." He shrugged off the rest of his statement.

Rachel's heart flipped at the unspoken suggestion. Still, she found herself shaking her head. "How could I leave Mother? I don't even know if she is well or safe or . . ." She tried to draw in enough air but couldn't seem to find it. "A couple of days isn't nearly enough time to see to her and prepare." She pulled her hand out of his. "Think of what you are asking." She couldn't go. She may be ready to accept that the future would inevitably bring difficulties and she could make the most of them; but that didn't mean she was ready to throw away everything she'd ever known and walk into something as unknown as the East Indies.

"I'm not asking you to leave England forever."

"No, only for several years. And who knows what might happen to Mother in that amount of time?" One could never be certain when one left for that long who would still be living upon their return. Mother's parents had both passed at a young age—Rachel had to be beside her mother to see the same didn't happen to her.

Moreover, life seemed to take particular enjoyment in robbing her of those she most loved. She'd be foolish to tempt the fates by leaving Mother for half so long.

Still, when she looked at him . . .

There was hurt in his eyes, sadness in the slump of his shoulders.

Could she not go with Christopher? The man who played the pianoforte with her, the man who shared her love for books, who listened to her worries and concerns with patience and understanding? How could life be so cruel as to force her to choose between the two people she loved most in the world? Then again, when had life cared two straws for her or her wounded heart?

But did she care for him *more* than Mother? Rachel's hand went to the locket about her neck. Certainly not. She could never care for anyone more than her own mother. Had she not determined as much on the very carriage ride when first coming to Curio Manor? Rachel took a half step back. "I'm sorry, Christopher." Blinking back the tears that she knew were coming, Rachel turned and hurried back to the house.

CHAPTER TWENTY-TWO

Rachel kept her head down as she hurried through the house. Hearing voices coming from further down the corridor, she turned left. It really didn't matter where she went, she only didn't want to see anyone just now. She pushed deeper into the manor, her turns based only on which direction seemed to take her away from anyone who might cross her path. Finding herself in the middle of a long corridor, with voices coming from either side, Rachel pushed open a door and slipped into a room.

"Rachel?"

She whirled about.

Dinah and Charlotte sat on a settee near a low-burning fire. Rachel blinked a few times, glancing about the room. She'd found her way to the drawing room. Standing up straight, Rachel tried to appear unaffected.

"Good morning to you both," she said.

"Morning?" Dinah said. "It's nearly dinner time."

Was it? Never mind. Rachel placed a hand on the handle of the door she'd just entered in. "I didn't mean to interrupt. I'll leave you both to your tete-a-tete."

Rachel turned the knob and pulled the door open, but before she could slip back out, Charlotte stood.

"Is everything all right?"

Still holding the door halfway open, Rachel froze. No, everything was certainly not all right. But, she didn't want to discuss it. She didn't want to explain why the thought of Christopher leaving for the East Indies caused her to feel as though she were losing her home all over again. She didn't want to explain why she refused to go with him.

"My dear," Charlotte called again from the center of the room. "Why don't you come sit and talk with us?"

If she sat, she might not be able to keep her composure. Still . . .

Oh, heavens, she was so tired of losing people. Her hand dropped away from the doorknob. She was so tired of life stripping away, bit by bit, everything she most loved. Slowly, she turned and looked over at the two women.

Two women Rachel knew loved her.

"Christopher is leaving," she confessed.

Dinah was by her side immediately, wrapping an arm about her shoulders and leading her back to the settee. Among tears and a few hiccups, Rachel explained Christopher's change in situation.

The good of it.

The bad of it.

All of it.

"And he didn't ask you to go with him?" Dinah asked as Rachel neared the end.

Apparently, her preference for Christopher had not gone unnoticed by her family. "He did," Rachel admitted. "I told him no."

"Whyever so?" Dinah blurted out.

Tears welled up once more, blurring the room about Rachel. When she answered, her words were so very soft. "I cannot leave Mother."

Dinah shook her head; from behind her tears, she appeared a wobbly, blonde splatter to Rachel. "I am certain my aunt will understand. She only wants you to be happy. Nothing would make you happier, I am certain, than—"

"Dinah," Charlotte said, reaching over Rachel and placing a hand on Dinah's lap to still her. "This must be Rachel's decision. Only she can determine what manner of happiness she wishes for her own life."

"Thank you," Rachel said. Yet—there was something about Charlotte's statement that niggled at her.

Only she could decide what *manner* of happiness she wished for.

What manner.

The statement buried itself deeper into her mind and heart, and she felt as though there was something in that statement she didn't fully understand. She'd always believed that returning home, going back to the way life had been when she was a child and happy was the only way to recapture peace and contentment. But Charlotte's statement left behind a niggling notion that perhaps Rachel had been wrong about that all along.

Charlotte's life had not turned out the way she'd wanted. Her own husband had died quite young—and yet, like Lady Fitzwilliam, she'd found happiness despite the sorrow. She'd chosen not to let her horrible sadness consume her—even going so far as to defy what others would call common sense and travel, alone, to see her own son whenever she so pleased. Rachel leaned her head against the woman's shoulder. It was Charlotte living her life in the manner that brought her the most happiness that had brought the marchioness into Rachel's life. She would be forever grateful for that.

"Dinah, sweet," Charlotte continued, "would you please go find your father and let him know I must speak to him immediately?"

"I am sure there's a footman about. Might we not send him?" Dinah said.

Charlotte only shook her head. "I wish to speak to Rachel while you are finding him."

The tears were drying a bit—at least for now—and Rachel could see Dinah's features clearly enough to notice that she pursed her lips and seemed a bit put out to be asked to leave.

"Very well." Dinah stood abruptly. "I shall see to fetching my father so that you two may speak without someone as naive and ignorant as myself in the way." With that, she stomped toward the door.

"I didn't mean—"

Dinah was gone before Charlotte could finish.

The marchioness blew out a long breath. "I swear she's becoming more of a handful by the week."

Rachel rested back against the settee. "She's always hated being the youngest of us three."

"Let us not worry about that now," Charlotte said, turning to face Rachel yet again. "Explain to me why you aren't going to the East Indies with Mr. Dunn."

Now it was Rachel's turn to purse her lips. "It is like I said. I cannot leave Mother."

"Forgive me, but that seems a bit paltry in comparison—"

"If you don't understand why I can't leave Mother, then you must not understand me at all." It was as simple as that. "I love Uncle Seth dearly, and he has given me much. But he has never been able to give me the happiness that I felt as a child. Since my father was taken, there's always been a piece of me that has been missing. If I lose my mother, I fear there will be nothing left of my heart." She turned atop the settee to face Charlotte more fully. "I have tried; please believe me, I have. But all the parties and pleasant company I've enjoyed only leave me feeling guilty that I have this, and Mother has next to nothing. I have even found a man I most desperately care for—yet I cannot fully open my heart to him because of the turmoil inside me. I know you asked me to start looking forward, to think more of my future. But I cannot see a way to move forward that would not also be moving *away* from Mother. If I marry a titled man, Mother would never be accepted in our same social circles. If I marry the man I care for, I will never have the means to be by her side as frequently as she needs." Rachel shook her head. "I cannot move forward. I must go back. I need to know Mother is all right. Perhaps, while there, I can finally find a bit of peace, a bit of healing."

"Oh, Rachel," Charlotte said, placing a hand against her cheek. "I had no idea you were hurting so much." Her hand slipped away and moved over Rachel's shoulders, encircling her in a hug.

They sat in silence for a time, and in not long at all, the drawing room door opened and Uncle Seth entered along with Eliza and Dinah. Eliza hurried to Rachel, sitting on the floor near Rachel's feet and taking her hand.

"I am so sorry," Eliza said.

Uncle Seth gave a soft cough and all eyes focused on him.

"After having recently learned of some changes in the present circumstances," he said slowly, "I believe it makes sense for Rachel to return to her mother's house as soon as possible, instead of in two weeks' time, as we originally planned."

"Truly?" Rachel said, standing. "I can go home *now*?"

His expression was sad, but he stood as straight as ever. "Yes." His voice was soft, barely audible.

Rachel rushed forward, throwing her hands about him. "Thank you."

Finally, she was going home.

Christopher watched most of the readying of the carriage from his bedchamber window. The Mulgraves would be gone within the hour. Blast it all, but no matter how much it tore at him, he couldn't bring himself to look away. One trunk, then a second were secured. Then Miss Mulgrave and Miss Dinah Mulgrave came out of the house speaking to one another and directing the footmen as they readied the coach. Lady Blackmore appeared on the scene next. Her commanding presence drew every manservant's attention, causing them to work that much faster.

Sir Mulgrave came around from the side of the house with two horses and one of the groomsmen. Christopher knew both Sir Mulgrave and his oldest daughter, Miss Mulgrave, were excellent riders. He hoped they met with clear skies and easy roads between here and their destination.

Christopher pressed his forehead tighter against the glass.

Everyone was present except Rachel. Was she waiting until the last minute before walking outside? If she were alone in the house right now, might he not be able to find her and plead with her one last time to change her mind and come with him instead?

He pulled away from the window, turning and looking over his own room. Clothing had been pulled from the closet. His few personal effects had all been carefully wrapped and packed away. He, too, would be leaving soon. Mere hours after the Mulgraves left Curio Manor if all went well.

He scratched at his jaw and the stubble he'd been too upset to shave away that morning. Might he not speak with Rachel one last time?

With his fists clenched, Christopher moved quickly through the room and out the door. Where might she be?

As soon as he asked himself the question, he knew the answer.

She'd be playing the pianoforte.

He found her there. But she wasn't playing. There was music set before her and she was atop the bench, and though her hands rested on the keys, they didn't move, and no sound reverberated about the small room.

"You could still come with me, you know," he said.

She didn't start at his voice; she must have known he'd walked in the room, just as he'd always known whenever it had been him at the pianoforte.

"Please don't ask me to," she said without turning around.

Christopher walked up to her and took one of her hands. "Very well, I won't." Though it killed him. "I understand why you can't. May I at least say it's one of the things I love about you?"

"What's that?" Her eyes finally came around and found his. Her dark eyes were tinged with a bit of red. Though she wasn't crying now, she had been recently.

"I love that you don't give up on those who mean the most to you."

"But . . . *you* mean so much to me, too," she whispered. "How can I lose one of you?" She blinked a few times, and tears appeared along her lashes. "What am I to do when I *do* lose one of you?"

Christopher tugged gently on her hand, helping her to stand. He placed an arm around her waist, pulling her close to him. She hiccupped and wrapped her arms around him as well, burying her face against his chest.

"Do you always hiccup when you're crying?" he asked.

She nodded, her head moving against him. Lud, but it felt heavenly to hold her close. What he wouldn't give to have the right to do this every day.

"Do you remember the first time we met?" he asked.

She pulled her head back without releasing him and looked up at him. "In the tree?"

He couldn't help but smile a bit at the memory. "Yes. I climbed down first, and do you recall what I said to you?"

"You said to go ahead and jump. You said you'd catch me."

"And then you said that I certainly would not be permitted to catch you. You were quite certain you could jump from that height without injuring yourself."

"And then you said, 'Or you can just trust me to catch you.'"

"Just so." Christopher pushed a dark curl behind her ear. "Rachel, my love, that promise still stands. I am still willing to catch you."

"This 'jump' you call it—leaving you to see that my mother is all right—feels far higher than the jump from that tree so many weeks ago."

"It does not matter if that means you come with me now, or you join me in the East Indies in a year, or if you wait two years"—gads, but that sounded like an eternity—"for me to return to England. I will always be here for you."

"You'll always catch me?"

"I always will."

Her head listed to the side. "You can't promise me that. The East Indies is a dangerous place. The trip there and back even more so."

She made a valid argument. Though most ships arrived in India without deaths, and most people did not succumb to disease or injury while there, the trip would certainly hold many dangers. She was right; he couldn't truly promise he'd return at all.

"I do promise," he said, "to do all that is in my power to come back, safe and sound, for you." The first signs of a little smile flitted across her lips, so he continued. "You are determined to see your mother again and, Rachel, I am just as determined to see you again."

Going up on tiptoe, Rachel pressed her lips to his.

Christopher froze, surprised at the unexpected touch. Then he melted. Tightening his hold around her, he drew her in closer still. If only this kiss could last. If only it could continue to go on and on for years. Her hands wound up his neck, cupping his jaw, her thumb stroking the stubble there. He poured all his longing and all his wishes into that simple, single kiss. How he loved her, how he wished she could be his now, not in some distant future.

And yet, he wouldn't demand she come with him now. He would respect her decision. How could he not?

He pulled away, ending the kiss before he was overcome and did anything truly foolish.

Hang it all, but he loved her. He wanted her.

"Goodbye, Christopher." Her words brought him back to the present, to the fact that she was leaving and they might never see one another again.

His voice caught and he almost couldn't get the words out. But they needed to be said.

"Goodbye, Rachel."

CHAPTER TWENTY-THREE

The rattling of carriage wheels taking Rachel away from him still rang in Christopher's ears. It had been nearly two hours since the Mulgraves had left, and already it felt far too long. Christopher climbed the last stair and looked down the long corridor. Would Fitzwilliam be in his bedchamber? He'd checked the entire rest of the manor and hadn't found the man. There seemed to be nowhere else to check, and Christopher was not about to leave Curio Manor without telling his good friend farewell.

Christopher knocked on the bedchamber door. "Fitzwilliam, you in there?"

"Enter," his lordship replied. It was immediately followed by a low thud, and then the sound of something being scraped across the floor.

Brow creased, Christopher pressed the door open. "Fitzwilliam?"

The room was not at all how Christopher had last seen it. There were clothes strewn about every which way, and no fewer than four large trunks were open on the floor. Indeed, Fitzwilliam had one by the handles and was dragging it yet closer to his bed.

"What the devil are you up to?" Christopher asked.

Fitzwilliam let go of the trunk, turned to his bed, and yanked all the bedding off it in a single pull. Wadding the linens up most unceremoniously, he dropped it all inside. "I'm packing," he said, even as he slammed the trunk shut and did up the clasps.

"Packing for what?"

A footman hurried into the room from the connected closet, the largest pile of clothes in his arms that Christopher had ever seen.

Fitzwilliam turned toward the footman. "I'll bring them all." As the footman bowed—somehow managing not to topple the load in his arms—Fitzwilliam turned back to Christopher. "A man has to look his best while in the East Indies, after all, and we shall be there for quite some time, I understand."

Christopher watched the footman carefully fold and place each bit of clothing inside one of the many trunks. "You're . . . coming with me?"

"Of course!" Fitzwilliam sat down on his bed, placing an elbow on his knee, and leaned forward. "Spoke with my grandmother this morning and she agrees. You can't honestly consider your employ finished, nor my education done until you've shown me the East Indies. That you never thought of such before now *does* give me cause to question your capability as a tutor. But, seeing as the problem will shortly be remedied, I have decided to overlook my concerns on that front."

Christopher was touched. He ran a hand through his hair. Fitzwilliam was up and leaving England, to go to the East Indies of all places, just for Christopher.

"Henry," Fitzwilliam said to the footman, quite as though he wasn't upending his life for a friend, "will you run down and see if Cook could make us a bit of something for the road? Mr. Dunn is wanting to leave before dinner, I believe."

"Right away, my lord." The manservant, who'd just finished with the large pile of clothing, bowed and left the room.

Christopher shook his head, his gaze moving over all the disarray. He walked over to Fitzwilliam and extended a hand. "Thank you."

Fitzwilliam took it, standing once more, and slapped Christopher on the back. "I couldn't stand to see you leave alone."

Christopher nodded, his throat closing off and preventing him from speaking. Alone he most certainly was.

"Did you propose?" Fitzwilliam asked, still standing shoulder to shoulder with Christopher, both of them looking at the room instead of each other.

"In a manner of speaking."

"So, you left it up to chance? Your monumental, life-altering moment came, and you went into it with nothing more than a prayer?"

Christopher scowled at the half-packed room. And here he'd been thinking Fitzwilliam was a friend.

"Now who's the fool?" Still his tone wasn't haughty or mocking.

"There's more to being a gentleman than looking good on horseback."

When Fitzwilliam spoke again, his voice was softer, more sincere. "I know. It's about taking responsibility. It's about seeing to the wellbeing of those you are master over. It's about making sure those you love know it."

Christopher glanced over at his lordship. Fitzwilliam met his gaze, an earnest smile on his lips.

He waggled his eyebrows. "Being a gentleman is about all that— or so my tutor has taught me. Well, that *and* looking good on horseback."

Leave it to Fitzwilliam to assume the best medicine would be to encourage Christopher to laugh at his own pain.

"I can't make light of this one just yet," Christopher said, though he did feel the weight lift a bit.

"Then it is a good thing I'm coming," Fitzwilliam said, "because sooner or later, you're going to need to."

Perhaps. But Christopher didn't see himself doing that anytime soon.

"Now," Fitzwilliam said, taking hold of one of the trunks again. "Go see the carriage is brought around post haste. I am determined

I shan't slow you down a bit. We'll be out of here within half an hour; you have my word."

Rachel had hardly slept last night—it had been her first night not at Curio Manor in nearly two months. Though she'd moved from one place to another before, last night had been particularly hard. Not that she was in any danger of falling asleep at this point in their travels. She could suffer through dozens more nights like last night and still be wide awake.

They were only minutes away from home, and Rachel was nothing but nerves.

"Sir Mulgrave felt you would prefer to reunite with your mother on your own," Charlotte said, once more sitting on the same bench as Rachel. Dinah slept on the opposite bench. They were all as they had been when they'd first traveled to Curio Manor.

Heavens, but so much had happened since then.

"Rachel?"

She drew in a breath, willing her mind to stay focused. "Yes," she said to Charlotte. "That would be much appreciated."

"Very well," the marchioness said. "We shall leave you to visit with your mother and continue on to Sir Mulgrave's house. We'll send a carriage back for you in a few hours."

"Thank you," Rachel said. Uncle Seth only lived half an hour's carriage ride away from Mother, so she didn't feel guilty since she wouldn't be putting her uncle out much.

Charlotte patted Rachel's hand, giving her a reassuring smile, and the carriage fell into silence once more.

Rachel's gaze traveled back to the window and the road just outside. They'd reached the part of the road that was not just vaguely familiar, but very familiar two hours before. Rachel had been counting each tree, each landmark ever since. The carriage turned right and there it was.

Home.

Rachel kept her gaze on the small cottage as they approached. As the old adage went, the place certainly *did* look smaller than she remembered. The shutters hung a bit more lopsided, and the flowers out front had clearly not been seen to for ages. Of a truth, the closer they drove, the more neglect became apparent. Rachel's stomach tightened. Mother had always been so proud of the flowers out front. And the fence . . . gracious, it looked ready to topple over.

The carriage came to a full stop, but Rachel couldn't take her eyes off what had become of her home. All her concerns for her mother's well-being came back, pulsing through her entire being stronger than ever before. She'd been right to come back, to *insist* Uncle bring her here.

The carriage door began to open, and Rachel had to pull back or else tumble out and land on her face.

The footman lowered the stairs and handed her down.

"Will you be all right?" Charlotte called, still inside the carriage.

Rachel glanced back at her. Charlotte, in her very elegant carriage, with her finely quilted squabs and family crest emblazed on the side, was a stark contrast to the home Rachel had just pulled up to.

"I shall be quite fine," she reassured Charlotte.

Rachel bid her family farewell and then, before any of them could question her further, lifted her skirts and hurried up the front walk. Weeds covered most of the stone walkway and nearly tripped her twice. Nonetheless, after all Rachel had been through, a few weeds were nothing in comparison.

She didn't bother knocking but twisted the knob and pushed the door open. It gave with a discontented moan.

"Mother?" Rachel called out. The entryway was dark, not a single candle in any of the holders or sconces lit. Neither was there any answering reply. Rachel's brow dropped and she shut the door behind her.

"Mother?" Rachel called again, walking past the front parlor, where they had once entertained many visitors. She moved beyond the dining room, the table and chairs covered in dust.

Rachel froze, suddenly realizing what she should have noticed the moment they pulled up.

The place was empty.

Uncle Seth said Mother had taken on *more* boarders. Where were they? The dust about everything only proved that not only was no one staying here now, no one had for weeks. Possibly months.

Possibly . . . not since Rachel had left for London.

Partway down the corridor was a small side table, which appeared to be covered in papers. Rachel reached it easily enough, but in the darkness had to study what was before her to make anything out.

Letters. The side table was piled high with letters.

Rachel lifted one. The seal was unbroken. She flipped it over. That was her handwriting across the front. She picked up a second. It was the same.

She rifled through the pile. They were all her letters, and they were all unopened.

She couldn't believe this. Someone had brought them into the house and placed them on this table; yet, Mother had not bothered to open or read a single one. Her heart fell.

Slowly, Rachel spun about. She couldn't seem to put the random pieces together.

An empty house.

Unanswered letters.

Uncle Seth had promised her that Mother was healthy. But, he'd also said the house was full of boarders. Had Mother been *unable* to read these letters? Suppose she'd been hurt? Grown seriously ill? Mother still had a part-time maid-of-all-work who came in twice a week, so it could have been she who placed the letters here. All this time, Mother may have been bedridden or worse.

Rachel hurried through the rest of the rooms on the main floor. No one. The only sign of life was a small fire in the kitchen hearth. Rachel returned to the entryway and looked up the stairs. It was only the bedchambers up there, and she hadn't heard anything since first walking in the house.

Still, Rachel hurried up. The door to one of the smaller rooms, which had once been hers, was shut tight. If the dust on the floor near it was any indicator, it hadn't been opened in years. Across the hall and down past several other doors was the one she most wanted. Her Mother's.

Rachel moved up to it. Soft voices floated out. The woman's voice she recognized immediately—Mother was home, after all.

Had she not heard Rachel, then?

Or was she unable to get up and greet her?

Rachel lifted a shaking hand. Someone else was in there with Mother, but she had no idea who it might be or what she might find when she opened the door.

Steeling herself against the worst, Rachel pushed the door open.

She moved her gaze to the bed first, praying she wouldn't find Mother there, pale and drawn and delirious with disease. But the linens were smoothed over the mattress, and no one was there. Rachel's gaze moved next to the small settee beside the fire.

There it stayed.

There was Mother.

Far from pale and drawn, she was smiling, and her eyes shone.

"Mother?"

Her mother turned atop the settee suddenly, her expression showing shock and then joy. Mother stood and hurried over to Rachel, wrapping her in a hug. She was still thin, but she seemed not as thin as when Rachel had first left for London.

"Darling." Her voice was strong, too. She appeared as healthy as ever. "We had not expected you for another day or more still."

Rachel hugged her mother tightly. "I convinced Uncle Seth to bring me back sooner."

Mother squeezed tighter and then let her go. "Well, I'm glad you didn't arrive any sooner than this. We only arrived ourselves yesterday."

"We?"

Mother's smile brightened. She stepped back, motioning toward the other individual, still sitting on the settee, with a grand sweep of her arm.

It was a man. A man of some years, with a full beard. Both it and his head of long hair was mostly gray. His left arm was bandaged and secured across his chest. Who was he? Why would he be here, in Mother's room? Rachel's eyes caught his. They were a dark brown, just like her own.

A memory sparked somewhere deep in her mind.

The man stood. "Hello, my little songbird."

CHAPTER TWENTY-FOUR

"Father?" Rachel uttered the words, her voice so broken it was barely more than an indistinguishable sound.

Mother wrapped an arm about Rachel and squeezed her tightly. "That's right."

Rachel looked from the man who was smiling at her—the man who was her father?—then back to Mother. "I don't understand." He'd died while in prison years ago. Rachel blinked a few times and reached for something to steady herself. Was Mother trying to trick her? Had she gone so far as to find someone who resembled her late husband and convinced him to take on the assumed name? Perhaps Mother was more ill than Rachel had originally worried.

The man walked around the settee, coming closer to both Rachel and her mother. He walked with a bit of a limp, and on closer inspection, he wasn't just thin, he was emaciated. There were dark circles under his eyes. Wherever Mother had found this man, he certainly *looked* as though he'd spent the better part of the last two decades in debtor's prison.

He took hold of her hand; his fingers were rough and bony. Still, one would have imagined that such a touch from a complete stranger would feel unwanted. Yet, Rachel found it to be warm and caring. She looked to his eyes once more. Their dark depths *were* familiar, she couldn't deny it.

"But, how?" she asked feebly.

The man's smile quirked to the side. "I think it best you sit down before you faint, my dear."

Rachel nodded, though even that sent the world shaking more than it ought. The man pulled a chair up close to the settee and Rachel took it. She watched her mother closely as she and the man sat closely together. Mother was happy. Truly, utterly, completely happy. Though Rachel still could not understand what it was she was seeing, neither could she not feel overjoyed to see her mother doing so well.

Mother turned to her, the smile on her face faltering a touch. "First, I need to ask your forgiveness."

"Whatever for?" Rachel asked. If it was whatever led to Mother being so entirely happy once more, Rachel was quite certain she could forgive nearly anything.

"I believe you were old enough when your father left to under-stand why," Mother continued. The man seemed content to allow her to tell the story and simply sat back and watched.

Rachel nodded; she'd understood that their store had fallen on hard times, money had been lost, and he'd had to leave because of that.

"You must know that it wasn't your father's fault." Mother's hand went to the man's knee and rested there. It was a subtle act of affection, but one that Rachel couldn't look away from. "After he'd been in Marshalsea for almost a year, I received word that he had died of an illness."

As Mother spoke on, Rachel's gaze moved from the hand on the man's knee, up to the man's face. He was watching Mother speak. Though he seemed uninterested in interrupting, his eyes shone like a man clearly in love.

"You were so heartbroken," Mother said to Rachel. "I was as well. Money grew tight and your uncle began sending me funds to help cover costs here."

Rachel hadn't known that Uncle Seth had begun helping

Mother *before* she'd gone to live with him. Then again, she'd been quite young at the time.

"Then I received another letter from Marshalsea. This one informed me that many prisoners had died the past winter and that some of the bodies had been incorrectly identified."

Rachel's heart skipped a beat. "Incorrectly identified?"

Mother nodded. "The previous letter—the one saying your father had died—was a mistake." She turned to the man sitting beside her, a bright smile lighting up Mother's face once more. "Your father was still alive after all."

Rachel grew lightheaded. Then, it truly was her father sitting beside Mother. "Why didn't you tell me?" All this time, she'd believed her father was gone.

Mother's brow dropped. "That is why I must ask your forgiveness." She shook her head sadly. "You'd already grieved for your father. I'd seen the pain and heartache you'd endured. As much as I was overjoyed at knowing he still lived, I also knew it would probably only last until the following winter."

Father spoke up. "Marshalsea is a harsh place. Most do not survive."

"I couldn't tell you he was alive, only to have you mourn him again," Mother said softly. "Please say you understand and will forgive me."

Rachel only nodded. Someday, she most certainly would. For now, she wasn't even sure how she felt about the whole thing. It was rather too much to take in.

"After that . . ." Mother picked up the tale once more, her voice returning in strength. "I knew I had to somehow scrape together enough funds to see him released. So I spoke with my brother once more."

"That's why Uncle Seth had me come live with him," Rachel surmised.

Mother rolled her lips inward and let out a long sigh before nodding. "I hated to do it. First to have your father taken from me and then you? It was almost more than I could bear. But I knew Seth would see to your every need in a way I couldn't, no matter how much money he sent me. I couldn't both take in the odd job and raise you properly. A boarding house is no place for a young lady to grow up. Moreover, in having you go, I could save even a greater sum of money. As Seth's business grew, he was also able to not only see to your comfort but also contribute even more to my savings. Then," her smile broke through once more, shining like the very sun itself. "When he was knighted and sold his business, he used most of it to take you girls to London for a season. After all, though we both wanted you to have your father back, it wasn't worth sacrificing your future over. Still, Seth is a smart man. He was able to gift me a substantial sum. Between all that I'd saved until then and that amount, I finally had enough." Her free hand, the one not on Father's knee, wrapped around Father's uninjured arm. "I left the day after you left for London."

Father bent over, kissing Mother lightly on the top of her head.

Mother rested her head against his shoulder, turning back to Rachel. "We only just returned yesterday. My brother must have brought you here the minute he heard word that we'd returned."

Rachel simply sat, the emotions, the new information, swirling about inside her. For a minute, the room was silent. This was why Mother had lived in such poverty for so many years, why Rachel had been sent away, why not one of her letters had been answered.

It all made sense now.

Rachel drew a breath in and with it, some of the happiness that filled the room.

It made sense—wonderful, beautiful sense. It would take time for her to fully grasp all she'd been given back in only the space of an hour. Nonetheless, she moved over to the settee and sat on her father's other side. A conversation started up about the innate little things of everyday life. Mother spoke of her traveling to Marshalsea to free Father. Rachel spoke of all that had happened since she'd left for London. Slowly, as the sun sunk further and further in the sky, they moved back in time, Rachel speaking of life with Uncle Seth and her cousins and Mother speaking of all the various odd jobs she'd taken up in an effort to earn a bit more money.

It was amazing how hard her mother had worked to see her

husband free once more. And all the while, Rachel had never known. This whole time, Rachel had been wanting to go back— back to when Father was free, back to her home and her parents. Yet, her own mother hadn't been looking back at all. She'd been looking forward, working for the day when they could be a family again, working to create the future happiness she desperately wanted.

When the carriage came around for Rachel, it wasn't empty as she expected. Uncle Seth, Eliza, Dinah, and even Charlotte had come to welcome her father home. They enjoyed a lovely dinner together and afterward when her uncle and cousins were ready to leave, Rachel chose to stay behind. She'd lost many years with her parents, and she wasn't ready to give up even a night's sleep here at home.

Rachel stood at the front door, her arm wrapped around Mother, as they waved goodbye. Father—how strange to use that word—had chosen to remain in his seat by the fire. Though he hadn't said so aloud, Rachel rather guessed he struggled to stand for long periods of time.

"We are very blessed to have family," Mother said to her.

Rachel nodded. "I must confess to being quite angry at my uncle for the better part of these past few months."

Mother's lips pursed. "So he told me." She pulled Rachel back into the house and they shut the door. "I am so sorry for all the worry and heartache I've caused you, both these past few months and these past many years." Arm in arm, they began walking toward the parlor together.

"I am most specifically sorry about not writing you since you removed to Town," Mother continued. "When I finally had the money needed to see your father released, I was so elated, I'm afraid I wasn't thinking straight. I should have written you then, told you I was leaving for a time and not to worry if you didn't hear from me. Instead, I wrote to my brother and asked him to see you didn't worry, returned unfinished sewing and still dirty laundry to their owners, and sent all my boarders packing. After that, I was traveling from place to place, and your letters never reached me. I had no idea you were on to my little white lie until I returned home and found a letter from Seth waiting for me."

"And by then we were already on the road to meet you."

"Exactly."

"I suppose I ought to apologize to my uncle. He did keep saying I ought to trust him." Rachel truly should have—he'd known the whole of it the entire time.

"Oh, heavens, that man." Mother cast her gaze heavenward. "I *told* him to make sure you wouldn't worry. I should have foreseen that he would go about it in the worst way possible." Mother laughed softly, and Rachel found herself joining in with a giggle.

"Every time we talked," Rachel told her, "I became more convinced he was keeping something from me. I started coming up with the most horrid theories. You were sick and dying. You thought our connection would hurt my chances of making a good match. You were working yourself to the bone and would pass early as your parents did. I told Uncle Seth all my concerns but all he would say was 'trust me.'"

"He did bungle that terribly, didn't he? Never ask an honest man to lie—that's the lesson we should learn here. That, and never underestimate a daughter's intuition to know when something is off." Mother leaned in and kissed Rachel on the forehead.

Rachel closed her eyes and breathed in the feel of being home once more.

"We, neither of us," Mother continued, "had any notion when I first left that you would instinctively know something was up and go after it with such dogged determination."

"You taught me to cherish my family."

Mother smiled at her. "You don't know how happy I am to hear you say that."

They stepped into the parlor and found Father asleep in the large chair.

"Oh dear." Mother laughed, but quickly covered her mouth.

"Do we wake him?" Rachel asked.

"I sincerely hate to. Yet, I also hate to let him sleep there all night."

"I think waking him would be the lesser of the two discomforts."

Mother nodded and together they gently shook his shoulder until one eye opened. He smiled at seeing them and together, the three of them made their way up the stairs. Rachel's father kissed her goodnight with a whispered, "Sleep well, my songbird." She nearly cried for joy.

Lying in bed that night in her very recently dusted room, staring up at the plain ceiling, Rachel smiled to herself.

This time, life had not taken away.

This time, life had returned.

Christopher looked over the list of items Mr. Andrews suggested they purchase here in England before setting sail. It was long indeed. He flipped it over. The backside was a list of items Mr. Andrews suggested they leave behind—apparently warm, winter clothing would not be as necessary in the East Indies as it was here in England.

Christopher tossed the paper back onto the table before him. He could easily have everything he still needed purchased today—he probably could have had it purchased and ready yesterday. But his heart wasn't in it. The roads had been clear, and they'd arrived sooner than expected. The ship didn't set sail until day after tomorrow. There seemed little reason to be ready this early. Christopher picked up his cup and took a drink. The pub around him was quite full. No doubt, many of those he saw here were also readying for the same voyage to the East Indies. Perhaps he ought to ask around, get to know some of his fellow travelers.

But he couldn't find the heart to do that either.

Instead, he simply sat, drinking his port alone and trying desperately to not think about a certain engaging set of dark eyes.

"Still here?" Fitzwilliam sat down next to him. "Weren't you saying this morning that we had much to do today?"

He had, but the more he'd thought on it, the more it all felt so horribly pointless.

"I know this adventure has only just begun," Fitzwilliam continued, "but I must say that you are decidedly less fun now than when we previously journeyed abroad."

"Ah, yes, but this time we aren't traveling for pleasure, are we? We're traveling because if we don't, I lose my only shot at a home and at a life as my own master."

Fitzwilliam screwed his lips up on one side. "I suppose that would put a stop to the merriment, wouldn't it?"

Christopher didn't bother responding.

"I don't think it's the prospect of selling your grandfather's estate in the East Indies that is troubling you," Fitzwilliam said.

Christopher gave his friend a flat stare; a fool could have deduced as much. "Don't tell me you're going to criticize my proposal again."

"Of course not." Fitzwilliam leaned over the table. "The problem wasn't your proposal—unpracticed though it most decidedly was. The problem is that you're *leaving*."

Christopher slammed his cup down on the table. "Don't you think if there was any other way, I would be taking it now?" He was done being the calm, polite tutor. Fitzwilliam's grandmother could fire him for all he cared—he wouldn't be needing the position anymore, regardless. "Suppose I do what you say. Suppose I stay. What then? Perhaps I could convince Rachel to marry me, though she'd be smarter not to. Because what can I offer her?" His voice grew in volume as he spoke his frustrations aloud. "As a tutor, my home is the room next to the nursery, or a spare bedchamber no one else is using, or even sometimes a small place in the servants' quarters. That's *all* I have to offer a wife. More still, if by some miracle Rachel deemed such a miserable life worth it, it isn't as though she'd actually be welcomed wherever we went. She wouldn't be connected to the master or mistress of the house, but neither would she be part of the staff. It would be beyond the pale. She's the ward of a knight, hang it all, and one with very high connections. She shouldn't be asked to take up work as a maid. Such would be decidedly below her station." He jabbed a thumb at his own chest. "*I* am below her station."

But that would change if he went to the East Indies. A couple of years and his affairs would be in order. Then he could return to England, buy an estate, and join the ranks of the landed gentry. *That* was a life he could proudly offer a wife; that was a future that was fit for a brave and caring Rachel.

Though, by then, he would undoubtedly be too late.

Blast it all; he'd run through this same circle over and over in his mind. There was no way out.

Fitzwilliam shrugged. "I'm sure there is another way, if only——"

Christopher stood so suddenly his chair toppled over, crashing against the floor behind him. "For you, there would be. For an earl, a viscount, a member of the gentry, yes there would be. But for me? A tutor? You don't understand, Fitzwilliam. Life for me is not so easy. I can't just propose to any woman, confident I can offer her the world and more."

Fitzwilliam's expression hardened. Slowly he rose to his feet, a calm, controlled fury in his eyes. "Don't ever assume my life hasn't been hard," he whispered tightly.

Christopher felt his own temper rising. "I don't care. It's still not the same." He pushed away from the table, blindly moving through the pub and toward the stairs which led to the rooms above. He needed time and space alone. He needed to lay down before he punched a certain smug baron.

Though they'd shared a room up until then, that night Fitzwilliam never showed up. Christopher supposed he'd decided to rent a different room altogether. Perhaps even in a different pub altogether. It was for the best.

The next morning, however, Christopher did feel a bit guilty. He hadn't meant to insinuate that Fitzwilliam's life had always been ease and bliss. He'd known the man long enough to learn otherwise. Still, his own frustration at not being able to marry the woman he loved burned.

When his morning coffee was brought to him, a note came with it.

And the handwriting certainly looked like Fitzwilliam's. Christopher shook his head as he opened it—probably just informing

Christopher that he'd secured other lodgings for the time between now and when the ship would sail.

Dunn,

I'll be back soon. Don't do anything stupid before I return—
Like board a boat to the East Indies without me.

F.

Well, he'd not only taken himself off to another nearby pub, it seemed he'd quit the county all together. Christopher tossed the letter aside and picked up his coffee. But instead of taking a drink, he simply swirled it about. With a sigh, he placed it back down none too gently, and it clanked loudly. Christopher pushed the drink away and stood. Part of him couldn't care less if the man made it back or not—but part of him sincerely hoped he did. Christopher was not looking forward to this trip to the East Indies and having a friend by his side would make a difference.

He moved toward a window and looked out at the road. His best chance at a future with Rachel required his departure. The sooner he arrived in the East Indies, the sooner he could plan his trip back. Regardless of Fitzwilliam and his presence on board, Christopher would be on that ship when it sailed.

CHAPTER TWENTY-FIVE

Rachel, with her arm through Father's good one, strolled into the front parlor.

"One of these days, I shall be able to stomach three solid meals a day, just you wait and see," he said, motioning for her to sit in one of the two seats on either side of the fire before he took the second.

"A little bit of coffee in the morning is not so bad," she said. Truth be told, seeing him only take coffee for breakfast put her in mind of another man she loved who did the same, one she missed dreadfully. Father must have noticed her sadness but mistook the cause of it.

Rachel's gaze dropped to her lap. Today was the day Christopher's ship was scheduled to sail. What would become of him during the next couple of years? Would he return to her well and whole? One could never be certain. Life had taught her that many times over.

But life wasn't all bad. She had made the most of the cards she'd been dealt. And now she even had her father back. Fighting the melancholy that she couldn't seem to shake, Rachel turned back to her father. He watched her closely.

"That you are with us again is all I care about," Rachel said. It was true. She was happier to have him back than she could ever express.

How was it that she could be both overjoyed and quite sad at the same time? She hadn't known a person could hold such intense, yet conflicting, emotions in one's heart at the same time. She'd always thought that in doing so, each emotion would balance out, decrease the severity of the other. That she might find an equilibrium somewhere in the middle.

But that wasn't it at all. Each only seemed to amplify the other by contrast.

In the end, Rachel constantly felt torn. Wishing she were somewhere else, wanting to be nowhere but here. Sincerely happy to be with her father once more, longing for another man to be sitting beside her. It was distressing in the extreme.

"Are you upset with your mother?" he asked.

Rachel blinked and came back to the chair she sat on, the low fire warming her feet, Father sitting beside her. "No, no I am not." She truly ought to do better at showing her parents how happy she was to have them both back or else they might mistakenly believe that she didn't care for them at all; and nothing could be further from the truth than that. "I do wish I had known you were alive all these years. But Mother was right in that I had already grieved your passing by the time she got word that you were alive. I was so young then, and the chances of you actually surviving a second winter were not high. I think, in the same situation, I probably would have done as she did."

Father reached out, taking hold of her hand. In only the two days since she'd arrived home, he already appeared to be doing better. It might be wishful thinking, but he seemed to be filling out once more. The dark circles under his eyes were fading. Though his hands were still as rough as ever, they felt less bony.

Being home was good for him.

It was good for her, too.

Or, it would be, once her heart accepted the fact that it would be many years before she saw the man she loved again—if he ever returned to England at all.

In many ways, she *was* facing the same future her mother had. Separated from the man she loved, knowing it would be years if not longer before they saw each other again, unsure if death wouldn't claim him first.

"How did you do it?" Rachel asked. "How did you wait so long?"

He gave her hand a squeeze. "I thought of you. I thought of all the good memories, of the first time I held you, of taking you swimming, of coming home and finding you elbow deep in the flour." He chuckled softly, though it came out more as a wheeze. Then it turned to a bit of a sob. His face seemed to be warring between crying and laughing.

Rachel waited patiently as he cleared his throat loudly and recovered his composure. Whatever his experience these past many years, it had not been easy.

He gave her an apologetic smile, then sat up straighter, seeming to wish the unexpected display of emotion ignored. "Mostly, it was your mother who is the hero. She never gave up on me. While in prison, I couldn't do anything to improve my own situation. But she worked tirelessly, day in and day out, year after year. She scrimped and saved, she entrenched and then entrenched yet more. She gave up meat completely, she gave up so many things. Not once did she stop working toward uniting us as a family."

Hearing of her mother's efforts warmed Rachel in a way she'd never felt before. It was a mixture of admiration, peace, and gratitude that surged from her toes fully up to her hair. Almost on its own, her hand went to the small locket about her neck. All this time, Mother had been sacrificing and working. Yet, Rachel had known nothing of it. She'd known her mother was living on next to nothing, but she hadn't realized just how much she'd given up, or why.

Could she do the same if it was asked of her?

Looking into her father's face, seeing the happiness Mother had brought into their lives, Rachel realized she could. She could because it would be worth it. Because she could rely on her mother's example and have faith that all would be well. She could shape her own future to be the one she wanted.

So—what did she want?

The moment she asked herself the question, she found she knew the answer. She'd known for a while now.

A knock sounded at the front door—an urgent, instant pounding.

Rachel's brow dropped. "That doesn't sound like Uncle Seth." It didn't sound like anyone she knew at all.

Father looked as confused as she felt. He and Mother hadn't been back in the neighborhood all that long. Rachel supposed it might be a neighbor coming to welcome Father back, but that knock —which sounded yet again—did not portend a friendly visit at all.

Mother came into view from the back of the house. She shot them both a curious glance as she wiped her hands on her apron and reached for the door.

"Hello?" she asked.

Whomever it was pushed past her and marched into the house. "I am Lord Fitzwilliam, and I am searching for Miss Chant. Is she here?"

Lord Fitzwilliam? Rachel stood abruptly. Was Christopher with him? But Mother shut the door and only his lordship stood with her in the entryway. So, no. It was only him.

Seeing her, Lord Fitzwilliam strode past Rachel's mother and directly up to her.

"Pardon me, my lord," Father said, rising to his feet as well, his tone a bit uncertain, even a bit wary. "May I help you?"

"No, I need no help," Fitzwilliam replied, his gaze still on Rachel even as he took hold of her hand. "I have been practicing these past two months for this very moment."

He swept his overly tall top hat off his head, placing the rim of it against his chest, and dropped to one knee. Rachel felt herself go still from utter shock.

Was he . . . again? Here?

"Rachel—lovely, kind, courageous Rachel—you are all a woman ought to be," Lord Fitzwilliam said, his voice as light and unaffected as ever. "You are willing to put up with one such as me, which is no small feat. More still, you play the pianoforte like an angel."

She hadn't known he'd ever heard her play. Rachel found she was smiling far too big and bit down on her bottom lip. Both her parents watched on, stunned into silence.

"You are all that is good and gentle. Since the moment we first met," Lord Fitzwilliam continued, "I have enjoyed each moment together—each *discussion*."

He clearly meant the many proposals. Rachel found she was near laughing. She hadn't mentioned to her parents that Lord Fitzwilliam had proposed repeatedly to her. That, and the fact she'd lost her heart completely to Christopher, had been the only things she hadn't shared.

Lord Fitzwilliam gave her hand a little squeeze and, for the first time ever while proposing, his voice dropped. A sincerity that had always been lacking before entered in. "In a way you are probably oblivious to, Rachel, you have helped me come to terms with losing my own parents. I know I often seem . . . like my life has never been hard. But that isn't true. Knowing you has helped me face that. I am a better man because I have known you." His smile returned and something mischievous sparked in his eyes. "What's more— Dunn will never survive without you. And so, loveliest Rachel, on behalf of our mutual friend, I ask that you agree to become his wife."

She looked from him to her parents, who appeared even more bewildered than before.

Leave them to be with Christopher?

She focused on her mother.

Sacrifice to create the future she wanted, as her mother had?

Choose her own happiness as Lady Blackmore had?

Focus on the ones she loves as the Dowager Lady Fitzwilliam had?

"Yes," Rachel said. "A thousand times yes."

Lord Fitzwilliam stood. "Thank the heavens. Between you and me, since you've left, he's become quite dull. I honestly don't know how I would stand sailing all the way to the East Indies with him in a stew. The very thought is most unpleasant."

Rachel swatted his shoulder. "Don't be so hard on him." All the same, she was glad Christopher had had such a good friend by his side. She hadn't known Lord Fitzwilliam had chosen to sail with him—

With *them*.

Rachel's brow dropped. "The ship was to sail today though."

Lord Fitzwilliam waggled his eyebrows. "Was it?"

He couldn't have stopped an entire ship from sailing. Could he?

"What have you done?" she asked.

He plopped his hat atop his head. "All I'm saying is that a ship that big can't sail without a full crew and if a few prominent members *suddenly* decided they had enough money randomly on hand that they'd rather head up to Scotland . . ." His voice trailed off and he shrugged.

"You paid off the crew?" Rachel blurted out.

"I'm not saying I did." He winked at her. "And I'm not saying I didn't." Then he clapped his hands and spoke to the room as a whole. "What I am saying is that at most, I've bought us two days. If we leave immediately and travel through the night, we might just make it in time." His face light up. "I *bought* us two days. Ha! Literally." Then his brow dropped. "And I have learned that buying time is not cheap. So we best make good use of it."

As Lord Fitzwilliam and her parents hurried about preparing for their quick departure, Rachel stood, stunned into stillness for some time. Their voices faded as they moved into the back rooms of the house; Lord Fitzwilliam seemed to be filling her parents in on the true nature of her and Christopher's relationship. Still, Rachel couldn't seem to make herself leave the front parlor. She was doing this—she was leaving England for the East Indies. She was going to be with Christopher after all. Once they were aboard, they could have the captain marry them before nightfall.

It was all too fast.

At the same time, she couldn't get back to Christopher fast enough.

Lifting her skirts, she hurried after the others, throwing things into the few trunks they owned and sending word to Uncle Seth, requesting use of a carriage. Rachel couldn't stop smiling the whole time.

They would make it to the ship on time.

Rachel was determined they would.

CHAPTER TWENTY-SIX

Christopher looked up at the grand white sails of the ship he
would soon board.

The departure had been mysteriously postponed directly after
Fitzwilliam had disappeared. It seemed too coincidental to be mere
happenstance. Yet, Christopher hadn't pried into the matter or sent
out inquiries. Whatever Fitzwilliam had done, he was too upset to
care anymore. Still, he had hoped his friend would have returned by
now. Fitzwilliam could be a handful, but he was, nonetheless,
Christopher's closest friend.

"Ready, sir?" Mr. Andrews said, walking up to him. When
Christopher didn't reply right away, he continued. "Your belongings
are all stowed away safely aboard, as are his lordship's." He shifted
from one foot to the other, clearly anxious. "If we're going to be
sure and make this ship, we need to board now."

The time had come. He was leaving England. Again. Christopher had moved from country to country so many times as a boy,
and not once had he felt as though he was leaving 'home.' Home
had been wherever he and his father were; then, after his father had
passed, home had been wherever his job had taken him. In truth,
traveling to new places had always been something he looked

forward to. Was his love of seeing new places not one of the main reasons he'd asked to become Lord Fitzwilliam's tutor to begin with?

But this time was different. *This* felt like leaving home.

Mr. Andrews was right, however; Christopher had postponed long enough. "Very well. Lead the way."

Rachel pushed through the bustling crowd filling the harbor. Gracious, were *all* these people traveling to the East Indies today? She had no idea a single ship could hold so many people.

"Your mother and I will check over by the offices," Father said, pointing to his right. "You and Lord Fitzwilliam look closer by the ship."

Rachel nodded and they split up.

"Don't you worry. We'll find him in time," Lord Fitzwilliam said as they pushed yet deeper into the crowd.

"I suppose I should just board the ship," Rachel replied. "At the very least, I'll find him there."

Lord Fitzwilliam shook his head. "I'm not letting you on that ship before we talk to him."

"But what if he is already aboard?" He very well might be, and if Lord Fitzwilliam was going with them, it wasn't as though she, an unattached woman, would be boarding alone.

Lord Fitzwilliam shook his head, nonetheless,

Ah well, Rachel would convince him if they didn't find Christopher in the next few minutes.

"I told him not to board the ship before I returned," Lord Fitzwilliam muttered, his pace slowing even as he turned around.

Rachel paused next to him. "Seeing as you are his student, not the other way around, I don't know if he would obey—"

There he was. His brown hair, glinting red in the sunlight. She would know that particular shade anywhere.

"Christopher!" Rachel broke away from Lord Fitzwilliam, barreling forward. She didn't dare take her eyes off him, and so nearly collided with other individuals twice. But finally she reached him.

Her hands went out, taking hold of his lapels and turning him toward her.

"Rachel?" His hands went to her shoulders, then up to her face, then around her back. He held her tightly to him. "Rachel, what are you doing here?"

She laughed slightly. "Lord Fitzwilliam proposed to me."

He pulled back slightly, and their eyes met. "Again?"

"On your behalf this time."

"The presumption." Yet he was smiling, too.

Lord Fitzwilliam reached them at that moment. "It is as I told you, old man. If one practices, one gets better. That last proposal was so perfect, even Rachel couldn't say no."

"Is that so?" Christopher didn't take his eyes off her. "I suppose he started with telling you that you're beautiful."

"Lovely, actually," Rachel said. "But that was to be expected. He does use that word frightfully often."

"Very true." Christopher cradled her closer, their foreheads touching. "Did he mention how wonderfully you play the pianoforte?"

"Yes, and I didn't even know he'd heard me play." She couldn't believe she was here, that he was here. That they were together.

"Ah, well, I may have mentioned to him in passing that one only needs to hear you play to know what heaven sounds like."

"Then it makes sense that he would stop by to find out." All the despair, the hopelessness melted at his touch. This was where she wanted to be. *Always.*

"Naturally. And what of your kind heart and gentleness?"

"Those were discussed as well."

Christopher's mouth pulled to the side and his brow dropped. "I am not sure if he's left anything for me. What about this?" Bending down, he pressed a light kiss to Rachel's lips. Though it was soft, it stole her breath. This truly was everything she wanted—this was the manner of happiness she desired.

After far too short a time, Christopher pulled back. "Don't tell me he's already done that as well?"

Rachel blinked her eyes open. "No." She couldn't find more words than that.

"You mean to tell me," Lord Fitzwilliam's voice broke in, "that all this time, the only thing I was missing was a good kiss and she would have said yes?" He reached for Rachel. "Here, let me try it again."

Christopher shoved him off. "Your proposing days are over."

"I wouldn't be too sure; I hear the East Indies are full of women who are desperate for a husband."

"Oh dear," Rachel said with a light giggle. "I'm not at all certain the East Indies could handle one like Lord Fitzwilliam."

"Either way," Christopher said, taking her fully in his arms and drawing her closer once more. "He's not my responsibility any longer." He kissed her yet again. This time far more soundly. Rachel's hands moved over his chest and up to his neck. She wrapped her hands around him, her fingers finding the small curls at the nape of his neck, and she pulled him in, deepening the kiss.

For as good and kind and inspiring as he seemed to believe she was, Rachel found him to be equally good and understanding and supportive and . . . well, perfect for her. Whatever the future might bring, she knew with Christopher by her side, they could shape it into one of happiness and joy.

A deep, if slightly reedy, cough put an end to their bliss.

With a sigh, one that Rachel was not sure had come from her or from Christopher, they pulled apart. Still, Rachel kept her eyes closed, savoring the lingering feel of his lips on hers.

"I take it *you* are the man who's going to marry my daughter?"

Apparently, Mother and Father had found them.

Christopher placed a hand against Rachel's cheek, causing her to open her eyes. He looked down on her, all the love she felt for him echoed in his eyes.

"Am I, dearest?" he asked. "What do you say? Will you build a future with me? Face uncertainty with me?"

"Yes," Rachel breathed out. Going up on her toes, she placed a quick kiss on his lips. "I want nothing more than to become Mrs. Dunn." Her voice grew, all her conviction flowing into it. "Of a truth, I want it so much, I'm willing to go to the East Indies to see that I get it."

"If I know anything about Miss Rachel Chant," Christopher said, "it is that once she has made up her mind regarding what she wants, nothing can dissuade her."

Rachel lifted her chin. "Then there is no argument. I want you, regardless of the details. We shall be married. I am determined."

He laughed and pressed a kiss to her forehead. "Mrs. Rachel Dunn. Has a wondrous ring, does it not?"

"Excuse me, sir," a man Rachel could not recall seeing before said to Christopher, "but we really must be going."

This had to be the man of business Christopher had spoken of, the one who'd come from the East Indies.

Rachel turned back to her parents. She was going to miss them terribly. But seeing them smile at her, she knew they would understand. If only she'd had time to bid farewell to Uncle Seth, Charlotte, Eliza, and Dinah. Life truly could take away at times, but she was ever so glad for all it had given her as well.

"I am certain the captain can be persuaded to wed us as soon as we leave the harbor," she told her parents.

Mother brushed a hand over her cheek, wiping away a tear. "I had so looked forward to seeing you wed in the same church your father and I were married in."

Rachel gave her a reassuring smile. "I know, and I'm sorry."

Lord Fitzwilliam held up a hand. "No need for tears. Dunn and Rachel *will* be married in a quaint little church, of that I have no doubt."

Rachel felt her heart leap even as her stomach dropped. "I cannot travel for two months, unattached, with two equally unattached men who are of no connection to me." Lord Fitzwilliam had done some rather unwise things in the past, but this suggestion was scandalous even for him.

"Of course not," he said, shaking his head as though Rachel were the one being unreasonable. "*I* shall travel to the East Indies, and *you two* shall remain here. It's like this." He turned and bowed most properly to the man of business. "Good day to you, Mr. Andrews, allow me to introduce myself. I am Mr. Christopher Dunn, son of Mr. Richard Dunn and grandson of Mr. Adolphus Dunn."

"Fitzwilliam, what are you doing?" Christopher asked.

"I'm becoming you. Truth be told, we've spent so much time together these past two years, I rather believe I am the perfect man for the job."

Christopher shook his head. "You cannot possibly pass yourself off as me."

Lord Fitzwilliam's eyes lit up and his smile grew. "That sounds like a challenge."

"No," Christopher said, stepping away from Rachel and pointing a finger at his lordship's chest. "No, you cannot—"

Lord Fitzwilliam only skipped back a few steps. "A challenge that I accept."

Rachel couldn't believe it. If this meant what she thought it meant, she and Christopher wouldn't be going to the East Indies at all. They'd be staying here. She'd have both the man she loved and her parents.

Christopher opened his mouth as though to argue, but Rachel took hold of his hand and gave it a tug. He turned toward her, his lips in a tight line.

"Couldn't we let him?"

Lord Fitzwilliam spoke up, while still staying far enough away that Christopher couldn't easily reach him. "Think of this as my wedding present to you both."

With a loud groan that ended in a laugh, Christopher moved over to Rachel once more and wrapped his arm around her waist. "Just don't get into too much trouble."

Lord Fitzwilliam waggled his eyebrows. "Of course not." Then he turned toward Mr. Andrews. "Well, my good man, I believe we have a ship to board."

Mr. Andrews looked from Lord Fitzwilliam to Christopher.

Then he shrugged. "Very well, Mr. Dunn. I'll show you to your room aboard the ship."

The two moved away. Just before they disappeared, however, Christopher called out. "Fitzwilliam!"

Lord Fitzwilliam turned around.

"Thank you," Christopher and Rachel called to him.

His lips ticked up to one side and he threw them a salute before turning yet again and disappearing into the crowd.

"He's not a typical lord, is he?" Father asked.

Rachel laughed, taking hold of Christopher's hand and leaning her shoulder against his. "No, not in the least."

Christopher turned and looked down at her. "Are you certain this is what you want? I may have inherited a fair sum, but I won't have any of it for a couple of years at least."

Rachel stared up at him. "You know I don't care at all about that."

"We won't have a home for some time."

Mother spoke up, her words quick. "Rachel hasn't lived with us in some time. We certainly wouldn't mind if . . ." Her words slowed; she was probably embarrassed to find herself speaking of something so personal to someone she hardly knew.

Father smiled down at his wife, then turned toward them. "You are welcome to live with us as long as you like—but *only* if that is what you both want."

It wasn't usual for an engaged woman to wish to live with her parents even *after* her wedding, Rachel believed, but in her case, she hadn't lived with her parents for so long, she found the idea suited her quite well.

"Please?" she asked Christopher.

He let out a small laugh. "Oh, I know better than to try and stand between you and what you want." Reaching a hand out, he shook Father's. "Sir, it is an honor to meet you and your good wife. I hope your offer was sincere because I don't think any of us could sway Rachel now."

They all laughed as Rachel merely shrugged.

Who would have guessed the future would be so bright? That

after all she'd gone through, she would have her family back once more?

Arm in arm with the man she loved—the man who would soon be her husband—Rachel smiled as they made their way toward the carriage, bound for home at last.

Life, indeed, could be very good after all.

CHAPTER TWENTY-SEVEN

R achel let the last note of her song hang about the room. She breathed in the final refrains of the music and then lifted her hands from the keys.

She didn't have to turn around to discern the different claps sounding behind her. Mother's clap was quick and light. Father's was deeper and slower, made all the more so because his left arm was still in a sling, so he clapped by slapping his right hand against his thigh.

Christopher's clap came from closest to her, indeed, from the chair just to her right.

"That was beautiful, dear," Mother said.

Father's tone was full of pride. "My little songbird."

Rachel turned atop the bench and smiled at them all. "It was just a little something I learned at Curio Manor." Nothing filled her like being able to play for her parents—both of them. Gracious, her father being alive was still so new. Even now, looking at him as he turned his smile on Mother, Rachel nearly began to cry.

Who would have ever guessed that life could have turned out so well?

"And now," Rachel said, blinking quickly and standing, "would you play for us, Christopher?"

He leaned in a bit closer to her. "I have a distinct feeling that, while your parents like me, they'd much prefer to hear you."

"But *I* wish to hear you play." Moreover, she'd been playing for nearly an hour straight and her wrists could use the break.

As she and Christopher stood to switch places, Mother spoke to the room in general. "Wasn't it ever so generous of Lady Fitzwilliam to gift you two this pianoforte as an early wedding present?"

"Most generous, indeed," Rachel agreed. And, luckily, the pianoforte was the perfect size for the small front parlor in her parents' home.

But as she began to sit in the chair Christopher had only moments ago occupied, he took hold of her hand. "Why don't we play this?" he asked, holding out a sonata written as a duet.

Rachel rolled her wrists. "I have played several songs already."

"Come now," Father called from across the room. "Do one together."

"You aren't too tired, are you?" Mother added.

Rachel looked from Mother to Father—they looked so happy sitting side by side.

"Too tired to play for my dear Father?" Rachel asked, sitting once more atop the bench. "Never."

Playing the higher notes of the piece, Rachel began first. The first few measures were light and easy, but the piece quickly sped up, growing in both volume and vivacity. Christopher, who had the deeper notes at the bottom of the pianoforte, also kept the tempo with a steady rhythm. As they neared the hardest section of the piece, Christopher caught her eye and winked. Then, he began to speed up.

Rachel smirked. That was completely unfair.

She focused all her attention on the page before her. Christopher continued to go faster and faster, and Rachel's fingers were soon tripping over themselves trying to stay on tempo.

She giggled as she flew through an arpeggio and then shoved an elbow into his side as she had to shift down and start lower for the next long arpeggio. Christopher laughed as he lifted his elbow in response, keeping her from getting to the notes nearest his own fingers.

Among much laughter, Christopher was the first to throw his hands up and admit defeat.

"You win, you win," he conceded. Then, instead of settling his hands back on the keys, he wrapped his arms around Rachel's waist.

Rachel gladly gave up on the difficult piece and instead turned toward the man she loved. Only then did she realize that her parents had, at some point in the song, slipped from the room.

"How do you like being home, Rachel?" Christopher asked.

"It's even better than I ever imagined. But only because I was wise enough to follow sound advice and stop looking back."

"Speaking of looking forward." Christopher tipped his head down until his nose brushed hers. "Are you ready to become Mrs. Dunn?"

"Yes." The word rushed from her, all her excitement and joy resounding in one single syllable.

Christopher chuckled and kissed her lightly. "Just over twelve hours to go."

Rachel wrapped her arms around his waist—gracious, but it was heavenly to sit like this with him. "Are you sure you don't mind living here for a while?"

"Certainly not. I wouldn't dream of taking you away from your parents just now."

"And what of the days when you grow good and tired of living with your in-laws?"

"I'm more concerned for the days when they grow tired of me. Either way, my ship won't come in for a couple of years yet. At that point, we'll find somewhere close by. You'll be free to choose your own home, visit your mother and father as often as you like for as long as you like," he pulled her in close and whispered in her ear, "and return home with me every night."

"That sounds like perfect happiness." She sighed.

He kissed along her jaw, moving up toward her ear. "I'm determined we shall be perfectly happy."

Tingles erupted along her skin. "I thought *I* was the determined one here."

He pulled back slightly and shrugged. "You're already rubbing off on me."

Taking hold of his lapel, she pulled him down until their lips touched. She gave him an ardent kiss. "I love you, Christopher."

"I know." He kissed her back. "And I love you."

EPILOGUE

Whispered conversation drew Lady Charlotte Blackmore's attention away from the grand wedding breakfast all around her and toward the corridor. Not only were Rachel and Mr. Dunn celebrating today, but Eliza and Lord Lambert were as well.

A double wedding. Nothing could have been more delightful.

It was to be the perfect diversion before returning to London. Here, in the small neighborhood where the girls had grown up, both Rachel and Eliza were wed. Charlotte—who never shirked any responsibility—had done her own research well before today and found both grooms to be quite respectable men. She was ever so pleased that two of her new 'daughters,' as she found herself thinking of them more and more often, were settled and happy.

Well, she would have been *fully* pleased, if only Dinah's pouting had not distracted Charlotte so. Pushing away from the table, Charlotte made her excuses to those sitting on either side of her and walked casually toward the corridor. As she reached the doors which led out of the dining room, the voices became easier to hear.

"Are you certain?" a deep, masculine voice asked.

"Of course," Dinah replied. "Only, we ought to find a more isolated room before we continue."

Every ounce of protective, mothering instinct flared to life inside Charlotte. She spun on one heel and marched toward the two forms, mostly concealed in a dark corner.

The man drew in closer to Dinah. "Excellent. What say you to—"

"Dinah?" Charlotte called. "Dinah, dearest, please return to the dining room."

The man spun at her voice, keeping his back toward Charlotte, and hurried away, much like a shadow slipping back into the dark.

Dinah smoothed down her skirt and faced Charlotte, quite as though nothing untoward in the least had happened.

"Who were you speaking to?" Charlotte asked. She and Sir Mulgrave had hoped that time away from London would help Dinah come to her senses and stop encouraging fops and rakes. But it seemed the time at Curio Manor had done nothing of the sort.

"Who, that man?" Dinah asked, all innocence. "I cannot seem to recall his name." She walked by Charlotte, her head held high.

"Dinah," Charlotte called. "You know you cannot do such a thing."

Dinah turned, her eyes wide. "I cannot do what?"

Charlotte's lips pursed tight. "You cannot be caught whispering in the corner with a man who isn't your intended."

Dinah lifted a single eyebrow. "Suppose he was, though?"

"Was what?"

"My intended?"

Charlotte shook her head, lifting her skirt and walking up close to Dinah. "Don't press your luck. Your father has had about as much matchmaking madness as he can stand." If she so much as suggested the name of a gentleman she deemed worthy of the last Mulgrave daughter, Charlotte wasn't at all sure Sir Mulgrave wouldn't spirit the man and Dinah off to Gretna Green himself.

"Oh, don't worry," Dinah said, once more walking away from Charlotte. "I am sure Father won't ever catch me in a corner with a man. He rarely thinks of me enough to catch me at anything at all."

"That's not true."

Dinah didn't stop but continued on into the dining room without a word.

What *was* true was that Dinah often felt neglected and overlooked. Charlotte hadn't realized how much before Curio Manor, but she could see it plainly now. But if Dinah knew even half of the conversations she'd had with Sir Mulgrave, she'd realize how wrong she was. It was hard to convince a dramatic young woman of that fact, however. Charlotte glanced heavenward and sighed.

Regardless, they would be returning to London in a few days' time. The Season was not over yet and if the warning in her stomach wasn't wrong—and it never was—the worst was only just beginning.

The End

The romance continues in
The Fearless Miss Dinah

**He's been waiting months for her to finally notice him.
Except suddenly, he's not the only one vying for her hand.**

Download the short story for free at:
www.LauraRollins.com

DISCUSSION QUESTIONS

- Rachel's love for her mother prevents her from being able to look forward and see the opportunities around her. Have you ever found yourself so wrapped up in worry that you've become blind to the good in life? What has helped you step away from the worry and see the good again?

- When you hear the word "courage", what other words come to mind? What ideas? What feelings? Does it take courage to choose happiness, to work to make the most of your given circumstance?

- In what ways is "enduring a circumstance" different than "choosing happiness" or "working to make the most of it"?

- Christopher's father chose a hard life to pursue what he was most passionate about. The word "passion" has its roots in Latin and has been interpreted to mean "what a person is willing to suffer or sacrifice for". What are some of your passions? What are you willing to work for, to take the hard path for?

- Fitzwilliam and his grandmother have focused their

entire lives on looking past heartache and finding the joy in life; but to first meet them, one might believe they were silly and perhaps even shallow. Have you ever known someone who appeared silly and shallow upon first acquaintance, but later you learned there was much more to them? Do you suppose there are people in your life now who you are making incorrect assumptions about?

ACKNOWLEDGMENTS

No book is ever written without much encouragement and support from any number of people. I am forever thankful to my husband and children, as their patience and love is the reason I get to do this.

Special thanks go to my writing groups, for their advice and help. Also to Jenny Proctor and Emily Poole; without your suggestions and edits this book would not have been half so good.

Lastly, thanks to my Father in Heaven, for giving me a beautiful life and the opportunity to create.

ABOUT THE AUTHOR

Laura Rollins has always loved a heart-melting happily ever after. It didn't matter if the story took place in Regency England, in outer space, beneath the Earth's crust, or in a cobbler's shop, if there was a sweet romance, she would read it.

Life has given her many of her own adventures. Currently she lives in the Rocky Mountains with her best-friend, who is also her husband, and their four beautiful children. She still loves to read books and more books; her favorite types of music are classical, Broadway, and country; she'd rather be hiking the mountains than twiddling her thumbs on the beach; and she's been known to debate with her oldest son over whether Infinity is better categorized as a number or an idea.

For more books, updates,
and a free short story, check out:
www.LauraRollins.com

Printed in Great Britain
by Amazon